Smoke Screen
(A Miranda and Parker Mystery)
Book 7

Water Brothers Books
31208 Five Mile Rd.
Livonia, MI 48154
(734) 524-1163

Linsey Lanier

Edited by

Editing for You

Copyright © 2015 Linsey Lanier
Felicity Books
All rights reserved.

ISBN: 1941191231
ISBN-13: 978-1-941191-23-1

Copyright © 2015 Linsey Lanier

All rights reserved. Without limiting the rights under copyright reserved above, no part of this publication may be reproduced, stored in or introduced into a retrieval system, or transmitted, in any form, or by any means (electronic, mechanical, photocopying, recording, or otherwise) without the prior written permission of both the copyright owner and the above publisher of this book. This is a work of fiction. Names, characters, places, brands, media, and incidents are either the product of the author's imagination or are used fictitiously. The author acknowledges the trademarked status and trademark owners of various products referenced in this work of fiction, which have been used without permission. The publication/use of these trademarks is not authorized, associated with, or sponsored by the trademark owners.

SMOKE SCREEN

Fulfilling your destiny…one killer at a time

Striking out on her own after a gut wrenching fight with Parker, Miranda is ready to prove she's an investigator in her own right. Problem is…she has no clients.
So when a scary dude from her past walks through the door and wants to hire her to find a missing exotic dancer, she's forced to take the case.
Meanwhile Parker is done with Miranda and the pain she puts him through. But if he can find whoever sent her those threatening texts on her cell phone weeks ago, he could prove to her he was right about her disregard of danger.
Little do they know they're both in danger—and about to face the most terrifying killer of their lives.

THE MIRANDA'S RIGHTS MYSTERY SERIES

Someone Else's Daughter
Delicious Torment
Forever Mine
Fire Dancer
Thin Ice

THE MIRANDA AND PARKER MYSTERY SERIES

All Eyes on Me
Heart Wounds
Clowns and Cowboys
The Watcher
Zero Dark Chocolate
Trial by Fire
Smoke Screen
The Boy
Snakebit
Mind Bender
Roses from My Killer
The Stolen Girl
Vanishing Act
Predator
Retribution
Most Likely to Die
(more to come)

MAGGIE DELANEY POLICE THRILLER SERIES

Chicago Cop
Good Cop Bad Cop

OTHER BOOKS BY LINSEY LANIER

Steal My Heart

For more information visit www.FelicityBooks.com

CHAPTER ONE

Life is like a symphony, don't you think?
The mood ever changing? The tempo of one movement so different from another? The ebb and flow of the music the conductor controls with a single sharp rod? Fast, then slow, then fast again, ending in a frenzied exhilaration like the timpani of a long guttural scream.

I can never decide which I like better. The look of terror in their eyes or their screams.

Their eyes are all so different. So fascinating in their variation. Some catlike and blue as the sky, some round and brown as chocolate marbles, some large and inky green—like the foul-tasting medicine Mother used to give me to calm me down after one of my fits. But even the green ones are so pretty when they fill with the watery tears that inevitably drip down the sides of their faces.

But the screams, the sounds…Yes, the screams are what truly drive me.

The shrillness reverberates through my body, making every nerve come alive. The never ending tears, the long, drawn out wailing. Oh, how it all spurs me on.

Amazing that their voices are as varied as their eyes. Some soft and pleading. Some hard and commanding. I don't like those. They remind me of Mother when I ran from her touch.

The pitches of their screams are like the pitches of the instruments in an orchestra. I wonder if Mother would think so. She would, I'm sure. But she isn't here to hear them.

And in the end all the voices grow hoarse with the screaming, and then, of course, still. Like Mother. The symphony of life must end.

It's inevitable. Their fate.

As it is mine to make them scream. It isn't as if I have a choice.

I always begin each project the same way. I waste no time invading her most private parts. Just the way Mother used to invade mine, rubbing her clarinet against my most sensitive spots. I tell her how shameful she is. Just as Mother used to tell me how shameful I was when I didn't get my lesson right. I tell her she must be punished. Just as Mother punished me. And as I begin the punishment I tell her what she is.

Whore. Whore. Whore.

Just the way *he* taught me. He was a much better teacher than Mother.

I hated her so. And I hated him, too. They both took so much from me. Mother took my innocence. *He* took my only love. It happened one night in December in a house full of flames.

The night I got my new name.

Now they call me—Smoke.

A wisp here. A wisp there. And suddenly I'm gone. Soon I will be gone for good.

Soon, very soon, I shall have the one I've been waiting for so long. The one I've been watching for almost a year. The only one who has managed to slip through my fingers. At last I will have her and the whole purpose of my life will be complete. I cannot wait to touch her.

The one who got away.

CHAPTER TWO

Miranda Steele sank into the creaky office chair she'd bought at a nearby thrift store and put her head in her hands.

She stared down at the check before her on the plasterboard desk she'd gotten from the same place and grunted out loud. She tightened her fists, wanting to smack something.

Note to self: Buy a punching bag.

Wait.

Amendment: Can't afford punching bag. Go to the local gym.

Teeth gritted, temper fuming, she glared at the check. The large neat handwriting seemed so full of confidence. So solid. So…trustworthy.

But, no.

Hank Lauderdale, her very first client—for the very case she'd gotten on her own—had screwed her over.

She could still see the teller at the bank two blocks down the street as she pushed the check back across the faux mahogany counter.

"I'm sorry Ms. Steele," she'd said in a prissy southern voice. "This account is closed."

Turned out Mr. Lauderdale had withdrawn his funds and closed the account that very morning.

Damn.

Hank Lauderdale was a fifty-something entrepreneur whose twenty-something bride of two months, Luella, had been cheating on him. Or so Lauderdale thought. He wanted Miranda to find out for sure.

After three days of following Mrs. Lauderdale around as she shopped, chatted to her friends on her cell, and met them in pricey midtown bars for dirty martinis, Miranda had decided Lauderdale was paranoid.

Then around nine on the third evening she'd spotted Luella Lauderdale leaving the marital home and heading to a local hotel. A real swanky spot. There Luella had met a tall, good-looking man about her age dressed in a casual shirt and shorts. With wavy blond hair and a deep tan he'd looked like a surfer.

Miranda had sat in her car and watched through the lens of her new high-powered camera, snapping photos as they played footsie and kissy face in the hotel's fancy restaurant.

Then she'd followed them upstairs, stood outside their door, and recorded their moans and grunts and f— me cries on her cell. Back in her car, about ten the next morning, she'd caught the happy couple sauntering out of the hotel's front door arm in arm—wearing the same clothes and an unmistakable afterglow.

She'd snapped photos like crazy.

Then she'd rushed home, grabbed a shower and a short nap, called Lauderdale, and arranged to meet him in a coffee shop. They had a light breakfast and she'd handed over the pictures along with her bill. He'd handed her a check.

The one now on her desk.

No wonder Luella had cheated on him. In fact Lauderdale might have been the first one to stray from the marriage. When it came to paying his bills, he was sure a cheat.

It had to be a mistake, Miranda told herself for the twentieth time. But she'd already called Lauderdale on the way out of the bank and her call had gone to voice mail.

"Shit!" she cried into the empty space.

Same thing she'd said to the bank teller when she'd told her the account was closed.

She got up and paced around the room. "Look Lauderdale," she said to the air. "I don't know who you think you're screwing with, but this is Miranda Steele here and I don't take this crap lying down."

But no one heard her.

The check in her hand she plodded into the tiny waiting room. It was just as empty.

She'd painted the room a minty green with the vague idea of setting clients at ease. The sofa she'd gotten from the local thrift store was rust colored leather with some fancy carving on the trim. The middle sagged a little, but she'd fluffed it up as best she could. There were a couple of chairs that almost matched, a floor lamp, and a coffee table with a leg that had fallen off as soon as she got it out of the shop.

On the walls she'd hung some inexpensive paintings. A picture of some large, weird looking orange flowers, a white cat licking its paw, a canoe marooned on a deserted shore. She'd even sprung for a fake plant.

Too bad nobody had seen the place.

Feeling drained she took a seat on the sofa and sank into its faltering cushion. As if they had a mind of their own, her thoughts drifted back in time three weeks.

Hard to believe it had been that long since her last day in the Parker mansion. She'd woken up that morning in one of the guest rooms with a crick in her neck, a throb in her head, and an ache in her heart like a knife wound.

She got out of bed telling herself Parker had to have changed his mind overnight.

He hadn't.

When she found him in the kitchen that morning he was as cold as ice. He barely spoke. He refused to discuss any options at all. He was closing their partnership, Parker and Steele Consulting, and that was that.

So she'd done what she had to do. She left.

She hadn't pitched a fit. She hadn't ranted and raved—though she'd dearly wanted to. Instead she calmly went upstairs, packed her things and left. She took her jeans and T-shirts, work clothes, shoes, and underwear. Mostly things she'd paid for. She'd left the party dresses Parker had bought her. Couldn't see herself needing those again.

She found her checkbook in the bottom of a drawer and confirmed the balance. The money was from her earnings at the Parker Agency, so she figured it was hers. She'd saved a good bit of it. Except for the cost of clothes and lunches and gifts for coworkers and friends, and payments for the mansion that she still insisted on keeping up. She'd thought it was a decent sum. Enough to get her started.

So she'd grabbed her bags and headed down the grand mahogany staircase and out the majestic front door for the last time.

The terrible, roiling pain in her heart had threatened to consume her, burn her to ash like a roaring fire. But she'd refused to give in to it. Refused to let herself grieve.

Not over Parker. Not over the friends she'd left behind. Not over her fourteen-year-old daughter she'd found last year after so long a search. Mackenzie had little use for her these days anyway.

If she let her feelings take over, she didn't know what might happen to her. Parker had been the only man she'd ever truly loved. The only man who loved her back, who cared about her, who really got her. Or so she'd thought.

But he didn't get her any more.

So instead of falling to pieces, she got to work.

She'd taken the Corvette ZR1 Parker had given her as a wedding present and traded it in for a light tan Acura with good mileage. She'd gotten screwed on the deal but she didn't have the luxury of shopping around.

She'd found an apartment in a two-story building off GA-10 on East Avenue in midtown, with a view overlooking a dumpster. Not a great place to live. Not a great place to walk around alone at night. Yet it was still pricey. The office space she was renting cost a bundle, too.

The second story in the back of an abandoned Mexican restaurant named *Plato Caliente*. She knew it had been called *Plato Caliente* because three people she'd hoped were new clients had stopped in to ask what happened to it.

Both landlords wanted two months rent in advance.

And then there was the furniture, the paint, business cards, accounting software, investigative equipment, and those ueber expensive database subscriptions she had to have to do business. And the sign she stuck in the window—*Steele Investigations, walk-ins welcome.*

After everything, she barely had two months living expenses left in her account.

She held up Lauderdale's bad check. "And now this."

The rent on both the apartment and the office were due in a week. It had taken her forever to get the office in shape and get this one client and now she had to do collection, too? Damn.

She dug out her cell phone and dialed his number again. He'd answer this time for sure. Be nice, she told herself.

But once more the call went to voice mail.

She hung up and stared into space. What if she couldn't make this guy pay? What if she couldn't find another client? She should take out one of those pricey ads in the *Atlanta Journal Constitution*. But that might break her.

And if it did—then what?

Back to road work? A construction job?

She didn't want to go back to her old life. She had meaning now. She wasn't going to give it up. But she might have to postpone it for a while. The idea made her sick. But she wasn't giving up that easy. If she had to take a job laying floors or pounding shingles for awhile to make ends meet, she would.

Suddenly she had a vision of Parker standing before her, his strong, muscular body clad in one of his fancy blue suits with a red silk tie. She saw the sexy salt-and-pepper of his styled hair, the distinguished lines in his to-die-for face, the piercing stare of his gunmetal gray eyes.

He shook his head at her as if to say, "I knew you couldn't make it on your own."

Lip curling, she shot to her feet growling. "Like hell I won't, Wade Russell Parker the Third!" she cried into the empty air.

Then she marched back into her office, yanked open the squeaky top drawer of the filing cabinet, and took out the only folder in the hanging files to find Lauderdale's work address.

She'd just go pay that sonofabitch a visit.

"Miranda."

The sultry voice behind her made her whole body go stiff. As did the provocative roll of the r in her name. And the smell of exotic cologne.

Slowly she turned around.

There he was, standing right there in the doorway of her office. She hadn't seen him in over a year but she knew him right away.

She took in the thick black curls, heavy with gel. The well-defined widow's peak. The well-trimmed beard and mustache. The skintight leather pants and glossy purple shirt over a body that had been through years of street fights and won, the muscular neck decked with gold chains. And those deep black eyes that sent a frigid North Pole chill straight through her.

Carlos Santiago.

"*Plato Caliente* is out of business," she told him as if he were a stranger.

His dark eyes narrowed. "Do not pretend you do not know me, *cara*."

Cara? Oh, she knew him all right.

Carlos Santiago, a local Columbian drug lord who ran the streets in this area. He had a rap sheet as long as the I-20 Corridor, but he'd weaseled his way out of everything he'd been charged with. She'd gone motorcycle racing with him one night when she was on a case for the Parker Agency.

Actually, it had been a case she'd taken on herself, and Parker had been pissed about it. That was when she'd learned about Parker's first love, Laura, a girl he'd fallen head over heels for when he was in high school. She'd died a violent death and he'd never quite gotten over it. She should have seen the handwriting on the wall back then.

"What do you want, Santiago?"

"My, my, we have grown churlish since our last encounter." He took a step toward her with the same confident swagger he'd used when they were locked in a jail cell together.

Suddenly she noticed a piece of paper in his hand. "Is that what I think it is?"

He held it up, the gold rings on his fingers catching the light. "I saw this posted on a convenience store window. You are on your own now?"

Sure enough, it was one of her flyers.

She'd posted them around midtown Atlanta, everywhere she could think of, after she'd taken out a Craigslist ad and gotten no response.

"Yeah, that's me. And yes, I'm on my own." She sat down in her chair to dismiss him. She wasn't in the mood for his gloating.

He stepped to her desk, laid the flyer down on it. "This is why I'm here, Miranda."

She opened a drawer and pretended to search for client papers she didn't have. "You want to turn me in for littering, Santiago? That would be calling the kettle black."

She heard his low, sultry chuckle and looked up to see him shaking his head at her.

She cocked her head at him with a you-still-here? grimace. "What?"

His smile disappearing he thumped a finger on the desk over the flyer. The ruby ring on it flashed as if sending out a warning signal. "Are you really working on your own as a private investigator?"

"Trying to." Why did he care? Was he going to make her pay protection money? Good luck with that.

"Answer me." He spoke so sharply he made her jump.

She eyed her lower drawer. She kept her Berretta in there—something else she'd taken when she left Parker. Now she wished she'd kept it in a shoulder holster.

"Okay, you got me," she said in the tough voice she used to use in bars. "Yes, I'm really working as a private investigator on my own. What of it?"

He grinned and a diamond twinkled on his front tooth. "I seem to recall you owe me a favor."

She swallowed hard.

That night in the Fulton County jail he'd given her some vital information on a case. Then he'd stepped in close, wrapped a strand of her hair around a finger—and asked what she could do for him in return.

"That is why I came to see you, Miranda."

He was here to collect a favor?

"Oh, yeah?" It was all she could do to keep her voice from squeaking.

She shivered a little, remembering how close this violent criminal had come to her that night. Almost as close as he was now, leaning over her desk. So close she could feel his breath.

Her skin turned cold and every hair on the back of her neck stood in attention when he spoke the next words.

"Miranda Steele, I want to hire you."

CHAPTER THREE

Wade Parker sat at his glossy desk in his corner office on the fifteenth floor of the Imperial Building and stared out the window at the building next door. His head throbbed, his body ached, his face was raw from the first shave he'd had in three weeks.

And his mind was a blank.

Why had he bothered to come into the office today? He was utterly useless here. He'd sat at his desk all morning and produced nothing.

What was the point?

Three weeks ago Miranda Steele had walked out on him and he hadn't been the same since.

He hadn't gone after her. He knew that would do no good. Instead he'd cursed. He'd roared and ranted and raved. He'd smashed things. He'd drunk to excess. He'd roamed about the empty mansion he'd grown up in, a whiskey bottle in his hand, until he'd dropped onto the floor somewhere in a dull stupor.

Friends had come by to find out what was the matter. His father, his daughter had come, too. They all said they were worried about him.

He'd told them to leave him the hell alone.

He ran a hand over his chin. Its smoothness felt strange. He felt strange. Like a creature from outer space inhabiting a human body for the first time.

And all he could think of was the sound of the front door shutting when Miranda walked out of it for the last time.

He rubbed his temple to ease the pain. He couldn't ease the pain in his heart.

What a fool he'd been to fall so in love with someone so headstrong. So willful. So obstinate. She'd been right. It could never work between them.

And yet he ached for her. For what they'd had together. Or what he'd thought they had.

But, no. Her foolish need for danger and risk would always set them at odds. She'd chosen it over him. Over their life together. Over their marriage.

His first inclination had been to send someone to watch her. He knew where she was. He'd traced her credit card and discovered she'd rented a room in an unsavory part of town. Just like her to be so reckless. And an office, as well. She was actually trying to set up an investigation business. That had stunned him.

Not that she couldn't handle cases on her own. He had every confidence she could. She had natural instincts for the work. She was as quick a learner as he'd come across in his twenty year career.

But at what cost?

He shook his head. There she goes, he thought, living a dangerous life and taking few precautions. But he'd decided against round-the-clock surveillance. She would easily make any tail he put on her. She was too good at what she did. He had made her that good.

And when she did, it would only prolong the breakup. Better to make the break clean. Besides, if she got into trouble and came back to him, it would only prove he'd been right. The work, the cases she craved were too dangerous. Would she learn that lesson? Would she come back?

His gut quivered at the thought, the anger brewing again. If she did, she would not get a second chance from him.

He was done with her.

Slowly he opened a drawer in his desk and eyed the device inside it. Miranda's old cell phone. The one with the anonymous text messages she'd kept secret from him. For some reason he'd brought it into the office this morning and stuffed it into this drawer. Force of habit, he supposed.

He picked the phone up and scrolled to the messages.

I know who you are.
I know where you are.
I know what you are.

Miranda had insisted they'd come from some crank caller, someone who'd merely been looking for attention. Someone who was no real threat. He'd thought the source was more sinister. Perhaps she was right. There had been no more texts since the last one. Since there had been no response to the calls, the person had moved on to other thrills.

But if she wasn't right?

A few weeks ago in Chicago he had tried to find the person who'd sent his wife these messages. He knew now he'd taken the wrong approach. But every case, especially the tough ones, had several angles to attack from.

A new one began to form in his mind about this one.

What if he did find the mysterious texter? What if the source wasn't as innocent as Miranda had assumed? Parker envisioned himself hunting her down in her office, showing her proof this person was dangerous and she should have listened to him.

Then he would turn away and walk out.

He turned the phone over in his hand, his mind coming to life again as he considered the next step.

Familiar footsteps echoed in the hall. A rap on his door followed.

He glanced up and saw his daughter, Gen, standing in the open door, looking concerned.

She wore a straight line silver business suit that showed off her tall, athletic figure, as well as her short crop of white blond hair.

His heart filled with pride for her. As his office manager she was more than competent. She could take over the business side of the Agency one day. Perhaps one day soon. Judd could handle the field work.

She put a hand on her hip. "You're late."

He frowned.

"The meeting with Judd?"

"Oh, yes." He had called for it this afternoon to catch up on business and review the new recruits for the next training session he was offering later that year.

Ironically, he had pretended he was recruiting new employees to Miranda and he hadn't even started.

When he didn't move Gen came over and sat down in his guest chair. "You okay, Dad?"

She wasn't usually so gentle.

"I'm fine."

Her lips drew into a thin line. She shook her head. "I still can't believe what that woman did to you."

Parker raised a hand. "Please, Gen. I don't want to talk about it."

"And on your anniversary."

"It was the day before the anniversary," he corrected.

"I know that. It was the day Joan and Coco and I worked our butts off to throw you and her a nice party to celebrate." Her voice dripped with bitterness.

Parker rubbed his temple again. He'd hated disappointing her and he'd especially hated disappointing Joan Fanuzzi, who'd been a loyal friend to both Miranda and himself. He'd called her personally to apologize that day. Joan had not heard from Miranda.

He appreciated his daughter's feelings but he didn't want the drama right now. "How's our bottom line for the quarter looking so far?"

She gave him a smirk at the change of subject but her demeanor instantly turned professional. "Good. Collections are at an all time high. As are worker's comp cases."

"Excellent." The Agency was in good shape. It could run without him. Good to know.

"Do you want me to ask Judd to come in here for the meeting?"

Parker shook his head. "No. I'll join you in the board room."

He got to his feet.

Gen rose and moved to the door. Then she turned back to study him.

"What is it?" He hoped he looked presentable, though he felt like the grease on the pavement under a leaky vehicle.

She folded her arms. "I know you might not like this idea and you can say no, if you want."

He sat on the edge of his desk and frowned. "What idea?"

"What if I hook you up with someone?"

"Hook me up? You mean a date?"

"That's exactly what I mean. I have some friends in town. I know someone who's really nice. You could go out, have some drinks."

Parker scanned his internal list of social contacts and wondered who Gen had in mind. He was about to say no. Then he changed his mind.

Why not go out on a date? It wasn't a lifetime commitment after all. He was single now, or would be soon. Why not enjoy some female companionship? Why not pick up where he'd been when Miranda came into his life?

He could find his own date, but why not let his daughter pick someone out for him? Let her feel she was helping him, though he didn't need it.

"That sounds like a good idea."

She flinched in surprise. "Really? I thought you'd balk at the idea."

"Not in the mood to balk this afternoon."

"Well," she grinned. "Good for you, Dad. I'll get started right after this meeting." She turned and scampered down the hall.

As Parker started to follow her, he realized Miranda's phone was still in his hand. He paused to stare down at it.

Gen was right. He needed to start a new life.

He would not take Miranda back. He would not make himself vulnerable to this kind of pain again. She wasn't made for long term commitment. He should have listened when she told him that. And maybe he wasn't looking for that kind of relationship any more, either.

No, he would not take her back. But he would find whoever had texted her and teach her a lesson.

Gen's voice rang out from the hall. "Dad? Are you coming?"

For the first time in weeks Parker smiled. "Yes, Gen. I'm coming."

He put the phone into his pocket and followed his daughter to the conference room.

CHAPTER FOUR

"You want to hire me?" Miranda stared up at the expensively dressed Hispanic drug lord hovering over her cheap thrift store desk and rued the night she'd met him and his fancy streetfighter motorcycle. "What for?"

Did he want her to investigate a rival gang? Keep the cops away from some drug deal that was going down? Or maybe he thought *his* girlfriend was cheating on him.

He straightened as if satisfied she was finally taking him seriously. "One of my dancers is missing."

"Dancers?"

"May I?" without waiting for her to answer Santiago settled into her only guest chair—a padded polyurethane deal with a steel tube frame that looked cheap but had cost her fifty bucks. He positioned his elbows on the armrests and steepled his fingers. "I own a nightclub off Piedmont Road. I employ dancers. One of them is missing. I want you to find her."

Miranda blinked and let out the breath she'd been holding, feeling it singe her lungs. "A dancer? At a nightclub?" She could just imagine what kind of joint that was.

"A gentleman's club," he said smoothly in his low, rich accent.

Slowly she nodded, his words sinking in. "A strip club."

Santiago made a face and shook his head. "That is such a crass term. We are a high end establishment."

Okay, so it was a high end strip club. No doubt with high end strippers. And one of them was missing.

"I need to find her. I have top dollar customers asking for her. They want her back."

So it was the money that made him so concerned about this dancer.

"Have you gone to the police?"

The gangster just stared at her with his coal black eyes.

Bad joke.

This club was only one of Santiago's many businesses. A semi-legitimate one, but God only knew what illegitimate activities went on under its roof. Uncomfortable, Miranda shifted her weight in her chair. She wasn't going to look for a gangster's missing stripper. That was no way to start a detective business.

"Uh, can't your customers get those 'services' from," she waved a hand in the air, "someone else at your club?"

Catching her drift, Santiago scowled darkly. "The customers adore her dancing and are willing to pay to see it. The 'services' you are referring to are not offered in my establishment."

Yeah, and the Easter Bunny left chocolate eggs under her pillow every spring. But that wasn't getting this guy out of her office.

She decided to humor him before kicking him out. "When was the last time you saw your dancer?" There was a reason the police waited forty-eight hours before declaring someone missing. People usually showed up during that time.

"This past Thursday. We had a special show for some local sports figures. I stopped by to make sure things were going well."

"And did you see her then?"

He nodded. "I watched her perform. She was excellent."

Took her clothes off in an extra special way that night? "Have you seen her since?"

"No one has. She did not come to work the next day."

"I see." Okay, it was now Monday so that was almost twice the requisite forty-eight hours. Miranda shrugged. "Maybe she decided to quit and didn't bother to give notice." Maybe she was trying to get out of having to take her clothes off in front of horny men.

"Most girls do not quit. Someone like Nitro would not quit."

"Nitro?"

"That is her stage name. We call her that because when she steps on the stage, it is as if an atomic bomb went off." He made an explosion gesture with his hands, grinning greedily, his tooth diamond flashing.

She just bet. "So…why do you think this…uh, Nitro wouldn't quit?"

"For one thing, I pay very well. For another she enjoyed her work. It was a creative outlet for her."

Spoken like a true man. "What's Nitro's real name?"

He thought a moment. "Hannah, I believe."

"Last name?"

He lifted a shoulder. "I do not recall."

So a young girl goes missing from a club and the owner—who can't recall her last name—wants her back. Did something bad happen to her? More likely she was hiding—from him. Miranda didn't want to work for a notorious drug lord who dabbled in what she thought this was. Especially not if he wanted to drag the girl back into a life she was trying to escape from.

She let out a calculated sigh. "I don't know Carlos."

Thick dark brows drew together in a menacing look. "You do not know what, Miranda?"

"Whether I can take your case. I'm pretty busy right now." She gestured around the room.

Santiago wasn't stupid. He could see the office was empty, as was her desk. His lips curled up in a sensuous smile. "You will take my case, Miranda," he said in that sultry, demanding voice, trilling the r in her name again.

Then he reached into a pocket.

She jumped, heart pounding. Was he going to pull a gun on her? But, no. Instead he drew out a fat stack of bills.

Without counting them he laid them on the desk before her.

Miranda gulped, stared at the wad of money. It was all hundreds. It must have been at least three thousand dollars.

The gangster patted the stack as if it were a pet. "Let us call this your retainer. There will be twice that much when you find Nitro."

Feeling dizzy she put a hand to her head. Six thousand dollars? Carlos Santiago was offering her *six thousand dollars* to find a missing dancer? This Nitro must really be something.

Her mind started to race. Six thousand dollars would give her time to get her business started. Six thousand dollars would allow her to advertise better. Six thousand dollars would give her some breathing room. She wouldn't have to take a side job.

But she couldn't take money from a man like Santiago. Didn't want to take it.

She opened her mouth to say no thanks, then stopped.

On the other hand, what if Nitro was in trouble? What if she really was hiding from him? What if she were holed up somewhere in the city, scared to death Santiago was going to find her and teach her a lesson for leaving him.

If Miranda got to her first she could help the girl get away.

So far, Santiago hadn't been very forthcoming. He didn't even know her last name. How was she supposed to work with that? She needed more information.

"Is there anyone who can give me more details about this girl? Maybe a picture of her?"

He nodded. "Yolanda. She manages the club."

"Any way I can talk to her?"

He glanced at the heavy classic Rolex on his wrist. "We do not open until seven, but she is there now. Shall I drive you?"

She'd been hoping for a phone call, but it would be good to check this place of his out. "I'll follow you."

Santiago rose and made a gesture toward the cash on her desk. "And so you will take my case?"

Miranda picked up the bills, stuffed them in the bottom drawer and took out her Beretta. She locked the drawer, slipped the gun in her waistband behind her back and under her jacket.

Then she turned to Santiago with a smile. "I'll let you know after I talk to Yolanda."

CHAPTER FIVE

She followed Santiago and his driver in his shiny black BMW up Piedmont, past the billboards and the auto repair shops and the strip malls. Suddenly Miranda's stomach took a hard dip. They'd just rolled under the I-85 bridge.

She glanced at her new Acura's GPS map.

Sure enough, the Imperial Building was just three miles north. She was right in the neck of the woods of the Parker Agency. Less than two miles from the Parker mansion.

She was on the doorstep of her old life.

Was it some kind of cosmic joke that her first case would be here? Her first paying case, anyway. Not only would she be working for a notorious criminal, but she'd be doing it in the shadow of the Parker Agency.

The idea made her bristle.

It didn't matter, she told herself, jutting out her jaw. Business was business and she was here to do a job. Parker wasn't the type for strip clubs anyway. He'd never know.

They turned down a side street, cruised past a strip mall with a pawn shop, a tattoo parlor and an all-night diner, then made another turn.

On the side of the building a sign in fancy lettering read *Exótico* with an arrow pointing toward a door in the back.

Miranda rolled her car over the gravel parking lot, turned it off and got out.

Santiago shot her a follow-me look and headed for the side door. Shielding her eyes from the blaze of the late August Georgia sun, she followed him inside.

She stepped through a small space where IDs were no doubt checked during business hours, and then into the huge open space that was *Exótico*.

The air was winter cool and smelled of rose water and breath mints. The walls were painted solid black, giving the place a theater like feel. Along one side ran a row of windows where DJs and lighting crew worked their magic. At the opposite end sat a wide stage hung with a black curtain, where the dancers worked theirs.

The audience area was a study in sensual indulgence.

Long tufted divans of pink satin were bathed in lights flickering azure and rose. Wait staff scampered about busily decking oval shaped tables with flowers and sparkling glasses and silver decanters for champagne or other libation. There were menus, too, and she bet the food here was terrific. Miranda noted the tables looked sturdy and could be easily cleared for the dancer who wanted to give those seated around it a private show.

This place must really be something when it was filled with horny sports figures and businessmen, with the music and lights going. And, of course, the action on the stage. A perfect setting for modern hedonistic revelry.

"Yolanda is in the back," Santiago said and led her behind a row of divans to a door at the side of the stage.

On the other side of the door was a short hall, then a dressing area. An expansive row of large mirrors ran along the wall, counters beneath it were littered with lipsticks, powders, eye makeup, and several wigs mounted on Styrofoam heads. Mounds of fake jewelry lay scattered here and there. At the edge of the counters stood a rack of glittery costumes with lots of fishnet and feathers. Headdresses, outrageous high-heels, g straps, leotards.

Everything a girl might need for the show.

Maybe she was a prude, but Miranda couldn't understand how someone could put on one of those getups—much less take it off—for money. But maybe she'd been lucky she'd never been so desperate.

Up ahead Santiago came to a stop at a closed black door and gave it a sharp knock. "Yolanda?"

"Come in. I am decent." The comment sounded like impatient sarcasm.

He opened the door and gestured for Miranda to follow him.

She stepped into a small space that was only a little bigger than her new office. The walls were done in bamboo, giving the place an Asian prison camp feel. Another rack of costumes and a sewing machine stood along the back and made the space seem even smaller.

A thin, dark haired woman sat behind a stingy desk piled with papers, working on a laptop that was squeezed between the stacks. Paperwork and sewing? The woman must be a Jill-of-all-trades.

Her lifeless hair was teased and its texture said it had been dyed often before it had been left to go gray at the sides. Her skin had a sallow tone that might have once been olive. She wore a sleeveless black tank top that revealed the tight sinews of a scrawny neck. A gold chain hung around it, and a rose tattoo decorated one shoulder. Her eyes sagged with the weariness of a beaten dog and a cigarette hung from the side of her plum colored mouth. In the forest of paper on the desk, Miranda spotted an ashtray filled with lipstick-imprinted butts.

The woman looked like the definition of overworked.

"Yolanda, this is Miranda Steele," Santiago announced.

Yolanda looked up at him with her sunken eyes, then slid them toward Miranda. "So?"

"Ms. Steele is a private investigator. She is here to help us find Nitro." Miranda extended a hand.

Yolanda's hand was dead fish limp and felt just a bit greasy during a quick shake.

Then she took the cigarette out of her mouth, blew smoke up toward the ceiling with a curled lip and leaned back in her chair. "This is your PI?" Her voice was smoke hoarse and tinged with the expected Spanish accent.

So they must have discussed her.

"Yes, this is she. She has questions. Answer them."

Yolanda narrowed her eyes at her boss. Santiago wasn't the type of man you argue with, but Miranda had a feeling this woman had gone a few rounds with him in the past.

She flicked ashes into her tray. "What do you want to know?"

At last the woman had deigned to speak to her. "Let's start with a name," Miranda said, trying not to cough from the smoke. "First and last, preferably."

"Hannah Elizabeth Kaye. She's a student at Georgia Technical Institute."

Say what? Miranda knew some college girls took questionable jobs, but Georgia Tech? "Why would a Georgia Tech student work here?"

She'd been about to say in a dump like this, but caught herself in the nick of time. It wasn't a dump, after all. Just sleazy in another way.

"She needs the money. A lot of college girls do. And the boss here pays them well."

"Very well," Santiago added. "I also offer health insurance and a 401(k)."

Jeez. "But you must have a big turnover, right?"

Santiago scowled. "What do you mean, Miranda?" He was feeling insulted.

She tried to sound diplomatic. "Well, if your dancers are going to school, don't they leave after they graduate?"

"Most do," Yolanda said. "Some stay on with us. Dolly Winston, for example. She has been with us the longest. She graduated from Georgia Tech. An Astrophysics major, as I recall."

"And she decided to...dance instead?"

"It is good money. And with the economy the way it is now, many of them cannot find lucrative employment elsewhere. When was the last time you saw an ad for an astrophysicist?"

Yolanda laughed a hoarse, throaty laugh and Santiago joined in with his deep scary one.

A girl's gotta do what a girl's gotta do—and so you flush your self respect down the toilet along with your diploma. But she wasn't here to judge.

Santiago turned to her. "Well, Ms. Steele, have you heard enough? Are you going to take my case?"

Miranda hesitated a moment. "How can you be sure Nitro, or Hannah, didn't just get tired of working here and quit?"

Again Santiago chuckled while Yolanda grinned.

"No one quits that way, Ms. Steele," Yolanda said, reaching for her cigarette and taking another drag.

What the heck did that mean?

Santiago looked at her as if he were sorry she didn't understand. "As I said I pay too well. Now. The case?"

Miranda wasn't convinced Hannah wasn't in hiding somewhere. But if these two were right, and she didn't want to get away from her job, she could be in another kind of trouble. No doubt the bouncers here were good protection for the staff, but some drunken customer could have snatched her when she left the building after the show. She might be a prisoner in some weirdo's apartment somewhere.

And the money from Santiago was back in her office burning a hole in her drawer. Like he said, he paid well.

She didn't want to make a habit of working with someone like Santiago, but this time, she decided to make an exception. Now that she'd heard this much, Miranda knew she had to make sure this Hannah Kaye was all right. Might as well get paid for it.

She held out her hand to Santiago. "Okay, Carlos. I'll take the case."

He smiled in that unnerving way of his, his tooth diamond flashing. Miranda hoped she hadn't just made the biggest mistake of her life.

"I am very pleased, Miranda. You will keep me informed of your progress?"

"Of course. Right now, I have some more questions for Yolanda."

"Then I will leave you two ladies to yourselves. Let me know if you need anything."

"Will do."

He turned to go out the door.

But as she watched him saunter away in his skintight leather pants, the heels of his flashy shoes clicking against the floor, the sinking feeling in her gut only deepened.

CHAPTER SIX

"What do you want to know, Ms. Steele?" Yolanda asked, ribbons of smoke circling her head. "I have work to do."

And so did she. Now. "Do you have a number for Hannah?" Miranda decided she'd call the dancer/college student by her real name.

"A cell number. I have called it several times since Thursday. No answer."

"Let me have it."

Yolanda rattled off the digits and Miranda recorded them in her phone. For good measure, she dialed it herself and likewise got a mechanical recording. Okay, so that much was confirmed.

"Tell me when you last saw her."

"Thursday night when she showed up for the show." Yolanda stubbed out her cigarette in her tray and lit a new one. She seemed thoroughly annoyed with Miranda's third degree.

Miranda ignored the attitude. "Details. The very last time you saw her. Walking out the door?"

Yolanda took a long drag of her fresh cigarette, if you can call a cigarette fresh, and shook her head. "I didn't stay late that night. My niece needed help with her daughter. Her husband is in the hospital. I helped Nitro into her costume, saw her on stage and left for the evening."

So Yolanda's duties included herding the girls. "When did you realize she was missing?"

Yolanda lifted a skinny shoulder. "The next evening when she didn't show up for work. The girls get here around seven-thirty or eight. The first show starts at nine."

Good to know. It was the start of a timeframe, anyway. "Was Hannah usually late?"

"Never. She always got here early. She loved her work. She was really very good."

Punctual, loves her work. Either Yolanda was blowing some of that cigarette smoke up her ass or Hannah could really be in trouble. "Do you have any pictures of her?"

"I have a video. We were about to put it up on the website for promotion." She gestured toward her computer.

Santiago had a website for his club? Bet it got a lot of hits. "Let me see it."

Looking as if she wished Miranda would leave, instead Yolanda beckoned with her hand. "Come around here and grab a seat."

Miranda squeezed between the desk and the wall, pulled the sewing machine chair over to the desk. She checked the cushion to make sure there were no stick pins in it before sitting down.

When she looked up Yolanda already had the video up on her screen.

Miranda leaned forward as she hit Play.

Funky music with a sassy beat bounced through the speakers as a young woman pranced around a pole in a white sequined outfit decked with long fringe that swung out wide as she twirled. She had long blond hair. She swayed it along with the fringe in time to the music while flashing a gorgeous smile. Great figure. Lots of energy. Long legs. And super high heels that accented every well formed muscle of her calves and thighs.

"Our specialty used to be the classics," Yolanda explained. "Fan dances and balloon dances inspired by Sally Rand. But today everyone wants rock. Especially Nitro. She wanted the hard driving rhythms. Part of her image. It went over well with the customers, so I let her do it."

As if to demonstrate, the drumbeat from the speakers kicked into overdrive, and the girl on the screen began to gyrate as she peeled off her fringed top.

"Santiago mentioned she had a way with an audience."

Yolanda nodded. "They all love her. She was a real draw. That is why Carlos wants her back."

"Can you crop me out a still of her face I can put in my phone?" Miranda couldn't imagine showing this vid to passerbys on the street and asking if they'd seen her.

"If that is what you need." Yolanda stuck the cigarette in her mouth and went to work.

When she paused the frame, Miranda's heart stopped.

The young dancer with her pretty face, her long blond hair, her vivacious smile, suddenly took her back to her last case. The one she'd worked in Chicago with Parker three weeks ago. Though actually, she'd mostly worked it without him.

Hannah Kaye's image reminded Miranda of the victim in that case, Lydia Sutherland.

A young blond art student who had been murdered in her home in Lawnfield Heights. The murder had been covered up by a house fire that had left Lydia's body burnt to a char. And the killer had been none other than Miranda's psychopathic ex-husband.

The memory of that case still gave her chills. All Miranda had known of Lydia Sutherland was a photo of her with her long blond hair and eager-for-life smile.

A lot like Nitro's.

She hoped Hannah Kaye would not end up that way. Or anything like it. She hoped she'd run off with a boyfriend to get married or something.

"That good?" Yolanda said through her cigarette.

"Perfect," Miranda told her.

"Let me have your cell number."

Miranda gave it to her and the woman cropped the photo, converted it to a file and sent it to her phone. Yolanda was handy.

Miranda checked the screen. "Got it." She stood. "Do you have an address for her?"

Yolanda punched a few keys on her keyboard and brought up Hannah's employee record. Miranda scanned it, didn't see anything out of the ordinary.

"I'll print this out for you." Yolanda clicked her mouse.

"Thanks."

The printer whirred and soon Miranda had all the data she needed. The general stuff anyway. "I'll head to the school and see what I can find there. But I'd like to come back tonight and talk to some of the other dancers. Somebody might have seen something."

"I've already questioned them twice, but if you feel the need. You are the detective."

Miranda had a feeling Yolanda thought Santiago was wasting his money. She was going to prove her wrong.

"See you tonight then." Miranda folded the paper in her hand and headed out.

"Just tell the doorman you know me."

"Will do. Thanks for your help."

"My pleasure." Yolanda's smile was thin and unconvincing.

Knowing the woman was lying through her smoke stained teeth, Miranda turned and found her way out of the building and back into the sun.

CHAPTER SEVEN

She hit rush hour traffic, which wasn't so bad since she was heading south on the expressway, but it still took her over thirty minutes to make the five mile trek over to the Tech campus.

During the drive she checked out Hannah Kaye on social media. The last entry had been two months ago. She had a busy life.

Miranda's navigation system ended when she reached the Registration building so she drove around through the shady lanes of the grounds a good while, hunting for the right facility in the endless rows of boxy red brick buildings situated every which way in the name of design. She went to the East Campus and was told she should be on the West Campus. She overshot her turn and ended up near a golf course. She made another wrong turn and nearly ended up on the freeway.

When she'd finally located the hall where Hannah Kaye lived she decided she was far too dependent on GPS. She needed to retune her sense of direction.

The parking deck was expensive and crowded so she had to drive around some more to find a spot on the street—and still ended up having to stuff quarters in a meter. No wonder it cost so much to go to college.

At last she got her bearings. A pass card was required at the gate so she pretended she'd forgotten it and waited for a group of students to stroll by. She followed them in. Acting as if she belonged here, she began to make her way over the curvy walkway.

It was still in the low nineties, typical for the early fall in Atlanta, and humid. She could feel the sweat beading up on her back, staining her good blouse under her suit jacket. Just what she needed. Another cleaning bill. She hadn't intended on spending the money from Santiago on that.

She was probably overdressed for campus, but she hadn't had time to change. Maybe the students would think she was a professor. Hah.

As a rule Miranda didn't care much for institutions of higher learning. All those teachers and textbooks and tests made her skin crawl. Not that she didn't have something of an education herself. She'd attended college here and there around the country in her wanderings, mostly community colleges with practical studies like carpentry or welding. But she'd never stuck with any program.

In her whole life the only thing she'd ever stuck with was detective work.

Actually she hadn't been to a college campus since she'd gone to Cambridge with Parker a couple months ago on a case. She recalled driving through the ancient cobblestone streets of the university while Parker sat behind the right-sided steering wheel, giving her an overview of the famous school's history.

The image of him came back to her. His low, aristocratic Southern voice, the gleam in his gray eyes, his sexy smile. It made her heart stutter.

London. Where they'd promised not to lie to each other. That had worked out well, hadn't it?

She recalled saving his butt on that case. She'd done that a few times. Yet he couldn't believe she could take care of herself. They had been so good together. Why did he want to throw it all away?

She shook off the depressing thoughts of Parker as she reached the old red brick apartment building she'd been looking for.

This wasn't London. This was Georgia. And right now, she was on a campus filled with brainy nerds working her first solo case. She didn't need memories of Parker messing her up.

Hoping she would blend in enough to look like a resident she started up the steps. She found the number on the employee sheet Yolanda had given her on the third floor.

She knocked on the door. And waited.

She knocked again. And waited some more.

She was wondering if it was too late to check the dean of student's office when she heard the sound of flip-flops coming up the stairs.

Soon a young woman appeared carrying an overloaded basket of laundry. She had on short-short jeans and a yellow T-shirt with what looked like the school's logo on the front, though it was hard to see behind the clothes. Her hair was short and black, and a pair of dark tortoise shell glasses was perched on her nose. She was so engrossed in whatever she was reading on her cell phone, she nearly bumped into Miranda.

"Oh, excuse me," she said blinking as if coming out of a dream. Then she frowned at her, realizing the stranger was standing at her door. "Do I know you?"

"Probably not," Miranda said. "I'm here looking for Hannah Kaye."

"She isn't here." She looked down at her cell again.

Obviously. "But she lives here, right?" Miranda gestured toward the door. "Are you her roommate?"

The young woman tore her gaze from her cell and eyed Miranda up and down as if her photo had been on the news last night. "Why do you want to know that?"

So much for blending in. The truth would be quicker. "I'm a private investigator. My name is Miranda Steele. Hannah's employer is concerned about her."

The young woman's nose wrinkled as if she'd just peeled an onion. "You mean that strip club owner?"

"Does she have another employer?"

Bewildered at the question the young woman shook her head. "No. Did he hire you or something?"

"Something like that. Do you know where Hannah is?"

The woman stared at Miranda a long moment before deciding to answer. "She hasn't been home since Thursday. I thought she might have crashed at Marty's place."

"Marty?"

"Her boyfriend."

There was a boyfriend? And the roommate hadn't seen her since Thursday either? This was getting interesting. And this visit was going to take some time.

Miranda nodded toward the door. "Okay if we go inside and talk?"

Again the woman blinked at her, no doubt mentally reviewing the nightly news stories she'd recently heard.

Miranda dug her investigator's ID out of her pocket and held it up.

The woman studied it, still looking uncertain. But at last she opted for youthful trust. "Yeah, sure. Give me a minute."

Miranda decided to be neighborly and held the laundry basket while the roommate got out her key and opened the door.

After a bit more fumbling and cell phone juggling, Miranda followed her inside the student living area.

It was what you'd expect of a place where busy college girls lived. A faint smell of stale coffee and trash that needed to be emptied in the air. A cozy light colored kitchen nook with a counter overlooking a living room, a plain gray sofa facing a window overlooking the campus. Décor was sparse. A Tech poster on one wall, another of some frenzied rock star smashing his expensive guitar on the opposite side.

Clothes and books and papers were strewn everywhere. A laptop stood open on the far arm of the couch.

Miranda's new hostess put the laundry basket down in a corner, grabbed the laptop and began shifting books and clothes. "Find a seat. Sorry it's so messy."

Miranda eased herself onto the spot she'd just cleared on the couch. "What's your name?"

"Bonnie," she said reaching for an empty fast food cup and a matching bag of trash on the coffee table. "Bonnie Pinksy."

"And you're studying…" Miranda tilted her head to read the title of a textbook on the table.

Bonnie picked up the book and closed it. "Discrete Mathematics. I'm in my third year. So far, it's a bitch."

"I can imagine." Miranda smiled, trying to put her hostess at ease. "I don't know what numbers have to be discreet about. The secrets of the universe maybe?"

Bonnie only frowned.

So much for friendly banter. "What's your roommate studying?"

"Hannah's in the COA—the College of Architecture. She's a junior, too. We've roomed together since our first term. We're a good match. I'm the quiet one, she's the talky one."

"Talky?"

"You know. She never met a stranger? She'll talk to anybody."

Overly friendly. Not a promising trait in this situation. "How long has she worked at *Exótico*?"

At the mention of the night club Bonnie wrinkled her nose again. She dropped a stack of books on the floor and plopped into the chair across from the couch, her thin body not taking up half of it. She sat knees together, flip flop clad feet apart as she straightened her T-shirt over her stomach.

"She started this summer. We both signed up for summer session, hoping it would get us into grad school sooner. Hannah's dream is to build hospitals for the underprivileged. She said she needed extra cash for tuition and the job paid really well." Bonnie sat forward and pointed to herself. "She wanted me to do it, too, but I said 'no way.'"

Smart move.

Bonnie rolled her eyes. "I've got too much to do with my assignments and labs. I've got two classes with the hardest professors on campus and the workload is killing me. I don't know how Hannah keeps up."

So the shy Discrete Math major, who seemed pretty talkative to her, was too busy to notice her roommate might be missing? But Bonnie seemed too genuine to be involved.

"Where's Hannah from?" Miranda asked.

"Her parents are from Gainesville. She thought about living at home her first year but the drive is too far."

Gainesville was about fifty miles north of here. That would be a heck of trip every day. But maybe the girl had gotten homesick. "Do you think she went home to see her folks?"

Bonnie pushed her glasses up her nose as she considered that idea. "Maybe. The last I saw her was Thursday morning. I was rushing out the door on my way to my Abstract Vector Spaces class. God, I hate that professor. He makes you stand in front of everyone and apologize if you're late."

"What a hardass," Miranda agreed. "What time was that?"

"Uh, let's see." She glanced at her cell to prompt her. "That class starts at nine, so probably at least eight forty-five."

"In the morning?"

"Yeah."

"And you didn't see her at all again that day?"

"We usually don't run into each other until the evening. Sometimes we go to dinner or study together. But not always. And not Thursdays through Saturdays. That's when Hannah works at the club."

And Miranda had already confirmed the dancer/student had been at work that night. "Did Hannah say anything Thursday morning? Mention any plans she had for going away?"

Again Bonnie considered the question, frowning as if she were solving one of her math problems. Finally she blew out a breath that made her dark bangs fly up. "Not that I can recall. Do you think she's in trouble?"

Miranda kept her features still. "I haven't determined that."

She shuddered at how much those words sounded like Parker. But he was the one who'd taught her not to alarm people when you're questioning them.

What was she thinking of him now for? Maybe because he'd been with her on so many interviews.

She shook off the thought of him and continued. "And you didn't see Hannah Thursday night when she came home?"

"No. She hasn't been back here as far as I know."

"You said Hannah has a boyfriend?"

Bonnie nodded. "Marty Jenkins. He's a second year student in EE. Electrical Engineering."

"Second year?"

"Sophomore. He's a year younger than Hannah. She's twenty, he's nineteen." She did a back-and-forth gesture with her hand.

Twenty and nineteen? Lydia Sutherland, the victim in her last case, was twenty and the young man she was supposed to be in love with was nineteen. She'd been a college student, too. The pair had both been art students. During most of her investigation Miranda had suspected the lover of killing her.

Bonnie popped up from her chair. "Oh, I've got a picture of them." She pranced into the kitchenette and returned a moment later with a photo in her hand. "Hannah kept this on the fridge. It was taken last year. A couple of weeks after I introduced them."

Miranda took the picture and studied it.

Hannah with her long blond hair, blue eyes, and winning smile cheek-to-cheek with a guy dressed in a white band uniform holding a clarinet. He had a head of thick, curly dark hair half covering a narrow face, a pencil mustache and an overly long nose. The guy was no bodybuilder. Like Bonnie, he was skinny as a rail and his features screamed "nerd." An odd match for a beauty like Hannah, but maybe she was attracted to his brain.

"What's with the getup?" Miranda asked.

"Oh, Marty's in the marching band. He plays at the games. You know?" She pumped a limp fist in the air. "Go Yellow Jackets?"

She'd heard of them. The rivalry between the Georgia Tech Yellow Jackets and the University of Georgia Bulldogs was not something you could miss around Atlanta.

"You said you introduced them?"

Bonnie nodded. "Marty was in some of my classes and he seemed like a nice guy so I hooked him up with Hannah. They went out and hit it off right away."

"Did Marty ever go to see Hannah perform?"

"At that club? Yeah, I think so. Once or twice. But he's really busy. He wants to graduate early, too. His dream is to design medical machinery and he can't wait to get started. His father's a surgeon in Boston and he's got some good contacts. I think that's what attracted Hannah to him. You know? Building hospitals and designing medical machinery?"

A match made in heaven. "Where can I find this guy?"

Behind her glasses Bonnie's dark eyes grew round. "Marty? I don't know. I don't have his schedule." She rubbed her nose. "Maybe he's at band practice? I think there's one tonight."

"And where would that be?"

"The Burger Bowl."

"Burger Bowl?"

"It's right over there." She pointed out the window toward the campus. "Just this side of the CRC—the Recreation Center. You can't miss it. Just follow the band music. If he's not there he might be in the library. Or…I don't know. He lives off campus. Around Atlantic, I think."

That narrowed it down. "Do you have his cell number?"

"No. Hannah never gave it to me."

The carelessness of college life. When Mackenzie went off to school, Miranda was going to insist she send her a list of phone numbers and addresses for everyone she met. Especially males.

Miranda got to her feet. She had her work cut out for her hunting this guy down on a campus of over twenty thousand students.

She held up the photo. "Mind if I keep this?"

"No. I guess Hannah wouldn't mind." Bonnie stood and rubbed her arms. "She's all right, isn't she?"

"Let's hope so."

But as Miranda let herself out and headed back down the steps, she had a feeling things hadn't gone so well lately for the explosive Nitro.

CHAPTER EIGHT

Bonnie had been right about the band music.

Miranda followed the sound of thumping drums and blaring horns down the stairs to the sidewalk, past two more blocks of red brick buildings to an open meadow.

She made her way under the leafy foliage of maple trees, slipped between two cement planters, and came to halt on a paved spot at the end of the field. Shielding her eyes from the late afternoon sun, she took in the sight.

A mass of students dressed not in uniform but in casual clothes marched briskly around the field in time to some rah-rah football fight song they were playing. Trumpets, cymbals, drums, tubas, and piccolos rang out in a staccato rhythm.

Boom, boom, boom, boom. Turn left. Turn right. March this way. March that way.

Instruments held high, they split in two and formed two perfect circles. Miranda bet the band members were calculating the circumference of the circles in their heads. They marched in place for a few bars then some of them started moving backwards, some sideways until they ended up in a formation spelling out "Tech."

They were really good and it was fascinating to watch them. But how in the heck was she going to pick out Hannah Kaye's boyfriend in this throng of seventy-six trombones? There must have been a hundred students on the field.

Suddenly the music stopped and everyone raised a fist in the air. "Fight! Fight! Fight!"

At the other end of the field someone who must have been the band leader said some congratulatory words Miranda couldn't hear.

And it was over.

The students morphed back into the general melee and everyone began heading in a different direction.

Miranda glared down at the photo in her hand and scrutinized the students passing her. No one was a match. Damn. If she missed this guy, how the heck was she going to find him?

Suddenly she heard nerdy male laughter behind her.

"Hey, Marty. You going to the pool tonight?"

Marty? She spun around and saw two guys near some wooden bleachers packing up their instruments. The one on the right was a husky blond guy. The one on the left was a tall skinny dude with a pencil mustache and thick dark shoulder length hair. He had a clarinet.

Bingo.

"Me?" the skinny dude said to his buddy. "Naw. I've got a big Digital Processing exam tomorrow."

They picked up their cases and began moving out.

Miranda glanced down at the photo in her hand. Yep. That was the boyfriend, all right. She followed them as they headed toward the sidewalk and out to the street.

The buddy swung his arm over the kid named Marty's shoulder. "Come on, man. A guy's got to take a break once in awhile. Besides, you have time now. You got rid of that architect major bitch, didn't you?"

Marty uttered a nerdy snort. "Oh, yeah. I got rid of her, all right."

Got rid of her?

Miranda's ears started to burn. Chills broke out on her arms despite the ninety degree heat. But there was just enough sarcasm in the kid's tone to make her wonder what he meant.

Marty pulled out from under his friend's embrace. "C'mon Swanson. I'm a serious student."

The dude acted stunned. "Hey, me, too. But you know what they say about all work and no play."

"Forget it. I've got to ace this test."

"Okay." Swanson held up his cell. "But if you change your mind, text me."

"Sure, sure." Half ignoring his friend, Marty turned in the opposite direction and began shuffling across the pavement, head down, glancing up only momentarily to check traffic.

Miranda followed him across the street, down a long set of concrete steps to another sidewalk.

She stayed back, pretended to check her cell once in awhile so she looked like a student to the passels of kids who passed by in both directions. No one stopped her or asked what she was doing there.

But after a few minutes, she spotted Marty unlocking a white Civic. He shoved his backpack and clarinet case into the passenger seat and got inside.

The engine turned over.

Miranda's mind raced. Her own car was way back behind the apartment buildings, blocks away. She couldn't get to it in time to follow him. But he'd have to drive slowly on campus with all the students roaming around.

Maybe she could follow him on foot.

He pulled out into traffic, slowed for three female students crossing in front of him, then took off again.

Miranda hustled along the sidewalk. Brushing past laughing young men and women heading home after a long day of classes, she tried to look inconspicuous.

She kept up with the car until Marty reached the corner. He put on his blinker and turned left in front of her. Then he sped up. She started to run. The Civic moved faster. Had to be going about thirty now. This wasn't going to work. What had she been thinking?

As fast as she could, she stopped short, lifted her cell and zoomed in on the back of the car with her camera. She snapped the photo just before he made a turn onto the highway and cruised away.

She checked the photo. It was blurry, a little hard to read, but she could make out the letters of the license plate. It would have to do for now.

She turned around, saw several students watching her. One of the young men looked like he was about to ask for her ID.

Shoving the phone in her pocket she gave them a what's-it-to-you? look, got her bearings, and headed back to her car.

It was too early to go back to *Exótico*, she decided as she pulled out of her parking spot. She'd stop at the office first. She needed her laptop and to figure out what to do with that wad of cash from Santiago. Plus she had to see what she could do with Marty Jenkins' tag number. It was going to be a long night.

As worried as she was starting to feel about Hannah Kaye, the idea of working late gave her a little thrill.

CHAPTER NINE

It was about an hour before sunset when Miranda got back to her office, and rowdy looking dudes were already gathering on the street corner across from the former *Plato Caliente*.

Briskly she climbed the stairs to the second floor hallway and stepped inside her waiting room.

Her jaw dropped.

Standing across the room, hands on hips, studying the painting of the white cat licking its paw was Joan Fanuzzi.

"Reminds me of Wendy's cat, Inky. Except it's the opposite color." She turned around and gestured. "You know, you really ought to lock that door." Her Brooklyn accent echoed against the walls.

Her short, spunky frame was clad in a sleeveless apricot print blouse and sky blue Capri slacks. Her dark, shoulder length hair with its frosted highlights looked like it had recently been done. Over her shoulder she carried a big white straw purse that matched her summer sandals.

But her dark, scowling eyes and Italian featured face wore an expression that cut Miranda to the quick.

Not much here to steal, Miranda wanted to say. Instead she began to blubber with guilt. "Oh, God, Fanuzzi. I'm so sorry."

Fanuzzi shook her head at her. "You mean for ruining the anniversary party I planned for you?"

"What else?"

She put a finger to her cheek. "Let me think. Maybe for not calling me and telling me what was going on with you and Wade?"

Miranda winced.

In the year and a half since she'd come to Atlanta, Fanuzzi had become the best friend she'd ever had. She'd always reached out to her, always checked up on her. But Miranda had a bad habit of not returning the favor.

She gestured toward her office. "Let's go in here."

Without waiting for a reply, she crossed to the door—the one she did lock—and stuffed her key into it. "Come in and have a seat."

She didn't look back but Miranda heard the squeak of her friend's cork heeled sandals behind her. She hurried to the stand in the corner where she kept refreshments, wishing she had more than that cheap guest chair to offer her.

Fanuzzi settled into it, still giving her that eye of hers. Must be the one Brooklyn hit men gave to people who didn't pay up.

Miranda busied herself with the coffee pot. "How'd you find me, anyway?"

"I saw your Craigslist ad."

"Oh." Miranda hadn't realized she had a best friend who read Craigslist. She picked up a silver packet of grounds and gestured at the counter like a game show assistant. "See? I'm all set up. I even have a coffee maker. You want some?"

"Why not?"

Miranda emptied the grounds from the last pot into a nearby trashcan and opened the packet while she made a stab at small talk. "So what's up with you? How are the kids?"

Fanuzzi's dark Italian eyes narrowed. "You gonna tell me why you didn't call me?"

She finished with the pot and pressed the button. What was she supposed to say to that? Finally she raised her hands. "How could I? Your husband still works for the Parker Agency. You get a lot of your connections for your business from Parker."

Fanuzzi had a thriving catering business and many in Parker's ritzy circle had hired her for their fancy doings. She was an amazing cook.

"Don't you think I care more about you than about business?"

Miranda pursed her lips and turned her head away. The coffee machine was busy brewing away. She was on her own. She slunk over to her desk chair and sat down.

"I really am sorry about the party."

"Wade called me that morning. He apologized for both of you."

Miranda shuddered at the guilt washing over her like an ocean wave over a sinking life raft. Fanuzzi had been planning that party for weeks. Sending out invitations, picking out little paper favors and decorations—since paper was traditional for the first year, as she'd reminded her a dozen times. For the menu she'd planned to make some of her most delicious treats. She was even going to do the French croquembouche she'd learned to make in Paris.

Plus she was going to get Parker the gift Miranda hadn't had time to pick out.

Gift.

Miranda sat up. "What about the—?"

Fanuzzi held up a hand. "I got him a Rolex."

"A what?" That had to have cost a fortune.

"Couldn't think of anything else. I was going to have it engraved then decided that was going too far." She let out a sad little laugh. "Good thing I didn't. Took it back the next day so you don't owe me a thing."

Miranda couldn't have felt worse if her friend had dug out her heart with an ice cream scoop.

"I'm sorry," she whispered again.

Fanuzzi studied her for a long moment. "What the hell happened, Murray?" She said it with the softness of a mother. "You and Parker are made for each other."

Her words only made Miranda feel worse.

Made for each other. That's what she'd thought once. How could she explain it? Parker's paranoia about her had been there since they'd met. But it started in earnest after they began taking cases together as Parker and Steele Consulting this June. And then she'd started getting those crazy anonymous messages on her phone.

I know who you are.
I know where you are.
I know what you are.

They'd unnerved her, sure, but she'd trained herself a long time ago not to give in to fear. Not to be a wimp. Her mistake, she guessed, was in not telling Parker about them right away. But they'd just finished their first case together when the first text had come in and when she'd gotten the second one, Parker had been convalescing. She wasn't going to bother him over what might have been something trivial. Heck it was trivial. It was just a prank.

Nothing had come of those messages—except Parker's overreaction—which made him want to shut down Parker and Steele Consulting. Didn't he understand she couldn't live without this work? The work he'd introduced her to? Trained her for?

She glanced up at the pot. "Hey, coffee's done." Thank goodness.

She hopped up and returned to the corner. Picking up one of the mugs she'd gotten at the thrift store, she poured the hot brown liquid into it and handed it to her friend. "You get the sweet spot."

Taking it from her, Fanuzzi smirked. "This is cute."

"What?"

Fanuzzi pointed to the image on the cup. A tiny gray kitten asleep in a basket next to a big blue ball of yarn.

Feeling her face redden a tad, Miranda shrugged. "This set was the cheapest in the store."

"I see. Got any sugar?"

"Sure." She danced back over to the corner, fished out a packet from the drawer and handed it to her.

"Thanks." Fanuzzi opened the packet, dumped it into the kitten mug, and stirred the hot liquid with the plastic spoon Miranda handed her next.

Miranda steadied her shoulders as she got another mug—this one with two gray kittens stranded on the branch of a tree—and poured herself some brew.

She took it black.

Fanuzzi sipped her coffee. "So it was so bad between you and Wade that you can't even talk about it with your best friend."

Miranda sank down in her chair again, holding the mug with both hands. Confession time. "We had…a really bad fight. Worst we've ever had."

"There's always making up afterwards. Dave and I have had some doozies. I'm Italian, you know."

"Are you?" she teased, smiling sadly. It wasn't the same. "You know Parker can be very stubborn."

"Yeah, so what was he being so stubborn about?"

The question told Miranda Parker hadn't been telling tales out of school. That made her feel a little better. At least he had that much respect for what had been their relationship. Then again it meant he had no one to confide in. As she was about to do.

"He told me he's closing down Parker and Steele Consulting."

Fanuzzi's dark brows popped up in shock. "Your partnership?"

"Uh huh."

"Without even asking you?"

Miranda set down her mug, feeling the familiar anger rising inside her. "Probably wouldn't have told me until it was done if I hadn't pushed it out of him."

"Jeez, Murray. I never thought Wade could be such a hard ass. He's always been nice to me. Chivalrous, even."

"That's the thing. He thinks he is being chivalrous. He thinks the cases have gotten too dangerous. He's trying to save me like I'm a damn damsel in distress."

Fanuzzi had to smile at that idea. Then she grew thoughtful. "Things did get pretty hairy in Paris. If your other cases were like that—"

"It's part of the job. Part of what you have to do for a client. To settle the score, set things right, for justice and all that."

"Yeah," she took another sip of coffee. "And so you're going to prove him wrong with all this?" She gestured around the office.

"I'm doing my own thing with all this. This is my life. I don't care what Parker thinks of it."

"I see. Well, Dave says you ought to come back to the Agency. A lot of people there want you to come back."

That was a nice thought.

"Mackenzie does, too."

She hated the thought that her breakup with Parker had upset her daughter. She'd had enough turmoil in her life lately. That was the main reason Miranda hadn't contacted her.

"How is Mackenzie?"

"Fine. She's started classes at Old Ferncliff Academy now."

Miranda slid her cup onto her desk. Mackenzie was in high school now. She was missing out on her daughter's life.

"Is she speaking to Wendy yet?"

Miranda had thought Wendy Van Aarle was her missing daughter when she'd first come to Atlanta. Nothing had made her happier than when Wendy and her real daughter had become real friends—after a toxic relationship. Now they were mortal enemies. Kids.

"Not yet."

Miranda blew out a breath. "It's going on a month and a half."

"I know, but you know how teenagers are."

Fanuzzi had been at the Chatham mansion the night Mackenzie and Wendy had had a knock down drag out over a boy. That was the night Mackenzie revealed she'd been searching for her father. Her real father.

Actually, it had been Wendy who'd revealed the secret. Another reason Mackenzie was furious with her.

"Yeah, I guess so."

They were silent a moment, the coffee in the kitten mugs growing cold.

At last Fanuzzi leaned forward. "Murray, is there anything I can do?"

"You mean to get me and Parker back together?"

"I mean anything. You need help with anything? Money? Company?"

Miranda smiled sadly at her friend, remembering the time she'd put her up when she walked out on Parker before they were married. That was different. She was different.

And maybe Fanuzzi had a point. Not about needing help. About proving herself. She needed to prove she could make it on her own as a detective. To herself. To Parker. To her former colleagues at the Agency. To anybody who gave a rip.

It was important.

"No, thanks. I appreciate the offer. Besides, I've already got my first client." Not counting the deadbeat Lauderdale.

"Really?" Fanuzzi looked surprised. "Anybody I know?"

"You met him briefly once."

"Who is he?"

Why not tell her? If she told Becker and Becker squealed it to Parker, so what? It would make him worry about her, but he was going to do that no matter what she did.

"Remember the night we went out for drinks?"

"We did that a few times."

"It was over a year ago. Before you and Dave got together. We did the Strip." The Strip was the main street in Buckhead where revelers and partygoers went on Friday and Saturday nights.

"I raced a guy on his motorcycle." Miranda added.

Fanuzzi's brown Italian eyes grew round. She was remembering, all right. "Are you saying—? Do you mean—? Your client is that drug lord? Carlos Santiago?"

"Only one I know personally."

Fanuzzi slapped down her mug and waved both hands in the air. "Jeez, Murray. Are you out of your fucking mind?"

She'd said the same thing the night Miranda went racing with the gangster. "Are you going to be like Parker and tell me I don't know how to do my job without getting myself killed?"

Parker had never actually said those words, but he might as well have.

Fanuzzi's mouth started to move but no words came out. "I—I don't know what to say. I just hope you don't. Get killed, that is."

"It's just a missing persons case. I'll be fine."

"A missing persons case?"

"A dancer from Santiago's club is missing. He wants me to find her."

"Dancer?"

"Exotic dancer. Actually, she's a college student."

Fanuzzi stared at her open-mouthed.

"From Tech." The thought of her new client reminded Miranda of the fat retainer he'd given her.

Behind the shield of her desk, she opened her bottom drawer, grabbed the wad of bills and stuffed them into the case that held her new laptop. The laptop had been another big expense. She didn't feel it would be right to take the Parker Agency's machine she'd been using, though the thought had crossed her mind. But Santiago's money would help defray that cost.

Slinging the strap of the case over her shoulder she got to her feet. "I hate to cut this short."

Fanuzzi looked up at her a bit crestfallen. "You need to go?"

Miranda didn't want to end the visit, but she had to get a move on. She had work to do.

"Yeah, I've gotta be somewhere tonight. You need a ride?"

Fanuzzi rose looking a little bewildered. "No, I've got my car." She glanced at her watch. "It's later than I thought. I need to get home. Dave and the kids are expecting my famous spaghetti tonight."

"Sounds good." Fanuzzi's cooking was to-die-for.

Fanuzzi smiled sadly at the compliment. "Don't suppose you can swing by and join us."

Miranda's shoulders slumped. Fanuzzi sure knew how to lay a guilt trip. "I can't. Maybe another night?" Though she sure wouldn't know what to say to Becker. It would be pretty awkward.

Miranda walked her friend out to the corridor, remembering to lock both of her doors, then they went down the steps together. Fanuzzi's car was around the corner or she would have seen it when she came in.

She walked her over to it.

"Take care of yourself, Murray."

"Sure. I'll be okay. Really."

"Yeah, I think you will. You're a survivor."

Glad somebody thought so.

"But be careful wherever you're going tonight."

"I will. Say hi to Becker for me."

"Will do." Fanuzzi shifted her weight back and forth from foot to foot for a moment, then she lifted her arms and gave Miranda a big hug. "And call me once in awhile."

"I'll try to," Miranda said.

She watched her friend get into her car and drive off, then headed back around the corner to her Acura.

Miranda was glad Fanuzzi had found her. And maybe she would call her up sometime and get together. But if nothing else, her friend's visit had convinced her more than ever that her life with Parker was over.

CHAPTER TEN

Miranda headed home to her tiny apartment, stuffed her laptop in the closet and stuck the money from Santiago under her mattress.

She microwaved a frozen diet meal that tasted only slightly better than its cardboard container, took a shower, changed into something appropriate for clubbing, and headed out a little after nine.

When she got to the parking lot for *Exótico*, it was already full and she had to park a block away and hoof it down an uneven sidewalk to the entrance. She'd had no idea Santiago's strip club was so popular. A line in front of the door snaked all the way around the corner and she had to muscle her way through to the entrance.

In the dark alcove a huge muscle bound dude in black with a thick neck blocked her way. He looked like a referee from the MMA.

"Twenty dollars," he told her, eyeing her getup.

She'd worn some spangled jeans and a low cut pink sparkly thing as a top—an outfit her friend Coco had picked out for her once. She didn't know how it had gotten mixed in with the things she'd taken from the Parker mansion, but tonight it had come in handy.

"She cut in line," some short guy behind her whined.

"You can't do that," MMA guy said with a grunt.

Miranda sighed and pulled a business card out of the tiny purple purse she'd brought. "I work for the owner."

Not buying it, the guy shook his head without looking at the card. Of course, it was too dark to read it.

Miranda's patience was wearing thin. She pointed a finger at MMA guy and struck her best tough chick pose. "Santiago is going to be pissed when he finds out you're impeding my investigation." Then she added, "I'm here to see Yolanda. She's expecting me." Maybe dropping that name would help. Remembering the manager had told her to use it.

It did.

The big guy's face went hard and he turned on a little flashlight in his hand and checked a book on a stand. "You're Miranda Steele?"

"That's the name on the card."

He gave a brisk nod and stepped aside. "Just head for the back. Do you need an escort?"

Hah. Too late to play nice. "I'll find my way," she snapped and moved into the main room.

"Hey, that's not fair," she heard the short dude cry behind her.

But soon his voice was swallowed up in the loud funky horn music that seemed to be bouncing off the black painted walls.

Colorful lights flashed like lightning over designs hanging from the ceiling and the pink satin divans below—which were filled with laughing, shouting, and clapping guests—overflowed. The food and the drinks at the tables were also flowing. And so was the money.

Most of the patrons were men, of course. There were more women out on the dance floor, but the males had hung back guzzling bubbly, throwing back shots, feeding their faces, and of course gluing their eyes to the action on the stage.

It seemed to be some sort of lion tamer's act.

A statuesque dark-skinned woman with heels so high they made Miranda's feet ache to watch her, strolled around center stage. Dressed in a peek-a-boo swimsuit version of a tuxedo with a tall stovetop hat encircled with feathers, she wielded a lacey black whip while four other dancers pranced around her on all fours dressed in animal costumes. There was a tiger, a leopard, a panther, and a zebra.

Must be short of cat outfits.

The tiger was first. With the snap of the ringmaster's whip, she spun around with her back to the audience, gave them a wink over her shoulder. She did some fancy moves with her arms and presto! The top part of her outfit was gone, leaving the tiger-striped legs and tail along with a pair of glossy black thigh-high boots.

Can't give it away all at once, after all.

She did a backbend, giving everyone a peek of a pair of rather large boobs. Stretching out her arms, her head upside down, she jiggled herself, and the guys in the audience turned into the animals, complete with roars and catcalls. The noise was deafening.

Miranda felt a press on her arm.

A waitress in another skimpy outfit was talking to her, her lips moving. She couldn't hear a word, but she must have been asking if Miranda wanted something to drink.

Remembering why she was here, Miranda shook her head and made her way past her and around the back of the divans to the little side door Santiago had led her through that afternoon.

Inside the hall there was some relief from the noise. But Miranda discovered she'd traded catcalls and loud music for the girlish chatter of a dozen or so twenty-somethings.

The dressing table Miranda had seen earlier was alive with activity. The leotards, headdresses and high-heels she'd noticed on the clothes rack now had live bodies in them. Everyone was adjusting straps or head pieces, or dabbing on powder or lipstick, or otherwise primping for their turn on the stage. The air was filled with a bouquet of rose-scented powder and hair spray.

Miranda caught sight of Yolanda at the far end putting stitches in a blue sequined cape a redhead was fussing over.

She pushed her way through the dancers to her. "Have a minute?" Miranda asked.

Yolanda took a straight pin out of her mouth. "Do I look like I have a minute?"

"I need to talk to some of these women."

The stage manager pulled a needle through the cape at the dancer's shoulder. "Bad time. You'll have to come back later."

This was the time she'd told her to come back.

The redhead twisted around, ruining whatever Yolanda had been doing to her cape. Her red hair sparkled with glitter and was piled high atop her head and woven around a shimmering headdress of orange and red feathers. She was clad in a fire engine red fishnet getup that didn't leave much to the imagination. Her big round eyes were decorated with a lot of sparkly, colorful makeup, including very long dark blue false eyelashes.

"What's this about, Yolanda?" she asked.

Stubbornly Yolanda put the fabric back on the dancer's shoulder. "Hold still. This is the PI the boss hired to find Nitro."

"Nitro? What's wrong with Nitro? I thought she was sick."

Yolanda looked annoyed with herself for letting the cat out of the bag.

"Bambi, you're up in ten minutes," someone called from the area that led to the stage.

The redhead turned to the manager. "I can talk to her for that long. Are you done?"

Snipping off the thread, Yolanda held the needle up and shook her hands in the air. "Do what you want. But do not mess that cape up again or there will be hell to pay."

"C'mon over here," The redhead said in a sweet feminine voice, ignoring her surly stage manager.

She beckoned Miranda to the darker side of the clothes rack where two empty chairs stood against the wall in the shadows. She took one, lifting the cape as she sat and gestured to the other for her new guest.

"What's your name again?"

"Miranda Steele." Miranda slid onto the seat, hoping there was nothing sticky on it. "And you're…Bambi?"

"My real name is Crystal." She didn't have a southern accent. Miranda wondered where she was from. "What's up with Nitro?" she asked, frowning with concern.

Names and IDs must be slippery around here. "When was the last time you saw her?"

"Me?" Bambi-Crystal blinked her frosty blue eyelashes. "I don't know. I guess it was Thursday. That's right. Friday night Dolly was complaining she had to fill in for her. I thought Nitro had that stomach flu that was going around."

Flu? Had she checked herself into the hospital? "Did Nitro mention she was feeling ill on Thursday?"

"No, but I hear it comes on fast."

Surely the girl would have called her roommate if she'd gotten sick. Miranda decided to start with the basics. "How well did you know Nitro, Crystal?"

"As well as anybody knows anybody here. Well, I guess a little better. I trained her. She was a fast learner. Picked up the moves right away and invented her own thing with them. She's really good."

"So I hear. How long has she worked here?"

"Oh, just since this summer. I think she started at the end of June. She's a college student, you know."

"Yolanda told me that. Did Nitro say anything to you recently?"

"Like what?"

"Did she mention any travel plans? A trip to see her folks, maybe?"

"Oh, no. If anybody wants time off, they have to get it approved at least a week ahead. We have to have time to learn their act to fill in or get a replacement. That takes even longer. Yolanda wouldn't have approved anything on such short notice. That's why Dolly's so upset."

"You mean because of that slacker, Nitro?" a low sultry voice rang out from the other side of the clothes rack.

The rocky music stopped and changed to something with a slower beat. Out on the stage someone began to sing. This was a real talent show.

Miranda looked up and saw the tall dark-skinned woman who'd been the ring master in the act she'd witnessed descend the stairs from the stage. Graceful as a ballet dancer on those stilt-like shoes, she moved over to the crowded space where Miranda and the redhead were sitting and began shuffling through the rack.

"Where's the fringe outfit?" she called over her shoulder.

"Nitro isn't a slacker," Crystal said to her.

"No, she's an egotistical bitch."

Friendly coworkers. Sounded like the competition for the top spot might be pretty keen around here.

Dismissing the remark, Crystal gestured at Miranda. "Look, Yolanda has a detective looking for Nitro."

Miranda eyed the tall ring master as she started to peel off her costume. "Actually, it was Santiago who hired me."

At the mention of the gangster's name both woman went silent and wide-eyed.

"You're Dolly?" Miranda asked, ignoring the reaction as well as the half naked woman before her.

"That's me." She found the white fringed outfit and pulled it off the hanger.

It looked like the one Nitro had been wearing in the video Yolanda had shown her that afternoon. Miranda wondered just how intense the rivalry was among strippers.

"I hear you were studying to be an astrophysicist, Dolly," she said.

Dolly stepped into the costume and eased it up her long body. "Yeah, I got a degree. But I needed to go to grad school to get a decent job, and it just got to be too much of a hassle. This gig pays well and it's fun. It's all I do now." She let out a low, sour sounding laugh. "Nobody ever whistled at me for getting an A on a Wave Mechanics test."

Sounded as if she were hiding regrets. "Did Nitro say anything to you Thursday night?"

"About what?" She pulled one thin spaghetti strap of the white outfit up her coffee-colored shoulder, then the other.

"Plans she had for going away? Anything that might explain where she is?"

Dolly shrugged and shook out the long fringes under her arms.

Miranda's stomach tensed. The lead dancer knew something. "Do you think she's in trouble, Dolly?"

The young woman was quiet for a moment, then she said, "I don't think so. Except maybe with Yolanda when she gets back from her fling."

"Fling?"

Crystal sucked in her breath. "You think she's with that guy?"

"What guy?"

Dolly glowered at Crystal as if she'd just revealed a trade secret. "There was a guy in the audience. He came here every night for a week. Sat right in the front row table."

Bambi-Crystal nodded. "When Nitro came out and did her number, he acted like he was in love. Drooled all over himself."

"You're exaggerating, Bambi," Dolly sneered. "He didn't drool. Nobody that good looking drools. And nobody in the audience falls in love with us. Not in a healthy way, anyway." Dolly smoothed the sides of her costume.

"You're wrong, Dolly. There was something about this guy."

"Yeah, like the night I saw Nitro talking to him in the parking lot. Bet he wanted a blow job."

Miranda's ears were prickling. "Who was this dude? Did you get his name?"

Crystal shook her head. "Nitro never told me. I teased her about him, but she was so closed lipped about her personal life."

"What kind of car did he have?"

Dolly shrugged. "I don't remember…a gray one, maybe? Or maybe it was white."

"Sports car?"

"No, something more ordinary. A Camry or a Hyundai. I'm not sure. Excuse me. I've got to freshen my makeup." Dolly turned away and sauntered over to the dressing tables.

Miranda turned back to Crystal. "Did you see this guy?"

The girl nodded.

"What did he look like?"

"He had curly dark hair. Oh, and a thin little mustache."

Miranda's heartbeat kicked up. Hannah Kaye's boyfriend had curly dark hair and a thin little mustache. She'd seen both herself that very afternoon. "Is he here now?"

Crystal looked a little lost. "I don't know. I peeked out and saw him in the audience a few times, but lately I forgot about him."

Maybe he was there right now. The boy friend, Miranda bet.

"Can you show me?"

"Sure." She rose, took Miranda by the hand and led her down a dark little cubby hole. "All you have to do is pull the curtain back just a little like this and you can see them but they can't see you."

Miranda watched as Crystal moved the curtain and peeked through it.

She pointed a finger. "See? That's the spot. Booth number three. Front and center. That's where he sat."

Miranda scooted up next to her and peeked through the opening. The crowd was getting even more rowdy. The singer on the stage was nearly finished with her number.

She squinted through the smoky air and counted tables. "Next to the chubby bald guy with the glasses?"

The man was guzzling what looked like champagne.

Crystal peeked through the curtain. "Yes that's the place, but—"

"But what, Crystal?"

"The seat where the guy sat? The guy who was in love with Nitro?"

"Yeah?"

"It's empty."

CHAPTER ELEVEN

Back in her apartment, Miranda paced back and forth, every nerve on fire. She'd never get to sleep tonight but that didn't matter.

She had work to do. She had a lead. Sort of.

Was the mystery man in the audience at *Exótico* Marty Jenkins? Hannah Kaye-aka-Nitro's boyfriend?

Miranda thought of Marty's words that afternoon after band practice. He told his friend he'd gotten rid of the "architect major bitch." Had he done that after her performance on Thursday? Left her body in a dumpster somewhere?

What was the matter, Marty? Had Hannah been too much of a clinging vine? Did she get in the way of your studies? He did seem to take his work seriously.

Still it wasn't much of a motive.

What if he didn't want her working at that club? And what if Marty had a violent streak that came out once in awhile? They had a fight over it. He demanded Hannah quit. She refused. Marty lashed out, maybe hit her. Maybe too hard. An accident. He had to cover it up.

She was deep into speculation.

But the guy in the audience had to be him, right? Curly dark hair. Thin little mustache. Plain, easy-to-forget car. Though Crystal had said he was good looking, and Miranda wouldn't have described the dude she'd followed from band practice that way. Well, maybe Crystal thought he was. There was no accounting for taste.

Miranda wished she'd brought along that photo of him tonight from Hannah Kaye's fridge.

Her thoughts racing, she paced to the card table she'd set up in a corner for a place to eat. The table where her laptop now sat. She paced back to her tiny kitchen and got a bag of tortilla chips out of the cabinet. She retrieved a saucer of leftover salsa from the fridge and sat down at the table.

She took out her phone and scrolled to the shot she'd gotten of Marty Jenkins' license plate.

Firing up one of her expensive database subscriptions, she keyed in the number along with make and model and waited. She reached for a chip, dipped it into the salsa, popped it into her mouth and chewed. It took several more chips before a result flashed on the screen.

Too long.

Silently acknowledging she'd been spoiled by Parker's fast sophisticated equipment at the Agency, Miranda studied the data.

Five year old Civic. Good car for a college kid. Purchased in Minnesota. Fit the description Dolly had given.

There was his local address. Off campus on May Street, just off Atlantic, as Bonnie had said.

Miranda did a little maneuvering on the keyboard to see if he'd ever gotten into trouble anywhere.

Nope. No priors. Not even a speeding ticket.

She drummed her fingers on the table. Pays to be thorough. She'd learned that lesson at the Agency. And a few others.

She stretched her fingers, then went to the school's website and did a little engineering of her own, courtesy of Parker's personal training. She played around for another fifteen or so minutes, following one link then another. Finally she entered a code—and cracked it.

Hah! She was in.

There sat Marty Jenkins' academic record right on her screen. She rubbed her hands together and reached for another chip.

He'd come from Rochester, Minnesota. His parents were research scientists at the Mayo Clinic. Only child. His high school record was outstanding. Graduated valedictorian of his class. Won a slew of science contests. Built a robot in his sophomore year. Smart kid.

At Tech the dude was pulling down a three-point-nine grade point average. Impressive. She bet he was upset it wasn't a straight four-point-oh.

The guy seemed squeaky clean but you never knew. Maybe after a while Hannah got tired of the academic perfection and wanted to break up with him. Maybe he couldn't handle it when she gave him the bad news and socked her one. Harder than he'd meant.

Someone with his scientific background could get creative about getting rid of a body.

She was grasping at straws.

Objectivity, Parker would say. Yeah, yeah. The kid could also be totally innocent. But if he was, what had happened to Hannah?

One thing was certain. This data wasn't going to tell her anything about Marty Jenkin's temper or what had gone on recently with his girlfriend.

For that she'd have to confront him.

The guy's class schedule was loaded with course titles covering subjects that were Greek to her. Electromagnetics, Software Fundamentals, VLSI Design. But there at the top was the Digital Processing class he'd mentioned to his buddy after band practice.

Nine a.m. tomorrow morning.

She'd be there.

With a big yawn she got up and stretched. Now that she'd made some progress, the adrenaline high was wearing off. Fatigue hit her big time. Better get some shuteye if she was going to make that class.

She shut down her laptop and plodded into the bedroom. As she was pulling down the covers she heard a crash outside.

She lifted the blinds and peeked through the window. On the opposite corner under the streetlight, three young men were tossing beer bottles at the dumpster under her window.

Punks.

Maybe she should go out and break up the party. She still had her Berretta in the handbag she'd carried to the club tonight.

For a minute she thought about calling the cops. Maybe she could get ahold of her old buddy, Officer Chambers. Except he wasn't a beat cop any more. He'd been promoted to Assistant Detective some time ago, thanks to her. Well, because of a case she'd gotten him involved in.

Maybe she should look him up. It was good to have a contact on the police force. But then she might run into Lieutenant Erskine. He was Parker's longtime friend at the APD. If she went to the police station, she might run into Parker. She didn't need the hassle.

On the other hand, maybe Parker would go through with his plans to retire soon. He'd told her he wanted to quit the Agency and go off with her somewhere peaceful.

The memory of him springing that idea on her without any warning made her blood boil. But she couldn't think about Parker now. She had to get some sleep.

Yet as she glanced at the empty bed, the thought of him only grew stronger. She remembered the smell of him, the feel of the silky sheets on the bed in the Parker mansion master bedroom, the touch of his skillful fingers over her skin.

Night was the time she missed Parker the most.

Oh, yes. She missed him. She could admit that. She missed his wry smile, his low sexy voice, the way he'd look at her with admiration when she least expected it. Why did he have to change? Why couldn't they have gone on as they were? She had no idea. But she wasn't the one who'd caused the problem.

The punks outside moved down the street.

Just in case they had spawns, Miranda took the Berretta out of her purse and laid it on her nightstand. She undressed, opened a drawer for a T-shirt to sleep in. As she pulled it over her head, something fell to the floor.

She bent down and picked it up. She gazed at its dull sheen.

The dingy ankle bracelet from her last case. The fifteen-year-old cold case of poor Lydia Sutherland. She watched the tiny gold heart with the engraved initials twirl in the lamplight.

A.T.

The cop she'd worked with in Chicago had used a search dog to dig up this trinket on Adam Tannenburg's old property. Like Marty Jenkins, he had been a brilliant, talented young man in love with a young blond twenty-year-old.

The two had been deeply in love. At least that was what one witness had told her. During most of the investigation, Miranda thought it had been Tannenburg who'd killed Lydia and started the house fire that had burned his lover's body to an unrecognizable char.

But she'd been wrong. Tannenburg had been innocent.

And a year later, Tannenburg's mother had died in another fire at his family estate, heaping tragedy upon tragedy for the young man. And after that Tannenburg had completely disappeared.

Miranda believed it was because he thought he'd eventually be accused of killing Lydia. The cops had brought Tannenburg in for questioning. He'd said he wasn't there that night, but a neighbor had seen him leaving the scene.

He must have been living with incredible grief all these years.

She and her police detective partner on the case had been unable to locate Tannenburg. He seemed to be literally in the wind.

Maybe she should start looking for him on her own. She might find him eventually. And if she did, she could tell him it was over. The case was solved and he could stop running now.

Bending down again she clasped the bracelet around her own ankle. She'd keep it as a reminder of the case. Maybe it would bring her luck with this one.

She finished changing her clothes, hung up the pink blouse and glittery jeans. And with thoughts of giving somebody in the world some relief, she climbed into the empty bed, turned off the light and went to sleep.

The heat and humidity in this town was oppressive this time of year, he thought as he stood in the shadows gazing up at the second story window where the light had just gone off.

And so now they were back here in Atlanta. The two of them. Back from the hunt in Chicago.

Except that now the pair had separated.

He chuckled to himself softly under his breath. How amusing. This one always kept him on his toes. He'd had to change his plans again because of her actions. It enraged and fascinated him at the same time.

Oh, she was going to be a delight under his hands.

He was already experiencing similar delights, though he was sure they would prove to be inferior. He hoped his current project wouldn't dilute the experience he planned with Miranda Steele, but he'd had to act. It had been too long since he'd killed. Much longer than usual since his last victim. In a way, Ms. Steele was playing him just the way he was playing her.

No, there was no need to fear. Nothing could dilute what he had in mind for that project. He'd been looking forward to it for nearly a year.

And just now all the pieces were fitting together so nicely. Better than he had expected. He was terribly pleased. But he was anxious, as well. No need to fret, he told himself, the way Mother used to after she'd given him another episode of unbearable pain and humiliation.

It would all come to fruition soon.

As soon as he finished with the current project, he could zero in. At last he would have her. The one he'd been waiting for.

At last the drama would all play out, spinning and weaving its exquisite pain until it ended in a musical scream. Such beauty. Such delight. Such terror.

He could hardly wait.

CHAPTER TWELVE

When Parker walked through the doors of the Agency the next morning he was amazed he'd made it into the office two days in a row.

For some reason he was feeling better, though his head still ached from a two-day hangover and his heart was still as raw as freshly ground steak tartare. Yet this state was an improvement. Didn't they say time healed all wounds?

Or perhaps it was the new quest he was on.

Without stopping at his office first, he headed for the lab. Once inside he scanned the cubicles. He found the man he was looking for in the far corner.

Dave Becker.

He watched him a moment as he busily ran queries and bounced back and forth between two screens, analyzing data. He was proud of his employee. But this man had become more than an employee to him.

He was a friend. And so was his wife, Joan.

This morning Dave had on well worn jeans and a baggy orange T-shirt with the logo of a candy store on the back. No doubt somewhere he'd taken the three children that he'd inherited when he'd married Joan Fanuzzi.

Parker knew from personal experience that Dave treated each of them as if they were his own. He was an excellent father.

His thick dark hair curled around his ears at the base of his neck, and though he wasn't facing him, Parker could still see the end of his rather large nose.

It was necessary to relax the dress code for his technical workers and though Parker would have preferred everyone in suits, he refused to be tyrannical about it.

His chair was elevated a bit to accommodate his short stature. But what Dave Becker lacked in height he made up for in grit and determination, when it was called for.

Suddenly Dave's back went upright and he swung around. "Sorry, Mr. Parker. I—I didn't see you there."

"It's all right." Parker smiled at the man's perpetually nervous ways. "I want to discuss something with you."

"Sure. Let me get you a chair."

Parker raised a hand. "I'll get it." He pulled one from the next cube and sat down. Then he took Miranda's old cell phone from his pocket and laid it on Dave's desk.

Dave picked it up and studied it, looking uncomfortable. "This again, huh?"

"Yes."

Dave was one of Miranda's closest friends at the Agency and Parker knew he hadn't taken the breakup lightly. What he was about to ask would be awkward for him.

Glancing down Parker couldn't help but notice the missing tip of Dave's little finger and remember their time in Paris. Once again Miranda had put her life on the line. But it had been for their friends, and he had done so as well. As dreadful as Dave's ordeal had been, right now Parker would trade a missing fingertip for the wound he carried in his heart.

Dave set the phone on his desk. "You never told me how it went in Chicago."

Parker grimaced. "Badly."

"You didn't find anything? Not even a clue?"

"No."

One cold night in February fifteen years ago in a neighborhood on the west side of Chicago Miranda had been attacked by an unknown rapist. Mackenzie Chatham, Miranda's daughter from that unfortunate union, had recently been looking for her birth father on the sly. When he'd discovered that fact and when he and Dave had learned the first text on Miranda's phone had come from Chicago, Parker had realized Mackenzie's search might have triggered the rapist to attempt to get in touch with Miranda.

He'd had a hunch the anonymous texter had been that attacker from fifteen years ago. The rapist.

And so he'd hunted down several men guilty of that crime who lived near the area where Miranda had been assaulted. But he saw now that had been the wrong tactic. He should have known better than to play such a wild hunch.

Parker sat back in his seat and put his fingertips together. "I feel a different approach is in order. An inverse methodology, if you will."

He watched his employee consider the problem a moment. "You mean instead of trying to find out where the call came from…find out how the culprit got the number in the first place?"

"Excellent deduction." Just the one he'd decided on yesterday.

Dave blushed a little at the compliment. "So how do we do that?"

"Figure out any and all possibilities." A phrase Parker had made sure was drummed into the head of all his trainees.

"Okay," Dave studied the phone some more, scratched at his head. "The first text came in on a Sunday in mid-June."

Parker nodded. It had arrived on Miranda's phone while they were in flight returning home from their case in Las Vegas. He bristled at the thought that she had deleted it without telling him about it. She had later undeleted it before giving it to Dave for analysis—behind his back.

"We know the first text came from Chicago…and you two had just come back from that case in Las Vegas." Dave pursed his lips back and forth in deep thought. "Wasn't Steele on TV there?"

Again Parker nodded. "She did a press conference for the sergeant at the Metro police station."

A conference he'd told her not to do, but she'd jumped in anyway and exposed herself.

Dave lifted his shoulders. "So maybe the guy saw her on the tube?"

Exactly what Parker had wondered. "Another outstanding conclusion."

His cheeks flushing crimson, Dave raised a brow. He'd been working with him long enough to know his boss was two steps ahead of him. "So what do we do? Call the television station and find out if they've got a record of anyone who called asking for the number of the Parker Agency?"

"That would be a start."

"They wouldn't have given it to him."

"They may have. We are a business."

"If they didn't get the number from the station, they could have looked up our website."

"Exactly."

"Or they might have skipped calling the station and gone straight to the website. Did Steele mention the Agency in her press conference?"

"She mentioned her name, my name, and the name of the Agency. The story went national. There were reporters from every major station there."

Dave turned a little pale. "So this guy could have called any of them."

"Or none of them." Parker smiled grimly. "I've already made a list. Would you mind looking into about half of them? I'll take the other half."

Dave glanced at his screen with a worried look. "Well, I've got this Peregrin case…"

"Ah, yes." A local car dealer believed his computer system had been hacked and had hired the Agency to determine what data had been compromised and to set up stronger security measures. "As you have time, then."

He was truly in no hurry. But he knew Dave would find the spare minutes to please him. He got to his feet. "I'll send the list to your email. I appreciate it, Dave."

"No problem. I can look at the hits on our website around that time and see what I can find, too."

"I'd appreciate that."

Dave was still staring at the phone.

Parker decided to leave it with him. "In the meantime, I'll give the sergeant in Las Vegas a call and see if anyone contacted the station."

"Sounds like a good idea," Dave muttered.

But Parker could see he was already lost in thought over his new challenge and how he would juggle it with the Peregrin case.

Parker stepped out quietly and went back to his office feeling satisfied. He intended to get started on his set of calls right away.

CHAPTER THIRTEEN

Miranda didn't hear her alarm the next morning and woke up half an hour later than she intended.

Cursing the stupid thing, the traffic she was about to face, and life in general, she hurried down the steps of her apartment with a travel mug of hot black coffee in one hand, briefcase in the other, and half a bagel in her mouth.

She was negotiating the stairs pretty well, she decided, given she was in her dress pumps. She'd had to wear them today because they went with the outfit.

She'd gone for a power look, opting for her slate gray suit with a silky white top. As she bundled herself into the car, she hoped it would be intimidating. And that she didn't spill coffee down her blouse before her faceoff with Marty Jenkins.

She buckled up, started her Acura and took off for the Tech campus, but she soon discovered she could have slept another ten minutes.

Traffic was at a standstill.

She adjusted the radio and learned there was a water main break and cars on I-85 were backed up all the way to the connector. Sheesh. It was two miles to the school, but she'd be lucky if she got there by the time Marty Jenkins' Digital Whatever class ended.

Lucky break for him.

After she'd gotten through with him, he wouldn't have done well on his exam. If he was still around to take it, and not in jail.

Trying to wake herself up she swallowed a bite of her bagel and took a big gulp of coffee. She hadn't slept well. Some bad dreams had her tossing and turning half the night. At least she didn't remember them.

She'd been having more nightmares lately. Since Chicago they'd been mostly of Leon, her wonderful ex, trying to kill her. That was the biggest impression the psychopath had imprinted on her subconscious, she supposed—the fact that he wanted to kill her.

She'd gotten to him first, but psychologically maybe he was having the last laugh, the sick bastard.

When they were in the hotel in Chicago, she remembered Parker telling her she'd kicked him all night. It was something about being in that city. The place where she'd grown up, where she'd lived with Leon, where all those horrible things had happened to her, that brought out the nightmares. She never should have gone there. Wouldn't have if she'd known it was a cold case. But Parker had been trying to "protect" her by giving her something "safe" to do.

A vision of him with his strong muscular legs—the ones she had kicked—popped into her mind.

"Shut up!" she shouted at her own brain.

She was about to scream at the traffic next when her cell rang.

"Steele Investigations," she answered after a huff.

"Miranda." The roll of the r told her it was Santiago.

"Good morning," she said, forcing herself to sound nice.

"Have you found her yet? My dancer?"

Miranda stifled a grunt of annoyance. "I'm working on it."

"What sort of progress have you made? Do you have any leads?"

She scowled at the phone. That was all she needed. A gangster client micromanaging her. "I have some ideas, but I have to follow them up."

"What are you following up?"

Things a client doesn't need to know about. She closed her eyes and thought of the bankroll from Santiago under her mattress. "Not sure yet. I'm checking out the boyfriend."

"Nitro had a boyfriend?"

Santiago didn't know about it? Well, yesterday he didn't even know her last name.

"Seems she did," she told him, regretting she'd let that detail slip. "Like I said, I'm checking him out. I'll get back to you when I know something definite."

"When will that be?"

Miranda drummed her fingers on the steering wheel. "I can't say, Carlos. These things take time."

"How much time?"

Give it a rest, she wanted to tell him. This guy was used to getting his way. But what worked in the drug dealing business didn't work in a missing persons case. Somehow she had to make that clear.

She let out a breezy laugh. "If I knew that, Carlos, I wouldn't have to work for a living."

There was silence on the other end.

She was just about to hang up when Santiago said, "Just make sure you keep me posted." His low, icy voice sent a shiver through her.

"I'll let you know when I get a break."

He disconnected.

Jeez, she thought. If someone had hurt Nitro, Santiago sounded like he wanted to take care of the dude himself. Didn't bode well for Marty Jenkins.

Wondering what she'd gotten herself into, she concentrated on the drive.

At last she reached the Tech campus.

She wended her way through the narrow streets and another collection of boxy red brick buildings. These had flat roofs and were arranged in a straight row. One after another, and another, and another—until she finally reached the white concrete structure where the Digital Whatever class was held.

Kids were streaming out of the doors, backpacks slung over their shoulders. She glanced at the clock on the dash. Just as she'd thought, the class was over.

Damn.

She peered out the window at the crowd of students roaming every which way like a swarm of ants. She couldn't hope to find Marty Jenkins in this throng but maybe she could beat him to his next class.

She slowed for a stop sign and looked down at her cell where she'd downloaded the kid's schedule. She scrolled up then down. Seemed he didn't have another class until after lunch. Nice hours. But the afternoon was filled.

There was a honk behind her. The vehicle behind that one gave three short honks. Another car joined in the honking.

She was ready to stick her hand out the window and give whoever was back there the finger when a white Civic turned in front of her. She squinted at the license plate.

Marty Jenkins' car. It was him!

At last her luck was turning.

Before the vehicle behind her could honk again, she cruised through the intersection and followed the boyfriend.

He drove straight for a couple blocks north of the campus then he made a right onto May Street. Down another block, another turn and up a street until he pulled over in front of a tiny single story house with a screened-in front porch. She searched for the number on the mailbox.

Yep. This was the house Marty rented with a roommate.

She drove past slowly, watching him get out, dark curly hair, mustache, and all. He locked the car and shuffled inside the house with his backpack over his shoulder.

She went around the block and pulled up behind the Civic.

A tingle climbed up her spine as she stared at the trunk. Now wouldn't that be a perfect place to hide the body of your old girlfriend? But it had been five days since Hannah had gone missing. The body would reek to high heavens by now. Unless he'd treated it. A bright engineering student might know how to do that.

Maybe he hadn't killed her right away. Maybe she was drugged and tied up in there.

Only one way to find out.

Miranda dug around in the briefcase that held her laptop and other assorted PI tools she'd purchased with her dwindling cash supply and found what she was looking for—her own pick set.

She zipped open the case and pulled out a thin metal rod. "Come to Mama, baby," she whispered and got out of the car with the pick hidden in the palm of her hand.

Casually, she inched over to the Civic, as if she were just going for a little stroll through the neighborhood. Yep, just passing through. Just checking out these wheels. Thinking about getting one of these cars, herself.

She peered at the nearby houses. Didn't look like there were any nosey neighbors. Luck was still with her. Time to make her move.

She inched over to the back of the Civic, flipped the cap that hid the lock. Standing so that the view of what she was doing was blocked to anyone in Marty's house, she inserted the rod into the hole and gave it a twist.

Nothing.

She didn't have a lot of practice with picking locks. Parker had usually been the one to do that. But he'd taught her how on their honeymoon—when she'd saved his butt from drowning.

She gave it another twist the other way and pulled up on the trunk. No dice. She needed to see what she was doing. She dared to lean over to get a better look at the keyhole.

"Hey! What do you think you're doing there?"

Uh oh. Her luck had just run out.

She turned around in time to see Marty racing out of his house wearing only shorts and flip-flops, his pale skinny chest flashing in the sun, an homage to nerdom.

Crossing her arms she waited for him to catch up to her.

"Are you trying to steal my car?" he screeched, waving his white arms in the air.

Watching the outline of his ribcage as he heaved, she wanted to tell him he should be wearing sunscreen.

"No," she said calmly. "I'm trying to break into your trunk."

"What? You—you can't do that." His voice was a nerdy squeak of panic.

His dark curly hair was like a lion's mane around his thin face. His pencil mustache was his most adult-looking feature. He had a wild look in his large brown eyes. He hopped from foot to foot, arms flapping like a flamingo. This may have been the most excitement he'd experienced in his young life.

He shook his cell phone at her. "I—I'm calling the cops."

"Go ahead. I'm sure they'd be real interested in a kidnapping case. Or is it murder?"

He stopped moving, and his eyes grew wilder. "What?"

Miranda eyed him up and down the way a cop would. "You know, those are pretty serious charges, Marty."

He blinked, surprised she knew his name. "I have no idea what you're talking about. Who are you, anyway?"

She reached for a card from her pocket and handed it to him. "Miranda Steele. Private investigator."

"Private investigator?" He turned and did a little panic move, bending over at the waist as he studied the card.

"I'm looking for your missing girlfriend, Hannah Kaye."

His whole body suddenly stopped moving, except for his eyes which stared and blinked at her as if she were a ghost. "Hannah's missing?"

"Yep. You want to open your trunk for me now?"

He just kept staring at her. "Hannah's missing?" he repeated, his squeaky voice going up another notch.

"Well, if you're not going to call the police, I am." She raised her cell.

Luckily, Chamber's number was still among those on her contact list. She'd taken her cell from the Agency with her when she'd left and switched the billing over to herself just so she wouldn't lose any of her contacts.

She scrolled to the number and pressed the dial button.

Her old buddy picked up on the first ring. "Chambers."

"Good morning, Officer Chambers. Or maybe I should say Detective Chambers."

He sounded confused. "Who is this?"

"Don't you remember me?"

"The voice sounds familiar," he said in his slow and easy rural southern drawl.

"About a year ago? Aquitaine Farms?"

"Miranda Steele? Is that you?"

She was relieved he sounded welcoming for a change. "One and the same. Say, I'm out here just off the Georgia Tech campus with a possible twenty-one." She was glad she'd had to memorize the local police codes back at the Agency.

"A what?"

"Didn't you hear me?"

"What are you talking about? A twenty-one? A kidnapping?" Chambers must have been surprised she knew the codes.

"Roger. Might be a forty-eight."

"A murder?" There was a pause and it sounded like he was crumpling paper. A wrapper.

Early lunch or a late breakfast? she wondered idly as she eyed the growing terror on Marty's face.

"I'm not sure what you're talking about, Steele. I just got out of court. Domestic dispute that got nasty a month ago."

Good for him but what did that have to do with the price of tea in Indonesia? "Look, Chambers. I'm working a case here. Can you help me out or not?"

Another long pause followed by more cracking, then a tired sigh. "You're at Tech?"

"North of Tech. I'm questioning a suspect." She gave him the address.

That changed his tune. "I'll be there in ten or so."

He was going to cooperate. Good deal. As long as he didn't get in her way.

"I'll be waiting." She hung up and turned back to Marty, who was still staring at her with his jaw nearly to the sidewalk.

She held up her phone the way he had. "That was a friend of mine at the Fulton County Police Department. He'll be here in a little bit to take you in, buddy."

His chest started to heave. "But why?" he squeaked. "I haven't done anything."

She thought he might hyperventilate.

She nodded toward the Civic. "Then why don't you open this trunk of yours and show me."

As if in a daze, Marty patted the pockets of his shorts until he found his keys. He moved toward her with ballet dancer like steps and opened the trunk with shaky hands.

Finally. She peered inside.

Spare tire. Jack. Assorted tools. Dirty laundry. No body.

Miranda picked through the clothes to make sure. No blood. No sign of anything but someone who didn't use a washer very often.

"Where is she?"

"What?"

She turned and growled the words at him. "Hannah Kaye, your girlfriend. Where the hell is she?"

Marty took a frightened step backward. "I—I don't know. We broke up a week ago."

She closed the trunk and leaned against it. "You really expect me to believe that?"

He looked at her as if she were crazy. Then he rubbed his face with his hands. "It was actually last Monday. I met her at the student center after my Bioengineering class to study, like we've done since we met. Only this time she didn't want to study. She wanted to talk."

"What about?"

"Personal stuff."

"What sort of personal stuff?"

He rubbed his arms and glanced around at the trees as if wishing he could fly up into one. Clearly he didn't want to talk about it. But he knew he had no choice.

"About us," he said, his voice breaking. "I mean, about the fact that there was no 'us.'" He made awkward quote marks in the air with his fingers. "She said I'd been deluding myself. That she'd never been serious about me." His voice cracked again and he sniffled through his nose.

Miranda almost felt sorry for him, but it could be an act. "So what did you do about that?"

"There was nothing I could do. She said she'd found somebody else. I think it was a guy who came to see her at the club."

"*Exótico?*"

He let out a snorty laugh. "Yes, that's right. That sleazy place she works at. We fought about that a lot. I told her she didn't have to dance there. I'd help her with her bills. She never listened to me. She didn't care what I thought."

Miranda drew in a breath. "But it was you who went to see her at the club, Marty."

"A couple of times, sure. I thought it would be cool to watch her in a place like that. It wasn't."

"You were jealous?"

"Sure, I was. Who wants to listen to a bunch of old men hooting at your girl? Only I guess she never was my girl." He sounded so sad.

She wanted to believe him but she reminded herself how smart he was. Smart enough to create a sympathetic story about how his girl broke up with him. "And so you decided to teach her a lesson, right?"

"Huh?"

"You are in school, after all."

He looked at her as if she were speaking Hindi. Wait. He probably knew Hindi.

"I really don't know what you're talking about."

She took a step toward him. "Hannah Kaye has been missing for five days. That's what I'm talking about, Jenkins. I'm talking about murder."

His face went white. "No. There's got to be some mistake. Hannah can't be…dead."

Either he was a real good actor or Miranda was starting to think he was innocent. "Were you at *Exótico* last week?"

"What?"

"Clean the wax out of your ears, Jenkins. Last week. Were you at *Exótico*?"

He had that wild look again. "*Exótico*? No. I went there about a month ago. Twice. I've only been there twice."

"Two of the dancers saw you there recently. They said you went there for a whole week. They said you had a seat right up front."

He shook his head violently. "No. They're mistaken."

Miranda was getting tired of this runaround. She was about to tell Marty she was taking him into the station herself when a dark blue Honda pulled up in front of the Civic.

After a minute Chambers got out. "What's going on here?"

He ambled up the sidewalk with that loose, I'm-in-charge-here stride she'd first seen the night he'd chased her down in the Van Aarle's backyard.

His short curly hair with that nondescript blondish-reddish color was neatly trimmed. Must have gotten a raise. He could afford a decent cut now. He wore a short sleeved blue cotton shirt with no tie and khaki pants. The casual police detective look.

Miranda gestured toward the nerd. "This is the suspect I told you about on the phone. Name's Marty Jenkins. His girlfriend's been missing for five days."

She saw Chamber's wide-set Kelly green eyes flash, but the perpetual questioning expression on his baby face remained unchanged. "Oh, really now. What can you tell us about that, son?"

Marty went into nerd overdrive, pacing and stuttering and waving his arms awkwardly while he explained everything he'd already said to Miranda.

She noted his story didn't change. A point in his favor.

"I've already looked in his trunk," she told Chambers. "No sign of her there."

Chambers acknowledged with a nod. "This is your house, young man?"

"I rent it. It's registered with housing on campus."

"Mind if we take a look inside?"

Marty's jaw moved but no words came out.

Miranda decided to keep up the tough guy act. Chambers could play the good cop. "Got something you're hiding in there, Jenkins?"

"No. No," he squeaked, doing a little dance again. "Go ahead."

They followed him up the walk beside some ill kept bushes and inside the little place. It smelled of stale pizza and dirty socks. The lighting wasn't good and there was student clutter everywhere. Books, papers, laptops. In the kitchen the sink was full of dirty dishes and a table in a corner was piled with circuit boards and electronic tools.

It looked like a freaky nerd laboratory.

They went through the whole place. Kitchen, den, hallway, closets, bedrooms. There was no sign of Hannah Kaye anywhere.

"Your roommate isn't home?" Chambers said, stating the obvious.

"No. Anil's not here."

"What's his name?" Miranda started to make a note in her phone.

"Anil Singh. He's got a Physics class now. He's an Industrial Design major."

Miranda didn't bother to record the name.

"I see." Chambers turned to Miranda. "What do you want to do?"

Marty Jenkins sounded truly genuine. But he was still her best lead. She was about to say she wanted to take him in when he raised his hand as if he had a question for the teacher.

"What is it, Marty?" Chambers said, indulging him.

"You said there was a guy at the club? And he went there for a week?"

"Right," Miranda answered, ignoring Chamber's quizzical look. She hadn't mentioned *Exótico* to him.

"Last week I was studying with my friend Cliff Swanson."

Swanson. The guy Miranda had seen him with yesterday.

"All week?" Chambers asked.

"Yes. I had a big exam today."

"But I couldn't get much done. Cliff likes to play loud music when he studies. And he's restless. Takes a lot of breaks. Jogging. Swimming. He's my friend. I went to high school with him but he's a Business major and he has trouble with the technical stuff. I'm trying to help him pass his Calculus class, but last night I'd just had enough of his goofing around."

Consistent with the conversation she'd heard. And maybe the remark about getting rid of Hannah had been sarcasm. Bitter sarcasm over a broken heart.

"What's your point?" Chambers said.

Marty raised his hands as if it should be obvious. "I was with him all last week. Every night. I couldn't have been at *Exótico*."

At the name of the club, Chambers' curly red brows shot up.

Miranda ignored the reaction. "Thursday as well?" she said to Marty.

He nodded. "Yes. Thursday and Friday. You can call Cliff and ask him if you want. I can call him. He'll come right over and vouch for me. He doesn't have a class right now."

Miranda looked over at Chambers. He shook his head slightly.

Her heart slithered down to her dress shoes. Marty Jenkins was a dead end. He'd been telling the truth the whole time.

She waved away his phone call. "Don't bother, Marty. You've got my card there, right?"

"Yes, I do."

"Don't lose it. Call me if you hear anything about Hannah."

The expression on his face turned to such relief she thought he might break out in tears. "Yes, ma'am. I certainly will. I do hope you find her. And I hope she's okay."

"We do, too."

She turned and headed out the screen door and down the walkway with the police detective at her heels.

Chambers inched up to her. "*Exótico*, Steele? You know who owns that club?"

Good to know it was on police radar. "Sure do. He's my client."

She heard a rumble in his chest. "You want to tell me about this?"

She'd only had a few bites of bagel in the car and she could use some fuel. "You want to take me to lunch?"

"Sounds like an even trade."

CHAPTER FOURTEEN

Heading east then south, Miranda followed her cop friend's shiny blue Interceptor to The Varsity, probably the oldest and best known hot dog joint in the city.

She opted for a chili cheese dog and a soda while Chambers got a Frosted Orange in lieu of food, confirming her suspicion he'd been eating breakfast when she'd called him earlier.

As he set a stack of napkins on the table and slid into the red plastic booth across from her, she opened her order and took a bite of the fare. It wasn't a Chicago dog, but the chili gave it a unique taste and as far as junk food went, it was up there on her list.

Chambers pulled the paper off a straw and stuck it through the lid with an authoritative air. "So what gives, Steele? Why are you working for Carlos Santiago?"

She reached for a napkin and wiped the chili from the corner of her mouth. "He hired me."

Eyeing her intently with that curious look of his, he took a sip of his drink. "And?"

She took another bite and took her time chewing and swallowing before she replied. "He's got a missing dancer. Her name's Hannah Kaye. She's also a student at Tech. Nobody I've talked to so far has seen her since last Thursday night." She summarized the details of what she'd learned so far.

Listening, Chambers moved his straw up and down through the lid of his cup, making it squeak. He didn't ask why she wasn't at the Parker Agency anymore. Though Parker was a public enough of a figure, especially with the ADP, for Chambers to know she'd married him last year, he didn't ask about that either.

Whether that was due to discretion or indifference, she didn't know. But she silently thanked him.

"Five days, huh?" he said with a grimace.

"Five days." Not a good timeframe. Odds were Hannah Kaye wasn't alive.

"Santiago could have killed her himself."

She reached for her soda. "I don't think so. He was making too much money off her."

"Maybe she ran away to get out of that…lifestyle."

"I thought that at first, but when I talked to some of the other dancers, they all said she loved what she did. The dancing, I mean. I don't think there was much hanky-panky going on on the side. And she was good at it."

The corner of his mouth curled. "The dancing, you mean."

"Yes. The dancing. The boyfriend was my first suspect."

Chambers took another swig of frosted orange and leaned back in the booth. "That guy wouldn't have the strength to kill anyone even if he wanted to. He looked like he was scared of his own shadow."

Miranda studied the sheen on the chili on her dog and thought of Marty Jenkins' skinny white hairless chest. "Yeah, I just picked up on something I overheard his friend say yesterday. It was just guy talk."

He gave her a smug smirk. Then he got serious. "Have you contacted the parents?"

"Not yet." She had been avoiding that move. All she needed was worried parents breathing down her neck along with Santiago.

Chambers set his empty cup down on the table. "She could be at her folks all this time safe and sound."

She crammed the rest of the dog into her mouth and washed it down with soda. "I know. I'll get to it. Haven't been on it twenty-four hours."

"Have you tried the hospitals? The Medical Examiner's Office?"

"Not yet." She balled up her wrapper in her fist.

Chambers was starting to annoy her. She didn't need a cop telling her how to run an investigation. She'd gotten the lead on the boyfriend, so she'd jumped ahead in the standard checklist. Would have been a brilliant move if he'd have been the killer. And even though he wasn't, it was the right move.

"I'll be working on all that this afternoon," she told him.

"Have you checked her car?"

She hadn't even checked if Hannah Kaye had a car yet. But it had crossed her mind that she must have had one to get to the club at the hours she worked. She just hadn't had time. She needed an assistant.

"Been focusing on the boyfriend," she said.

"I can run it for you."

Miranda stiffened. She didn't want a cop muscling in on her case and she was pretty sure Santiago wouldn't appreciate it, either.

She recalled how ambitious Chambers was. The only reason he'd responded to her call was because she'd helped him move up in the ranks a year ago. She wanted an assistant. Not a cop meddling in her case so he could make a name for himself in the department.

She gathered up her trash and slid out of the booth. "Thanks, but I'll take care of it," she told him with a smile.

Chambers gave her a long steady look that said he thought he could do it better. "If your girl does turn up dead, we'll be getting involved anyway." He got up and followed her as she moved to the trash receptacle.

"If she does, I'll call you in." She shoved the paper and cup into the bin and watched him toss in his drink. "I need to get back to the office."

They strolled out and he was gentlemanly enough to hold the door for her. Even that gesture seemed to have ulterior motives.

"Why don't you swing by the morgue first?" he said. "I can get you in quick."

Now that assistance she could use. She turned to study his expression. His baby face features seemed sincere.

What could he do, anyway? Nothing she couldn't handle. "Sounds good," she told him and headed for her car.

CHAPTER FIFTEEN

The Fulton County Medical Examiner's office was just a short jaunt of four miles away.

Again Miranda followed the tail lights of Chambers' Interceptor, this time back west and down Northside Drive, the Coca-Cola building and various bank buildings making a jagged line against the clear sky in the distance.

Chambers got her in through a back door and introduced her to three of the examiners on duty, which was cool.

But after a search of the databases and facilities, they could find no Hannah Kaye and no Jane Doe matching her description. So Chambers' smart-sounding move turned out to be as much of a bust as hers with Marty Jenkins.

Feeling vindicated, she said thanks and good-bye to the detective and headed back to her office.

She had just reached the dingy hall that led to her new digs when she stopped short.

Standing before her waiting room door was her daughter, Mackenzie Chatham.

The girl spun around to her, deep blue eyes burning. "Where have you been? I was just about to leave."

Miranda was stunned. "What are you doing here? Shouldn't you be in school?"

She rolled her eyes. "We had a half day. There's a teachers' conference."

"Already?" Something fishy about that story.

The girl shrugged.

Still, to add weight to her claim, she had a backpack slung over her shoulder, the tips of her thick ebony hair trailing over the top of it. Her hair had gotten longer since Miranda saw her last.

Dressed in a flowing sleeveless top in a pastel southwestern design, complete with embroidered shoulder straps, she looked very grown up. Except for the pale blue pair of boyfriend jeans with the fashion holes in the knees. Definitely something a fourteen-year-old would wear to school.

Mackenzie pushed her silky hair over her shoulder and gestured to the door. "Are you going to let me in, Mother?"

"Sure." Miranda got out her key and unlocked the door—she'd remembered to lock it this time.

The door rattled and squeaked embarrassingly as Miranda opened it, and they both went inside. Before the girl could take in much of the prints and the second-hand furniture in the waiting room, Miranda crossed to her inner office, unlocked it as well, and ushered her inside and into the same guest chair Fanuzzi had used yesterday.

And Santiago before her.

Well, if she was going to run a PI business there'd probably be a large assortment of strange butts in that chair. She'd better get used to it.

"All I have is coffee." She gestured toward the corner, wishing she had a fridge stocked with soda.

Mackenzie wrinkled her nose and perched on the chair as she lowered her backpack to the floor. "No, thanks." She glanced around the small room. "This place is nice."

Really. This from a girl who grew up in an oversized mansion? Miranda decided she needed something to wet her throat and since there wasn't any booze, she started up the coffee pot.

"How did you get down here?" she asked, tossing grounds into the filter. She didn't ask how she knew where to find her. Either she'd seen the Craigslist ad, or Fanuzzi had told Colby, and Colby had mentioned it. Or maybe it was the cheesy website Miranda had put together.

"I took Marta then I walked." Mackenzie's tone had the lofty air she used to use before they knew each other.

Miranda eyed the round dark spot on the side of the girl's neck. The one that had convinced her more than anything that Mackenzie was her daughter. "This isn't a very nice neighborhood, you know."

"Then why are you here?"

Miranda folded her arms and tapped her fingers against her elbows, willing the coffee pot to hurry up and brew. She needed something to do with her hands. She should have gotten one of those high-powered gadgets.

If she were honest with herself, she was thrilled to death to see Mackenzie. She could only hope the girl had dropped by to see how Miranda was doing, though she'd never admit it. But she wondered if there was another reason.

At last the coffee started to drizzle.

Miranda grabbed a mug and held it under the spout. "How's school?"

Mackenzie shrugged. "Okay."

Miranda replaced the pot, took the mug and sat down in her chair.

Mackenzie smiled. "That's cute." She pointed at the mug.

Miranda turned it around and saw the two gray kittens playing with a big ball of yarn. Part of the cheap set she'd bought at the thrift store. She wished she had looked at it more carefully when she'd picked it up.

"It's so you," her daughter said with a smile, meaning exactly the opposite.

Miranda ignored the comment. "So you're in high school now. Classes going well?"

"As well as can be expected."

She'd always made top grades. Mackenzie's adopted parents wouldn't allow any less. Miranda didn't expect that to change so she didn't press. "Are you still coaching?"

Mackenzie had been ranked among the top ice skating contenders in the nation last year, but that awful incident in Lake Placid had set her back. She'd turned to coaching in the meantime. Particularly, coaching Wendy Van Aarle.

"If you're trying to ask if I've made up with Wendy, the answer is no."

Sharp girl. "Aren't you two going to the same school?"

"So?"

"Do you have any classes together?"

"We manage to avoid each other."

That worried Miranda. Not just for her daughter and her stubborn refusal to make up with her friend but for Wendy. She'd had a hard time with other girls in school when Miranda first met her—actually that was pretty much of an understatement—and if Mackenzie dropped her, she might wind up on the bottom of the adolescent social totem pole again.

But she didn't push. She knew that would only make Mackenzie dig her heels in harder.

She took a sip of coffee and continued the casual third degree. "Does Colby know you're here?"

"She's at a club meeting. And Dad's working, of course. So no, he doesn't know either." There was a don't-you-dare-tell-them threat in her voice.

"Well, next time you want to talk, text me. We can do something together." Miranda just didn't want her getting hurt.

Mackenzie straightened her shoulders in a businesslike pose. "Actually, this isn't a social visit."

Miranda's first impulse was to smile at the girl's formality. But she had a feeling she knew what was coming next.

She sat up straighter, looking more grown up than she was, every pore oozing the poise her adopted parents had schooled into her. "Now that you're on your own, Mother, I thought you might want to work for me."

Miranda put her mug down. "Doing what?"

"You know what."

Of course, she knew. Mackenzie still wanted to find her father. Dear Lord. "Haven't we already discussed that?"

"I thought things might be different now." Her deep blue eyes, nearly the color of her own, sparkled like razors as they dug into her, asking the silent question. *What happened between you and Mr. Parker?*

"They aren't different."

"Of course, they are. You're—" she waved a hand around the office, "on your own now," she repeated.

Her gaze was unrelenting. *What happened between you and Mr. Parker?* There was accusation in those deep blue eyes and Miranda felt the full sting of it. Her breakup with Parker had to be unsettling for the girl. Miranda despised the chaos she'd brought into her daughter's life. Sometimes she wondered if it would have been better if she'd never found her.

Miranda shook her head in disbelief. "What did you think, Mackenzie? Because I work for myself now I'd change my mind?"

She blinked at her. "But you're…single again."

Single again? Nice way of putting it. And what did that matter? "Whether I'm married to Parker or not has nothing to do with how I feel about the man who raped me fifteen years ago. How could you think that?" Did she think it was Parker's idea not to go after her birth father? If she only knew.

"I thought you might need a case. I have money. I have my own checking account."

Now it was Miranda's turn to roll her eyes. "I don't need your money. I've got a client. And even if I wanted to take your 'case'—which I most definitely do not—I can't. The case I've got is keeping me busy round the clock." A little exaggeration, but not by much.

Her pretty mouth pulling into a thin line, Mackenzie's eyes bore into her. "You don't have a case."

"I do."

"Prove it."

Prove it? She didn't have to prove it. It was none of Mackenzie's business. But she found herself zipping open her briefcase and reaching for the file she'd started on Hannah Kaye last night.

She slammed it on the desk. "Here's your proof."

Her expression turning to surprise Mackenzie eyed the folder as if it were a mousetrap. "What is it?"

"A local college student is missing. Looks like she's in trouble and I have to find her. Hopefully alive."

Mackenzie's face turned grim. "How awful."

"Isn't it, though?" She gestured toward the tiny window. "That's why I don't want you walking around here. If you want to see me, text first. I'll come get you."

"But—"

"I'm not going to look for your father, Mackenzie, and that's final."

"But—"

"But nothing." Miranda got to her feet. "C'mon. I'm taking you home."

"You're not even listening to me."

"Home," Miranda snapped.

"I didn't think you had time," she sniped, eyes flashing with rage.

Miranda wished she could ground the kid. "I don't. So let's get going."

CHAPTER SIXTEEN

Parker stared at the screen on his office desk, feeling his eyes growing bloodshot in their sockets. The list of phone numbers seemed to stare back at him, mocking his efforts.

He had called every major television station in every major city in the country and several midsized ones. He'd had to use his best persuasion techniques to get through the gatekeepers to someone who could answer his questions and even then there had been more delays.

But no one had a record of a caller asking about Miranda Steele of the Parker Agency during the timeframe of the Las Vegas press conference.

This search was turning out to be as fruitless as the one in Chicago.

Scrolling down to estimate how much more time this would take, he heard a knock on his door.

He turned his head and saw Dave Becker standing in the hall, papers in his hand. Had he found something?

"What is it, Dave? Come in."

The man approached his desk with mincing steps. "Sorry to disturb you, Mr. Parker."

"That's all right. Have a seat."

He straightened his orange T-shirt, adjusted his jeans and sat down. After a swipe at his large nose with his damaged finger his gaze danced around the room then focused outside the window.

"Have you had any luck on that assignment I gave you?" Parker prompted.

"We had a bunch of hits on the Agency website the hours after Steele was on TV in Las Vegas. Nothing looks suspicious, though."

"And the television stations?"

Dave shook his head. "So far nobody called any of the stations I've contacted. How about you, sir?"

Parker leaned back in his chair ignoring the stab of disappointment he felt at the words, even though it was exactly what he'd expected. "I've had the same result."

Dave gazed out the window again, his thoughts drifting. "It's just that—"

"What, Dave?"

"I've been thinking."

A good sign. "Go ahead."

"Actually, I ran into Holloway and Wesson in the break room an hour ago. They asked what I was working on, so I ran it past them. I didn't tell them about the texts. Just the general details. Hope you don't mind."

Parker had wanted to play his hand close to his chest. Both Curt Holloway and Janelle Wesson had been Miranda's colleagues at the Agency. All four, including Dave, had graduated at the top of their training class. He wasn't sure where their loyalties lay, and learning of this side project might cause office gossip. He'd have to do some damage control—preferably before the damage occurred.

He did mind, but he decided to overlook it. "And what were their thoughts?" he said.

"Same as mine." Dave rustled the papers in his hands, lifted his head, daring to make eye contact with his boss. He looked extremely uncomfortable.

"Which are?"

"Well…I…don't want to bring up bad memories, but like I said, I've been thinking and…"

"Yes?"

Suddenly, he blurted it out. "Steele was on TV before you two went to Las Vegas."

True, Miranda had garnered some notoriety in the press here in Atlanta due to the cases she'd solved, but that wasn't a large enough reach.

"That was local," Parker told him. "And confined mostly to the newspaper and radio. Someone in Chicago wouldn't have seen or heard it."

Dave shifted his weight the other way and looked down at his running shoes. "That's not what I meant, Mr. Parker."

"What do you mean?"

He took a deep breath to fortify himself and said in a near whisper, "Lake Placid."

Lake Placid.

Parker's thoughts shot back to one of the most dreadful times of his life. The crowds, the police. He remembered the endless medicinal smells of the hospital, the hours he'd spent in its chapel, begging God for Miranda's life. And then vaguely, he remembered the reporters at the crime scene, others at the hospital he'd turned away. He'd been too distraught to speak to them. They'd gotten the story anyway. Dave was right. The coverage of that event had gone national, too.

Slowly he nodded. "Excellent work, Dave. We'll need to adjust our time frame then."

Dave looked down at the papers in his hand with a weary look. "And start all over?"

"I'm afraid so. Think of it as a fishing expedition. We both need to exercise a good bit of patience to get a nibble."

Rising, he nodded compliantly. "That's what I figured. Guess I need to get started on that."

"I appreciate it. If you're getting behind on the Peregrin case, I can pass it to Fry."

"Oh. I'm almost finished. I found the breach. One of the salesmen had a weak password. I changed it, added a block. Just need to finish installing the patches."

Parker couldn't help smiling with pride. Dave Becker hadn't shown a great deal of promise when he started at the Agency but he'd found his niche.

"Excellent," he told him.

"Thanks, Mr. Parker." And he shuffled out of the room.

Parker returned to his screen with a new surge of hope. Dave's point was a good one.

The Lake Placid event might have been the one that had attracted the perpetrator's attention. Still, it had occurred what? Eight months before the Las Vegas case? Eight months before the first text was sent.

That indicated planning.

And that the anonymous messages had not been sent on a whim, but were carefully thought out. It also indicated a great deal of patience. Definitely worth another pass through the phone list, starting in the northeast this time.

And if he were lucky he just might catch the bottom feeder they were after.

CHAPTER SEVENTEEN

From the car Miranda watched her daughter bounce up the curved granite steps of the sprawling creamy-white stucco castle that was the Chatham mansion and slam the ornate front door. Just the way she'd slammed her bedroom door over a month ago.

How Mackenzie had the energy to stay that angry for that long was a mystery to her.

At this rate the girl might stop being mad at her by the time she turned, oh, maybe twenty?

Feeling a headache coming on, Miranda stared out her windshield at the expansive emerald green lawn and felt a powerful wave of longing for what she'd once had.

It had been a mistake to come here, but what choice did she have? She wasn't going to let her fourteen-year-old daughter take public transportation home, even if it was only late afternoon. Mackenzie had led a sheltered life. She didn't have the means to handle any…trouble that might arise. Besides, didn't Miranda have enough to worry about?

The kid would be the death of her. Nearly had been already.

Miranda put the car in drive and slowly rolled down the long path to the iron gate. She'd spent the better part of thirteen years searching for her daughter just to know she was safe. She'd nearly died to save her. She loved her so much. And—she never would have found her if it hadn't been for Parker.

At the thought of Parker sudden tears sprang up out of nowhere to sting her eyes.

Dear Lord, why oh why had he turned out to be such a stubborn ass?

She wanted to tell him that. Tell him about Mackenzie's visit to her office to hire her to find the slimeglob that was her real father and say, "Look what you've done!"

But it wasn't Parker's fault. Mackenzie didn't even know he had been looking for the creep himself.

Parker thought Mackenzie's father was the one who'd sent her those crazy texts. Just because he'd learned the first one had come from Chicago. Talk about jumping to conclusions. And Parker had warned her Mackenzie would keep trying to find him. He'd been right about that one.

No, she didn't want to see Parker. Wouldn't know what to say to him if she did. They'd just get into a big fight. She was sick to death of arguing with him. There was no point to keep rubbing salt in the wounds they'd given each other.

And yet as she drove away from the Chatham place, she found herself heading for the Parker mansion.

Force of habit, she told herself. Too late to turn around, she told herself. Besides, she told herself, it didn't matter. It was too early in the afternoon.

Parker wouldn't be there.

So she'd just swing by for a minute and take a peek at the place. It would be a good reminder never to let herself get spoiled again. Yeah, a good hard reminder.

As she turned onto the curvy streets of Mockingbird Hills, her stomach felt as if she'd stuffed it with cotton candy. Dry, sick, overly sugared. She certainly had let herself get spoiled. Spoiled by luxury. Spoiled by love. Something she'd vowed never to do. But it was hard to say no to a man like Parker.

The first night he'd brought her here she'd been unconscious. It had been against her will.

But the heady lovemaking session that had followed wasn't. She remembered the passion of that night. The thunder and lightning bolts of his talented hands. How he made her feel things she never knew existed. How he'd left her breathless and stunned and wanting more.

She'd fallen in love with him that night, though she'd refused to admit it then. Deeply hopelessly in love.

And now?

She was just as much in love with him. But that didn't mean they could make it work between them. Apparently it took more than that.

She steered onto the lane she knew by heart and just before she caught sight of the live oaks rising over the mansard roof of the ten-bedroom edifice, the willows casting shadows over the lawn, the sprawling gray stone balustrade around the front, she saw the figure of a man standing in the drive, hands on his hips staring up at the place.

He had on a pricey light gray suit and a cobalt blue Ascot that made the shock of his pure white hair and neatly trimmed mustache look even more distinguished. She'd know that tycoon air anywhere.

Mr. P. Parker's playboy-slash-real-estate-mogul father.

His face wore an expression of deep thought tinged with a bit of worry.

She spotted a black Lamborghini parked along the curb and pulled up behind it. Like father like son, she thought, getting out of her car.

"Good afternoon," she called, taking in the smell of the freshly cut grass as she crossed the lawn.

He turned to her and his thick white brows arched in surprise. "Miranda. Have you come home?" The tenderness in his old-world southern accent bore into her heart like shards of glass.

For some reason, Parker's father had always liked her and had been delighted when she and Parker had gotten together.

"No," she said flatly as she reached his side.

His expression fell. "Russell isn't here." He always called Parker by his middle name. But today the quaint paternal habit didn't make her smile.

"I know. He's at work."

Mr. P gave his white mane a brief shake. "He's moved out."

"Out?"

"He's moved back into his penthouse downtown."

She vaguely remembered Parker had had a penthouse before they'd moved into the family estate together. She hadn't realized he'd kept it all this while. Had he thought their breakup was as inevitable as she had?

With a weary sigh Mr. P stared up at the house again. "Antonio and Coco are thinking of taking over the place. I stopped by to see what sort of condition it's in."

Antonio and Coco? She didn't know what to say.

Antonio was Parker's semi-adopted son. His surrogate son, she'd always called him. And Coco had been her friend, one of the few women she socialized with, such as her social life was. But Miranda hadn't been in contact with her since the breakup any more than she'd been with Fanuzzi.

The pair had run off and gotten married almost a year ago. And now they were moving into the Parker mansion? She should be glad for them. Coco deserved it, and Miranda had never wanted to live in such a grand house.

Instead she felt like Mr. P had given her a sharp jab in the gut.

"At least the place will stay in the family." He turned back to her, fixed her with his sharp crystal blue eyes. "Miranda, tell me the truth. What happened between you and my son?"

The same question Fanuzzi had asked her. The same one Mackenzie had asked with her eyes.

She stuck her hands in the pockets of her jacket and raised her shoulders. "It just didn't work out, Mr. P."

His gaze continued to bore into her. "Do you still love him?"

She couldn't believe he'd just asked her that. Her throat went dry. She swallowed, trying to hide her reaction. "Of course, I do."

"Then why can't you work things out?"

Stubborn man. The trait ran in the family. But he was also a kind man. At least he'd always been to her. Suddenly she felt she could confide in him.

"We just can't, Mr. P," she croaked out. "He won't let me be myself."

His expression said he didn't buy that at all. "I don't see how he could stop you from being yourself."

He hadn't. That was why she'd had to leave. How could she tell him that?

She couldn't believe she was standing on the front lawn of the Parker mansion, trying to explain to Parker's father what had happened between them. She didn't understand it herself. She was still reeling with bewilderment over it. And truth be told, she was as much in denial about it as Mr. P seemed to be. But facts were facts.

It was over.

She pulled herself together and blurted out the truth. "Parker's shutting down our consulting business."

His mouth moved wordlessly a moment as the shock overtook him. "The one that's taken you on cases all over the world?"

"That's the one."

"Why? You two are tremendous together."

Miranda didn't know her former father-in-law had followed their cases. He'd been travelling with his new bride most of the past year. But most of them had been on the news all over the world.

"That's what I thought, too," she said. "But Parker thinks the work is too dangerous. He thinks I'll get myself killed sooner or later."

Mr. P uttered a bitter laugh. "Isn't that ironic? I've been worried about Russell's safety since he took on his first case."

She lifted her palms. "Well, there you go."

Mr. P stood silent a long time as he took in what she had told him about his son. Robins chirped and hopped along the branches of a nearby willow while the afternoon sun bore down its last vestiges of fury before setting for the evening.

Slowly the older gentleman ran a hand over his face, just the way Parker did when he was frustrated—usually with her.

He murmured half to himself. "Russell says he's through with love, through with commitment. I've never heard such talk from him."

A nice follow-up solar plexus punch to the news about the house. Miranda almost doubled over. She wrapped an arm around her waist.

So Parker was through with her. Really through. But why shouldn't he be? He'd find someone else eventually. Someone more his type. A socialite like his first wife. Someone he could coo over and protect.

The thought made her sick.

She felt dizzy. Her ears rang in her head. Suddenly she realized Mr. P was still talking to her.

"There's the little matter of your mortgage."

"What?" she said, bewildered at the comment.

She hadn't given him notice when she left. Was he going to make her pay for the last month on the house? She'd have to dig into the money from Santiago.

"I—I'm not sure what I can give you right now, but—"

"Miranda." He reached out and grabbed her with both hands. "I'm not asking for payment."

"You're not?"

"No. I'm trying to tell you I've been keeping your payments to me in an investment account. The economy being what it is, it hasn't grown as much as I had hoped, but it's yours. I want to make arrangements to transfer it to you."

Now her head was really spinning. "What?"

"Do you want figures? Reports?"

"No, no." He'd been saving all the money all this time? It would be enough to pay for her new apartment for a year. But she pulled out of his embrace and shook her head. "No, Mr. P. I can't take that money. I owed it to you."

"Miranda. The whole deal was a ruse to get Russell to take the house."

"And look how that turned out."

"Nonetheless, the money's yours. Give me a voided check and I'll have it wired to your account tomorrow morning."

CHAPTER EIGHTEEN

So, Miranda thought as she took the ramp to I-85 heading south and into the heart of rush hour traffic. If she didn't find Hannah Kaye, aka Nitro, and Santiago wanted his money back, at least she'd have the cash from Mr. P to fall back on.

Cause to celebrate, right?

Not with the ache that still throbbed away in her heart like a deep open cut. Parker had moved out of his family estate. He said he was through with love and commitment. That didn't sound at all like the man she'd known.

She really didn't know him anymore, did she?

But what did it matter? What Parker said or thought or did was totally irrelevant to her now. She was on her own, as Mackenzie had put it. And she had a job to do.

A job.

Gritting her teeth she shook off the bad feelings, or attempted to. She had no right to wallow in her own self pity when a young woman's life could be at stake.

With a sheer force of will, she wrenched her thoughts back onto the case. And the first thing she thought of was the To-Do list the obnoxious Detective Chambers had ticked off for her.

No dead body in the ME's office. That left hospitals, checking out Hannah's car, and the parents.

The parents.

A sick feeling rippled through her. She didn't want to be the one to tell Hannah Kaye's folks their daughter was missing. But despite what Bambi-Crystal had said about permission from Yolanda, the dancer could have been up in Gainesville lounging around the family pool all this time. What if she was?

Miranda had the family's address and phone number. They were on the employee information Yolanda had given her yesterday as the emergency contact. She had thought it was odd for Hannah to have listed them. Did she think her parents wouldn't care she was working in a strip club?

Maybe she'd assumed, like most folks, that she'd never have an emergency. Well, she had one now.

An in-person visit would be appropriate. But it would take Miranda at least two hours to get up there in this traffic. She didn't want to waste the time.

And she really didn't want the parents involved yet. Yes, they had a right to know about their daughter, but as soon as they did they'd be calling the police, getting on the news, spreading flyers everywhere and that would only drive whoever she was hunting further underground. Besides, if some sick slimeball had kidnapped Hannah Kaye a news story could trigger him to kill her.

All she really wanted was to know whether Hannah was with her folks. She tapped her fingers on the steering wheel. How to get that information. An idea formed in her head.

The traffic slowed to a parking lot like standstill and she reached for her phone. She scrolled to the information and dialed the Gainesville number.

After three rings a woman answered.

"Yes?" She had a low, throaty voice, and sounded as if she'd just woken up.

Miranda cleared her own throat and tried to make herself sound like she was twenty. "Mrs. Kaye?"

"Yes. Who is this?"

"My name is, uh, Nancy…" She glanced around and saw a billboard for a local barbeque joint. Flynn's Ribs. "Flynn," she said. "Nancy Flynn. I'm a friend of Hannah's?" She raised her voice into a question the way young folks do.

Now there was throat clearing on the other end as well. At last the voice said, "What can I do for you, Nancy?" She sounded awake now. And on the young side herself.

"Well, I…uh…I missed my Discrete…Digital…Equations class last week?" Miranda hoped this lady wasn't a scientist. "And Hannah said she'd lend me her notes. But she doesn't have them. Did she by any chance leave them with you when she was home this weekend?"

There was a rustling, and a murmur. Then a male voice mumbled in the background. The father?

The woman came back on the line. "I'm sorry, Nancy. But Hannah wasn't here this weekend."

Miranda felt her heart sink. She'd been secretly hoping the girl was at home safe and sound.

"Nancy? Are you still there?"

"Yes. Oh. My bad. I wrote it down wrong. Hannah was with Marty this weekend." She let out a nervous girlish giggle and waited for the response.

"Marty?"

"You know. Hannah's boyfriend?"

"Oh. I've never met the young man."

"So she didn't call and tell you her plans?" Miranda bit her lip. Might have gone a little over the line with that one. But it was a good opportunity to find out about Hannah's family and how they felt about her.

"Hannah's a grown woman, Nancy," the woman said, sounding annoyed. "Charles and I have our life. She has hers."

Miranda blinked at the phone. Pretty cold for a mother. She had to get off the line. "Oh, okay," she said in her girlish tone. "Sorry to bother you."

She hung up.

Didn't sound like Hannah Kaye had the warm loving family relationship Miranda had assumed. Whether that had anything to do with the case or not, she didn't know. What she did know was Santiago had been right. Hannah Kaye was definitely missing. And it didn't look good for her.

A horn blared behind her. Traffic was picking up.

"Okay!" she yelled and stepped on the gas.

CHAPTER NINETEEN

Forty minutes later, Miranda was back in her crappy Midtown office, going through the list of local hospitals she'd dug up on her laptop. One after the other, she schmoozed administrators and nurses and clerks, giving a description of the girl, asking if anyone matching it had been brought in after an accident or an attack or any similar circumstance.

No match anywhere.

She hung up and rubbed her eyes. She stared at the rest of the list on her screen. She'd covered the city but there were dozens of medical facilities around the Atlanta area. It would take her hours to go through them.

She got up and poured out the coffee from Mackenzie's visit this afternoon and made herself a fresh pot.

As she pressed the button she forced her thoughts off her personal life and onto the young woman she was trying to find.

Missing for five days. Didn't show up for work. Roommate hadn't seen her. Ex-boyfriend hadn't seen her. Wasn't at home with her parents.

The car.

That was the thing to look for. From what she knew of the fickleness of young women, Hannah might have decided she wanted to be an actress and hopped a plane to LA. Her car might be sitting at Hartsfield airport for all she knew.

Chambers said he'd track it down. Hah. She didn't need his help.

Forgetting the coffee Miranda returned to her laptop and attacked the keyboard with a vengeance. She hacked into the school's website again, the way she had with Marty last night, and after a few false starts, got the license plate and VIN number of the vehicle registered to Hannah Kaye.

The dancer drove a cranberry red Toyota Corolla. Shouldn't be too hard to spot. She took a look at the police scanner software she had. Nothing even close. So much for Chamber's promise.

She had another app that would give her better information. Namely, the Corolla's current location. What did investigators do before GPS tracking?

Stretching her fingers, she grinned to herself. Let's see if this baby was worth the cash she'd shelled out for it.

She plugged in Hannah Kaye's vehicle data and clicked Search.

The slim blue bar began to move. Slowly.

Two percent. Five percent. Back down to three.

Crap. This was going to take forever.

In the meantime, might as well check out the background on Hannah's parents. She switched windows and opened another piece of software. She entered the data for the parents and this time was rewarded with a quick response.

The personal data for Charles and Jean Kaye was displayed on her screen in all its glory. Charles, age fifty-one, had been a top-ranking sales manager for a medical equipment company for years. Travelled all over the country, made the big bucks, spent lavishly on a nice home. Looked like Hannah was their only child. And Jean...? Not much about her. Stay at home mom? Wait a minute.

Jean Kaye had died three years ago of lung cancer. Charles had gotten remarried last year to a thirty-two year old woman named Athena West. That must have been who Miranda had talked to on the phone. Not much about her, here either.

Social media was the place to go, Miranda decided.

She logged on to the popular site Mackenzie and Wendy frequented and entered the woman's name. Her page popped up immediately. This was Athena West?

Wow.

In front of a gorgeous sandy beach a leggy beauty was stretched out in a silvery swimsuit that left little to the imagination. Long golden hair that glowed under rays of the setting sun draped over breasts that would make any man drool.

With one hand, she balanced herself. In the other she held a champagne flute. Her tongue seemed to move seductively over her upper lip in a come-up-and-see-me-sometime pose.

So this was Hannah Kaye's stepmother.

The bio said she was a model. Miranda wondered for what. It also said her interests were skiing, fine wine, and swinging.

Wait. Swinging?

A few clicks and eyefuls later, Miranda had the answer. Charles and Athena Kaye were active members of a partner-swapping club. They seemed to frequent it regularly. The club met at various resorts, members' home, and local hotels for periodical partner swapping. For a reasonable monthly fee you could screw anybody in the club you wanted.

Feeling a little queasy Miranda sat back in her chair. No wonder Hannah didn't mind listing her parents on her employment record for *Exótico*. She knew they didn't care if she worked in a strip club. From Athena's attitude on the phone, she didn't seem to care what Hannah did. Or where she was.

Miranda tapped her fingers on her desk.

Had Hannah been close to her real mother? Three years wasn't a lot of time to get over the loss of a loved one. Was Hannah's disappearance a desperate cry for attention from her father? A way to lash out against her swinging stepmother?

More unanswered questions.

A sizzle came from the corner. The coffee. She'd forgotten all about it.

Trying to sort out all she'd learned, Miranda made her way over to the pot and poured a cup into another cute kitten mug.

She'd just sat down with it when her cell rang.

She looked at the display. Santiago. Good grief.

Better answer or he might send someone to break her legs. "Hello?"

"You said you would keep me posted." His dark voice sent another shiver through her.

"I said I'd let you know when I got a break."

"What does that mean? What happened with the *hombre*?"

"*Hombre*?"

"The boyfriend you were checking out this morning. I have not heard from you all day, Miranda."

Taking her time to respond she sipped her coffee.

"Miranda?"

"He's not our guy."

"Our guy?"

"He has nothing to do with Nitro's disappearance."

There was a long icy pause. "How do you know?"

She let out a long breath. "They broke up a week ago. He's alibied for the entire time Hannah's been missing." She certainly wasn't going to tell him the details. And especially not that she'd gotten Chambers involved.

She could almost hear the rumble in Santiago's chest. He wasn't buying it. "I can send someone to question him further."

Miranda could just imagine what that meant. A vision popped into her head of one of Santiago's lackeys beating the pale, skinny Marty Jenkins to a pulp.

And it pissed her off. "Are you telling me I don't know how to do my job?"

"If I thought that I would not have hired you."

"Then believe me. The boyfriend wasn't involved."

She listened to him breathe a long time. At last he said, "Very well. What is your next step?"

At least she'd gotten him off the boyfriend thing. "I'm going through some standard checks. I'm not finished yet."

"What sort of checks?"

She fisted a hand and rolled her eyes. "Hospitals for one thing."

"Hospitals? Do you think Nitro was in an accident?"

"I don't think anything yet. It's something I have to check."

She had to get him off the phone. It was a waste of time. She didn't have anything else to give him and she never would with him breathing down her neck like this.

On second thought, maybe the pressure was just what she needed.

Suddenly she remembered peeking through the curtain during the show at *Exótico* last night and the pieces clicked.

Both the tall dancer named Dolly and the nice dancer named Crystal with the silly stage name of Bambi had claimed a man in the audience had come to see Hannah aka Nitro every night for a week.

Crystal said he was in love with Nitro. Drooled all over himself when she performed. She said he was good-looking. Dolly said she'd seen Hannah talking to him in the parking lot. The dude had sounded like the boyfriend, except for the good-looking part. Miranda had dismissed that. She'd been sure it had been the boyfriend at the club. But Marty Jenkins hadn't been there. Not last week, anyway. He'd been studying with his Business major friend who was flunking Calculus.

Marty's words from that morning came back to her. Hannah had broken up with him last week. She'd said she'd found somebody else.

"I think it was a guy who came to see her at the club."

Miranda had thought he'd been lying. A breezy chill fluttered down her spine.

Marty wasn't lying.

She needed more information on that dude in the front row table. Somebody at the club ought to know something.

"Carlos," she said into the phone.

"Yes, Miranda?"

"Can you get your staff together for a meeting tonight?"

"What for?"

"I need to question them. It'll be faster if they're together."

"Very well." He sounded relieved she was taking an action he could understand. "Can you come to the club early? I am meeting with them myself before the show tonight. My monthly pep talk."

She couldn't imagine Carlos Santiago giving a pep talk but that was irrelevant. "I'll be there."

"I will see you then."

She clicked off and turned to her computer screen. She had nothing to go on about the mystery man yet but a vague description of him and his car. Nothing she could search.

But by tonight, she would.

CHAPTER TWENTY

Parker stepped out of his office and headed down the hall along the cube bank, his temples pounding. For six hours he'd gone through that list of television stations twice, calling every last one of them, using every charm cell in his body to find anyone who might have called looking for Miranda either after her Las Vegas press conference or the incident in Lake Placid.

Once again he'd come up empty-handed.

Scanning the aisles, he headed for the break room. The workday was at an end, the smells and sounds of coffee brewing had given way to the pop and fizz of soda cans, which in turn had given way to the snap of laptop lids and a yawn and a stretch before heading home.

And yet he heard voices down one corridor.

He took it, moving past the empty cubes to a corner near Miranda's old space. There was no activity there. He'd told Gen to turn her cube into storage. He couldn't bear the sight of it.

He made another turn and found Dave Becker lounging over the side of the cube belonging to Detective Curt Holloway. Holloway had his feet on his desk.

Opposite Holloway, Detective Janelle Wesson sat in the guest chair, her shapely legs crossed at the knee. She wore a conservative business suit of robin's egg blue that went well with her long, cinnamon red hair. The determined spunk Wesson brought to her cases showed in her alert posture. It was a trait Parker both encouraged in his employees and respected.

"I think you're right, Becker," Wesson said.

"Right about what?" Parker asked.

All three jumped together. Dave shoved his hands into the pockets of his jeans. Wesson uncrossed her legs and sat up even straighter.

Holloway put his feet down and adjusted his sport coat and tie. "Hello, sir. Becker here was just whining about hitting a dead-end on the assignment you gave him."

Parker studied their faces. They were hiding something. Just now he didn't care what it was. "Exactly where I am as well."

Dave hung his head as if in shame. "Bummer."

Parker turned to Dave. "Have you told them what we're doing?"

"Not all of it."

If two heads were better than one, four were even better. Parker took Miranda's phone out of his pocket and scrolled to the insidious text messages.

He handed it to Holloway. "Miranda started receiving these about two and a half months ago. We're trying to find whoever sent them."

Holloway took the phone and squinted down at the screen. "These sound pretty ominous, sir." He handed the phone to Wesson.

Her red brows drew together in serious consideration as she studied the texts. "Creepy."

Parker took the phone from her and explained the progress, or lack thereof, he and Dave had made so far. "Do you two have any thoughts to contribute?"

Wesson turned to him in her chair. "You mean as a theory of how this guy got Steele's phone number?"

Parker nodded.

She thought a moment. "The Agency's website?"

"Dave has already checked that out."

"I haven't found any unusual activity," Dave offered. "But it's hard to tell."

Holloway shoved back the shock of light brown hair that habitually fell over his eyes. "It could have been a wrong number."

Dave shook his head. "Not three times in a row."

"But they stopped after the third text, right?"

Parker drew in a patient breath. "They did. And you're right, Curt. It may have been a misdialed number. I'm working off the worst case scenario."

Holloway nodded and fell silent.

Wesson reached for a can of soda on the corner of Holloway's desk. "We have people coming and going in here all the time. What if he just walked in?"

"You mean a client?" Holloway asked.

"Or someone posing as a client."

"You mean somebody might have come in here and strolled right up to Steele's desk?"

"Or asked Sybil for her number."

Holloway frowned in disbelief. "That would presume a pretty underhanded motive."

Wesson scowled back at him. "That's what Mr. Parker just said he was going for. Besides, those text messages support that theory. If I'd gotten them, I'd be looking over my shoulder."

Something Parker knew Miranda had not done.

Dave's eyes took on a faraway look. "What if somebody was going to try to get money out of Steele and chickened out?"

"All plausible theories," Parker said. "We simply need to figure out which one is correct."

"Simply," Holloway said with a smirk. Then his head shot up. "Hey, doesn't Sybil keep a record of visitors?"

Parker nodded. "She has a sign in sheet, yes. And a call log." But if Miranda had received an incoming call from a stranger, she would have been suspicious. It would have been the first lead she'd have used to track down those calls.

An in-person visitor with an ulterior motive was a possibility he hadn't considered. And with the dozens of clients who had come through the Agency's doors over the past months, it could very well be a viable possibility.

But how could a stranger access Miranda's phone?

She had been careless with it when she first got her cell phone, but once she became a full-fledged investigator she was never without it. Never.

Except…Parker remembered a time during her convalescence when Miranda had grown restless and had stubbornly come into the office for the day. Over his protests. He had been right. The strain had proved to be too much for her and she'd gone home—and left her cell phone behind. He remembered her begging him to bring it to her. And he had purposely pretended to forget so she could rest. She'd suffered a gunshot wound and had almost died. She'd needed quiet. The landline in the mansion was enough for emergencies.

He'd managed to keep it away from her for two weeks. But when she threatened to come back in to the office to get it, he'd brought it home. He smiled at the memory of her delight when he'd handed it to her. When had that been? January? February? And then another thought came to him.

Parker scanned the walls of the open space. "I had surveillance cameras installed here some years ago when some cash went missing."

"They're still working," Dave volunteered. "I've seen Fry check them every so often."

"That far back might have been purged."

"I don't think so. We have a couple of terabytes of storage."

"Let's go check that out," Parker told him. He turned to Holloway and Wesson. "In the meantime, would you two talk to Sybil about her logs?"

Wesson got to her feet. "Sure. I think she's still here."

Holloway hopped up as well, eager to help. "I saw her doing inventory in the back. We can find her."

Parker appreciated their enthusiasm. "Thank you. Let me know what you learn."

"Will do." Holloway saluted and went off with Wesson to hunt for the receptionist.

Parker turned to head back to the lab with Dave. He was nearly around the corner when he spotted Gen at the end of the aisle. She'd changed from business clothes into jeans and wore a form fitting green top that brought out the ashen blond of her short hair. Her demeanor was still every ounce a professional. She reminded him so much of her mother at times.

Gen carried a clipboard in one hand. Holloway had been correct. Gen and Sybil were staying late to take stock of office supplies.

She glanced at her watch and gave him a derisive look. "Dad, what are you doing here?"

Lifting a brow, he came to a halt in front of her. "Working."

She glanced at Dave and made an even odder face. "Don't you want to get going?"

He gave her an indulgent smile. "Why should I want to do that?"

"You know." She moved her eyes back and forth, then lifted the clipboard to the side of her mouth. "That *thing* we talked about?"

He had no idea what she meant. And as much as he loved her, she was impeding his progress at the moment. "I'm sorry, Gen. I don't know what you mean."

She rolled her eyes and whispered in his ear. "It's date night."

"What?"

"I set up a date for you tonight. Didn't you get my text?"

Parker took out his own cell. Apparently he'd been so engrossed in his project, he'd missed it. Gen had arranged for a date at Tamarind Gardens at seven-thirty tonight. His first inclination was to cancel. He wanted to follow through on this new lead.

But Gen's expression told him she'd be sorely disappointed if he did. Besides, he'd agreed to the date to turn over a new leaf. And at the moment, he didn't care if Dave knew about it. Or if through his wife, Joan, the news got back to Miranda.

"Who am I meeting at Tamarind Gardens?" he asked Gen.

She gave Dave another awkward glance, then said. "It's a secret."

Parker raised a brow. "A blind date?"

"Yes," Gen echoed, folding her arms defensively. "A blind date. I think you'll be pleased."

Not exactly what he was hoping for, but he refused to disappoint his daughter.

From the corner of his eye, Parker caught Dave's stunned expression. Ignoring it he turned to his employee. "Dave, can you get started on that project while I step out for a few hours? I'll be back later."

"I—I—." Dave's jaw went up and down until he shook himself out of his shock. "I mean, sure, Mr. Parker," he said finally. "I'll just call Joan and tell her I'll be late."

"I appreciate it. Let me know the minute you find anything."

Dave nodded vigorously. "Will do, sir."

Parker turned back to Gen. "I assume you'll be staying late as well?"

"As long as it takes. We're behind in inventory."

"Then I'll see you both later." And with that Parker turned the opposite way and headed toward the exit.

CHAPTER TWENTY-ONE

Tamarind Gardens had been one of Miranda's favorite dining spots, Parker thought, as he stepped into the establishment's understated foyer.

She'd loved their extra spicy sausages, he recalled, breathing in the aroma of basil and ginger from the five-star Taiwanese kitchen. He wondered if Gen had taken his history here with his former wife into consideration when she'd planned this date.

Perhaps that had been her intention.

The gentle tinkling of Far Eastern music reminded him of Miranda's laughter, of how happy they'd been the last time they'd come here. It was before Parker and Steele Consulting. Before Las Vegas. And after Leon Groth was gone. One starry night in May, they'd stolen a few quiet hours alone, just the two of them, to celebrate nothing in particular except the joy they had found in each other.

If only things could have stayed that way.

"Mr. Parker. How good to see you this evening." Chao Lao, the owner, stepped through an inner doorway to greet Parker.

Parker shook hands. "And you, Chao. How have you been?"

"Well, well. And yourself?" Dressed in a dark business suit as finely tailored as the one Parker had changed into, Lao was one of the hardest working businessmen Parker knew. He thought highly of him.

"I'm fine," Parker told him, stretching the truth. "The Agency is having one of its best years ever."

"Excellent." Lao nodded and smiled as if Parker's personal life was nonexistent, though he had to know something of Parker's breakup. It seemed everyone did.

Parker appreciated the discretion.

Without missing a beat, Lao gestured toward the dining room. "Your party is waiting for you. Please step this way."

Parker followed the man through the rows of diners to one of the better tables. It was far enough away from the table he and Miranda had always shared to be tactful. Again, Parker was grateful.

But when he spotted who was seated at the table, he nearly balked.

Her maple brown hair done up in a graceful chignon, she wore a simply styled deep gray chiffon sheath over the tall lean figure of a woman who jogged regularly. A single strand of pearls graced her long slender neck. Elegant as ever. Just as she'd been at every social event he'd seen her. As he approached she turned her head and fixed him with the sharp gaze of the top defense attorney she was.

Wilhelmina Todd. Antonio's associate at Chatham, Grayson, and McFee.

She'd been a social acquaintance for years. Apparently Gen thought she'd be a good match for him. Parker wasn't so sure.

"Hello, Wade," she smiled with her confident air. "Did Gen throw you off guard with this…arrangement?"

He slid into the booth across from her as Lao handed him a menu and silently slipped away. "I suppose she did."

"Then I can admit I'm feeling as awkward about this as you must be." She didn't look awkward. She looked as cool as the proverbial cucumber.

Still, her remark made him smile. "It's good to see you, Wilhelmina."

"And you, Wade." She reached across the table and took his hand in a warm squeeze of old friendship.

How long had he known her? Six, seven years? Since Antonio started at the firm. He'd often brought home stories of the young ambitious female attorney who was both rival and colleague. Both were eager to make partner someday. Wilhelmina had to be in her early thirties, like Antonio. Parker had never thought about her age before.

"How have you been?" he asked.

"Oh, busy as ever. I've been working two attempted murders and a narcotics case lately." She named one of the defendants who had been on the news.

Parker nodded politely. He hadn't watched much television the past few weeks.

"Plus Felicia's in her last year of high school. She'll be going off to college next year."

"Is that so? I remember when she started junior high."

"Time flies as they say."

But the last few years hadn't been fun for Wilhelmina. She'd lost a child. Shortly after Parker and Miranda had met, Miranda found the killer of Wilhelmina's younger daughter, Tiffany. Those were difficult days for the attorney. It had been when he was falling in love.

Awkward wasn't the word for this so-called date. He'd have to speak to Gen about her choice of companions for him.

He opened the menu. "Shall I order for us?"

She smiled her winning smile. "How chivalrous you are. Something with chicken, I think."

"Very well."

He selected rice wine, an oyster and ginger soup, and chicken and vegetables in sesame oil. He avoided the basil rolls with chili paste he'd once shared with Miranda, and especially the spicy sausage. He didn't think Wilhelmina was the type for a three-alarm pepper dish.

Not many women were.

The meal was served and they ate and chatted about mutual acquaintances. Though Parker avoided mentioning Wilhelmina's boss, Oliver Chatham. The chief partner in the firm was Mackenzie's adopted father. Talk of him would lead to talk of Miranda.

The thought of lawyers made him realize he'd have to be seeing one shortly. It wouldn't be Oliver, though, thank the Lord. Grayson was the one who handled divorce.

While she ate Wilhelmina kept up the conversation with small talk of local events and mutual acquaintances. Parker pushed the fragrant bamboo shoots around on his plate. He recalled how excited Miranda had always been when he'd introduce her to a new dish. Her culinary history had been limited and there were so many tastes she hadn't yet experienced. He had loved feeding her and watching her reaction. Wilhelmina wasn't the type to get excited over a meal.

And tonight he found he wasn't in the mood to eat.

Wilhelmina finished her entrée and sat back with her teacup. She had a wistful look in her eye. "There's a law firm in London that seems to be interested in my work."

That news was a shock. "A long way from home. Are you thinking of taking a job with them?"

"I haven't decided yet. And they haven't made an offer. We're just going through the preliminary dance, feeling each other out. You're the first person I've told."

Another surprise. But somehow he was flattered.

"It would be a challenge. And after Felicia's gone off to college, I'll need that."

Parker knew what she meant. Work was keeping him sane at the moment. And Wilhelmina had suffered a divorce from a cheating husband right after the death of her youngest. She'd had a hard two years.

He laid his napkin down next to his half finished plate. "I have some contacts in London, if you need them. Not that you would."

She gave him a wry look. "Is that a brush-off, Wade?"

He cleared his throat. Of course, if Wilhelmina went off to London there wouldn't be a chance to pursue a relationship. He wasn't usually so thoughtless. "Not at all, I—"

She laid her hand against his. "I'm being facetious."

"Yes, of course." Dear Lord, he was out of practice. He felt like an awkward schoolboy at his first dance.

Her gaze grew penetrating. "You're not at all yourself tonight, Wade. Not that anyone would expect you to be."

"I'm fine." Parker fidgeted with his napkin. They'd done so well avoiding a personal conversation. He didn't want that to end now.

Wilhelmina withdrew her hand and leaned her chin against her palm with a sigh. "You tell yourself that. You even believe it for a while, but it's a lie. The truth is it takes time to heal wounds so deep."

She and Isaiah Todd had been married a long time. Their breakup must have been excruciating for her.

Suddenly her words seemed to open the lesions Miranda had left in his heart, making them bleed and fester all over again. The attorney was right. He was far from healed.

He had to admire her honesty.

He studied her intelligent brown eyes. Wilhelmina was an attractive woman. A wonderful woman. Another time, there might have been something between them. But just now...she was right. He wasn't ready.

Wilhelmina picked up her cup again. "I'm so sorry it didn't work out for you. Miranda is one special woman."

"She was. She is. It's just—"

"You don't have to talk about it. I didn't mean to pry." Waving a dismissive hand she took a sip of wine.

Parker bolstered his strength. Certainly he could casually discuss his former wife with a friend. "I don't mind, Wilhelmina. Really, I am all right."

She gave him an of-course-you-are grin. "I'll just say that I admire her courage. I can't believe what she's doing now."

Parker stiffened. What did Wilhelmina think Miranda was doing? "She's opened her own investigation office."

"Yes, but to take on someone like that as her first client." She shook her head in disbelief.

Parker froze. "Client?" He wasn't sure what clients Miranda had managed to get. He'd told himself he didn't care.

Wilhelmina straightened. "Oh, dear. You don't know, do you? I should have kept my mouth shut."

"I haven't kept up with Miranda's activities."

"No, I don't suppose you would."

There was an awkward pause.

"Are you going to tell me who her client is?"

Parker had never seen such a sheepish look on the elegant attorney's face. "I shouldn't have said anything."

"But now that you have..."

She nodded in acquiescence. "It's someone I first told her about over a year ago. Carlos Santiago."

Parker put down his drink with a thump. "The drug lord?"

"That's the only Carlos Santiago I know."

Parker felt as if Wilhelmina had just shot him in the chest. He nearly doubled over. Not only with the shock of this news, but with the rage bursting inside him like a break in the Hoover Dam. Foolish, irascible woman. She was going to get herself killed.

Just as he knew she would.

His first impulse was to rush over to her office in that God-forsaken part of town and demand to know what the hell she thought she was doing. His second impulse was to put Judd on a twenty-four-hour watch on her. His third impulse—the one that came after several deep breaths—was to recall he no longer cared what happened to Miranda Steele.

If she wanted to be careless and impulsive and throw all reason and caution to the wind, it was up to her. If she did in fact get herself killed, that was on her, too.

He was no longer responsible for her.

He realized Wilhelmina had been talking to him. He hadn't heard a word. "I'm sorry. What did you say?"

She repeated it. Evidently Santiago had hired Miranda to find a missing dancer. A girl who was a college student at Georgia Tech. Wilhelmina had heard it from Antonio, who'd heard it from Coco, who'd heard it from Joan Becker. Joan had gone to see Miranda yesterday afternoon.

His pulse returning to normal, Parker fortified himself with the rest of his rice wine. He longed for something stronger but, no. He had no intention of regressing to the state he'd been in after Miranda walked out on their marriage.

He thought of Dave's more than usual awkwardness today when he'd asked him to work on tracking down the source of those text messages on Miranda's phone. He must have known all this then. No wonder he'd been so uncomfortable.

He thought of the secrets he'd sensed tonight between Curt Holloway and Janelle Wesson. They knew it, too.

Dave Becker. He'd left him searching through old videos for a man who might have visited the Parker Agency to get to Miranda. Or to her phone.

His resolve grew solid as granite. He would find this man. He would show Miranda Steele the danger she was in. He would prove it to her.

He would have the last word.

"I'm sorry, Wilhelmina," he told his date, if that indeed was what this dinner had been. "But I need to get back to the office."

She blinked at him in surprise, but her expression quickly turned to understanding.

He said goodnight and without making arrangements for another get-together with the attorney, he called for the check, paid it, and left the restaurant.

CHAPTER TWENTY-TWO

It was just after seven-forty-five p.m., about an hour before the show. Miranda scanned the two dozen or so pairs of eyes staring up at her from the red felt chairs and white-clothed tables of *Exótico's* back meeting room.

In the chairs sat the club's entire staff. Kitchen workers, waiters, waitresses, hostesses, busboys, bouncers. All dressed in the universal black of those positions. Plus the dancers who were in jeans and a rainbow of T-shirts, their colors blending together under the muted light of fancy wall sconces.

The air fairly smelled of the tension in the room.

Everyone looked miserably uncomfortable, not only because of the subject of this meeting but because they probably weren't allowed in this place reserved for top dollar customers, except as servants.

Most of the non-performers were Hispanic. Dark-haired, ruddy-skinned friends and relatives of Santiago and his gang members. Keep it in the family.

And since that was so, Miranda knew they'd be willing to help. Or at least she hoped so.

"According to Dolly and Bambi," she told them after Santiago had introduced her and told them to listen up and cooperate, "there was a man in the audience who seemed to be extremely fond of Nitro."

Miranda shifted her weight and watched the nervous faces watching her.

Instead of a glittery, glam outfit she'd worn her best suit tonight. A black skirt and jacket ensemble that was austere, dark, serious. She thought it might scare answers out of tight-lipped workers, but maybe it was too intimidating.

Before she'd gone home to change, she'd finished her calls to the local hospitals. No Hannah Kaye or Jane Does matching her description had come in over the past five days. The GPS tracker on Hannah's car still hadn't produced any results, either. Miranda had left it running, wondering if she could get her money back if it ended up giving her zip.

So this meeting was her best bet right now. Somebody here had to know something about the mystery man.

"This man," she continued, "always sat in the front row when Nitro performed. Booth number three. According to witnesses he couldn't take his eyes off her. But last night, that seat was empty."

Some of the workers glanced cautiously at each other. By now everyone knew Hannah Kaye, aka Nitro had been missing since last Thursday. They were starting to get the creepy picture she was painting.

"This man had dark, curly hair, and a dark pencil mustache. He might have been driving a light color sedan."

"What kind of sedan?" a big-armed man standing in the back wanted to know.

At least someone had spoken. "Midsized. We don't have a specific model." She didn't want to lead them. She wanted them to tell her the details. "What I need to know is who among you knows something about this man. Does anyone know his name, for instance?" Might as well go for the gold.

A young man with a chunky face and a hairnet over his straight black hair put up a hand. "I do not know anything about this man," he said with a thick accent. "But I know Ms. Nitro, she was a big flirt with the customers."

Snickers tittered up from the group.

"That's an understatement," murmured a dancer with strawberry blond hair piled in braids atop her head.

Miranda pointed at her. "What do you know about it?"

"Me?"

"Yeah, you. You seem to have an opinion."

Her cheeks turning pink the dancer glanced over at the chunky-faced man. "Matias is right. Nitro was here for the attention. She was always talking to customers. More than we're supposed to." She shot a brief glimpse at Santiago and her face turned from rosy to crimson.

Another dancer waved a hand in the air. "It's true what they're saying, Ms. Steele. I don't know about that particular guy, but there were a lot of guys who would have loved to go out with Nitro. She encouraged them. She always needed to be out in front. Like Ginger said, she craved attention."

Murmurs of agreement rippled through the group.

It made sense. After all, Santiago had told her the customers adored Nitro's explosive, atomic bomb dancing. Miranda thought about what Hannah's roommate Bonnie had said. She was the quiet one and Hannah was the talker. Apparently it went farther than that. Miranda wondered if Hannah's craving for attention had something to do with her new step-mother.

She pointed at the waiters. "Do any of you remember serving this man drinks?"

They looked at each other blankly and shrugged. "We serve lots of people every night," a young woman with sunken eyes said with a scowl.

A man on the side of the room said, "I do not remember anyone in the front row matching that description."

"I do not remember no pencil-faced man," said another.

Drawing in a slow breath, Miranda summoned her patience. "Witnesses state the man came here every night for a whole week. Surely somebody noticed him." It couldn't have just been Dolly and Bambi, who for some reason were absent from this meeting. And so was Yolanda for that matter.

She pressed on. "Who's assigned to that section?"

"We take turns. Javier had it last night."

It would help if she knew which week the guy had been there. "How about the rest of this week and last? How about the whole month?"

The big-armed man in the back raised a finger. "I can get you that information. I'm the floor manager."

"Okay, thanks. In the meantime, does anyone know anything about this guy?"

Nobody said a word. They were getting fidgety. It was time to get started or they wouldn't be ready for the show.

"Anybody?"

Silence.

Miranda was about to give up and let them go when a skinny guy with large ears, who barely looked old enough to be in this place lifted a hand. "I've worked that section, ma'am," he said in with a squeak that reminded her a little of Marty Jenkins.

Miranda put a hand on her hip. "And?"

"I think I remember that guy. He'd always come in early and stayed late. Always sat in booth three. I remembered he ordered Irish Whiskey, neat. No ice, no soda."

Miranda stopped breathing. Somebody who actually remembered the guy? Was she finally getting somewhere? "What else can you recall?"

"Like your witnesses say, he was very focused on the stage. Especially when Nitro was on."

She had a thought. "Did he pay with a credit card?" If they could track that down, they'd have all the information she'd need to find the guy.

But the waiter shook his head. "Always cash. And he was a big tipper."

Miranda dismissed the group and marched over to Santiago who'd been standing silently in the corner the whole time watching the proceedings. Under the muted lights the silver satin of his open shirt playing against the gold of his chains and rings.

"Where's Yolanda? And Dolly and Bambi?" she demanded.

The gangster's hardened face grew harder. He wasn't pleased with her lack of progress. "They are getting ready for the show. Yolanda said they had already spoken to you."

That didn't mean they didn't have anything else to contribute. But she knew better than to argue with the drug lord. Instead she turned on her heel and headed out of the room and toward the backstage area.

She found Dolly, Bambi and the stage manager in Yolanda's office.

The room was filled with tulle and satin and glitter and perfume and hair spray. Dolly and Bambi stood back-to-back in the corner on a tiny round platform. Yolanda sat on the platform, pins in her mouth, adjusting the short hems of the matching costumes.

"You three missed my meeting," Miranda announced gruffly. She wasn't in the mood for games.

Bambi's big eyes grew round. "There was a meeting?"

She was playing dumb. Her standard MO, Miranda was starting to realize. She put a hand on her hip. "What's wrong with you? One of your co-workers is missing, and you don't want to help?"

Dolly stared up at the ceiling as if Miranda wasn't here.

"If there's some crazy killer out there, one of you could be next."

Yolanda took the pins out of her mouth and glared at her. "They know better than to go off with a customer they barely know."

"Is that what happened to Nitro, Yolanda? How do you know that? What haven't you been telling me?" The woman was holding something back. Miranda knew it.

Yolanda's dark eyes went hard. She got to her feet and made a shooing gesture toward the door. "Out of here, you two. I want to talk to the detective myself."

The girls stared at each other a moment then scampered out without a word of protest.

When the door was shut, Yolanda shot Miranda a hateful look. "You have a lot of nerve coming in here and scaring them. They are under enough pressure."

"What kind of pressure? What kind of things do these girls have to do?"

"It's not like that."

"Isn't it?"

Yolanda went around to her desk, sat down and turned to her computer. "I don't have time to talk to you. I have work to do. The show will be starting soon."

Miranda stomped across the little space and slammed her palms down on the desk so hard, the butts in the ashtray jumped. "You're holding out on me, Yolanda. Tell me what you know."

Yolanda stopped typing and focused on her cigarette pack. She reached for one and lit it, no doubt wishing she could blow Miranda away with a puff of smoke.

"What is it you want, detective?" Sarcasm dripped from her lips.

"I want to know about the man in booth number three."

The woman frowned unconvincingly. "Booth number three? I do not know what you mean."

Was she going to play dumb, like Bambi now? "I think you know exactly what I mean."

Yolanda took an extra long drag of her cigarette and blew the smoke over Miranda's shoulder, just missing her face. "Very well. I do know about this man."

"Who was he?"

"A customer. An admirer of Nitro."

"His name?"

She raised a careless shoulder. "Chuck, Bill, Sam. They are all the same."

Not in this case. "Yolanda, what the hell was his name?"

Yolanda's dark eyes flashed with anger. "I do not know his name. All I know was that I overheard the girls talking about him. For a while he came every night to see Nitro. He was crazy about her."

Nothing she hadn't already heard. "Go on."

"The girls thought he had a crush on Nitro. So one night I went out to see for myself. I peeked through the curtain and observed him."

"And?"

She flicked ashes into her tray. "And it was true. He watched her every move. I know that look. He was completely smitten."

She'd been right. This guy was her man, but a funny feeling gnawed at the pit of her stomach. "What aren't you telling me, Yolanda? What the hell did you do?"

The woman put down her cigarette, turned to her computer again as if she had nothing more to say.

"What, Yolanda?"

Her fingers froze on the keyboard. For a long time she just sat there. Then at last, the admission came. "I encouraged Nitro to start up a relationship with this young man."

Dear God. "With a stranger? Someone off the street who could have been a complete psycho?" And who probably was.

"Nitro was a smart girl. She could take care of herself."

"Apparently not."

Yolanda looked away, her mouth tight. Miranda couldn't be sure, but it looked like the woman was having a stroke of conscience. She dug in.

"Did you know Nitro had a boyfriend?"

Her eyes flashed again, this time with shock. "No, I did not."

"Did you know she broke up with him because of this guy?"

She shook her head. "No. I did not know about her personal life. Except where this man in booth three was concerned."

"Who was he?"

"I do not know."

"A relative? Someone you paid?"

"I do not know. He was a customer. A stranger." She reached for her cigarette took another drag, her fingers now shaking. "Nitro, she was such a big flirt. So full of herself. She craved attention. More than anyone I've ever seen."

"So? Didn't that make her good at this so-called job? Didn't that bring in money?"

A strange expression came over Yolanda. Anger, bitterness, regret. Miranda couldn't tell which.

"Dolly deserved to be the headliner," she said through gritted teeth. "She was the popular one before Nitro came along."

Now it was making sense. "And Dolly is...?"

Yolanda glared up at Miranda, this time there were tears in her dark eyes. "She is my niece. My sister's kid by a third marriage. We scraped and saved to send her to college and then she dropped out."

"I thought she graduated from Tech."

"That is what we tell people. The truth is she went there for three years and quit. The pressure got to be too much. And she did not believe she could get a job without graduate school. We could not afford it."

So that was it. After a crushing end to her dreams of higher education, Yolanda wanted her niece to have the choice spot on the stage. She wasn't going to let some upstart take it away from her. It was a case of stripper nepotism.

Yolanda put a hand to her head. "I never meant any harm to come to Nitro. I thought she would fall for the customer. Marry him, get pregnant. I swear to you. I do not know who that customer was. He was just a guy."

So she let the dancer go off with some guy and nobody even knew his name. "If the man in booth three's got Nitro, this is on your head, Yolanda."

"Please do not tell Carlos."

"Tell me what?"

Miranda turned to see Santiago standing in the office doorway. On impulse she decided to cover for Yolanda. "Nothing. We were just having a little girl chat."

Santiago's bitter look told her he didn't believe a word of that, but he had other things on his mind just now.

He gestured to a young man at his side. "This is Rafael Rodriguez. He has something to tell you."

Miranda looked him over. Another youthful staff member dressed in black. He wore sideburns and had his dark hair cut in an attractive fringe over his forehead. His deep brown eyes were intense.

"What is it, Rafael?"

He leaned forward as he spoke, like a singer pouring his soul into his act. "I do not know who the man you are looking for is, but I know he was here at the club."

Miranda's heart sank. "We've pretty much established that."

His head went back and forth. "That is not all, Ms. Steele. I remember when he was here."

When? That could be helpful. "Last week?"

He nodded. "Yes. And the week before that. Every night."

Okay. She dared to get her hopes up a little. "What about the last Thursday night Hannah worked here?"

"Yes, then too. They went out to the parking lot several times that night during Nitro's breaks. Once I saw her get into his car."

Just like Dolly had said. The current star of the show must be going through a doozey of a guilt trip. But that still didn't give Miranda anything she could use to hunt down the dude.

She thought a moment, then turned to Santiago. "Do you have video of the parking lot?"

"I do. Not very good quality, I am afraid."

No doubt figured he didn't need it with his bouncers. Plus he wouldn't want whatever they did with rowdy customers caught on disk. "Maybe we can see the car on it. It'll take some time to go through it, but if there's a chance we can get a license plate, we can start tracking this guy."

Again Rafael shook his head vehemently. "That will do you no good."

"Why?" Miranda barked. She was getting a little tired of being second guessed.

He raised his palms as if exasperated she didn't understand him. "Because the man in booth three is no longer in the car."

Miranda folded her arms. "How do you know that?"

Rafael paced over to the corner and back again. Miranda was beginning to think he was one of Santiago's substance abusers. Through the walls she could hear rocky music pounding. The show was getting started. She didn't have time for these antics.

Rafael turned and glared at her, a wild look in his eyes. "Because when I came in to work tonight, I saw it."

"Saw what?" She'd had just about enough of the histrionics. One more wacky statement and she was going to tell the boss to toss this guy out.

That was, until it suddenly hit her what the emotional staff member was trying to say.

He gazed at her with a watery stare. "The car that belongs to the man in booth three. It is parked two blocks down from the club."

CHAPTER TWENTY-THREE

The block Rafael had indicated was a too-long walk down a series of zigzagging back streets lined with ominous looking apartment buildings and parking decks. Several streetlamps had been broken out and in some spots the sidewalk was pitch-black. But with Santiago, the waiter, two bouncers, and her trusty Berretta in tow, Miranda felt safer than in her own bed.

And considering where she was living now, she probably was.

Under a row of Chinese elms alongside a shadowy wrought iron gate, they found the car.

It was a Hyundai, all right. Light gray. Maybe three years old. A dent in the right rear fender.

"You sure this is the vehicle?" Miranda said to Rafael.

He nodded. "I am positive. I remember the dent. And the mirror." He pointed at the window to something shiny on the inside.

Through the windshield Miranda spotted a rabbit's foot hanging from the rearview mirror. The guy in booth three must have been superstitious.

She took out her phone, snapped a photo of the tag, then strolled around and peered through the passenger window at the glove compartment.

One of the bouncers fisted his oversized hand and began removing his jacket to wrap it. "We can get in there for you, Ms. Steele."

She held up a palm. "Not necessary."

A break-in would generate too many questions if the police got involved. Instead Miranda reached into her pocket for her picks. After her trip to Marty Jenkins's house, she'd decided to keep them on her.

She pulled out one of the thin rods along with a tiny flashlight. As she stepped toward the passenger side lock, instinctively Santiago and the bouncers turned their backs and formed a protective wall around her.

Must know the drill.

She bent down, worked at the lock and after another minute or two, popped it open. She was getting better at this, she thought as she used the tail of her jacket to open the door.

Inside the air was stale and warm from the day's heat, scented with the smell of citrus air freshener. She scanned the cream colored leather seats with her flashlight. Clean, new looking. No sign of blood that she could see. No signs of a struggle.

Again she used her jacket to pull down the latch of the glove compartment.

She reached into the space and pulled out a neat stack of papers. The guy was tidy. She sifted through the stack. Maps, brochures to local sights, a concert ticket, and finally—the motherload.

Not only the Hyundai's registration but a genuine Georgia driver's license.

Miranda was stunned at her sudden stroke of luck. Why would the guy leave his driver's license here?

She stared at the card. At last she had a name.

Thomas Anthony Drew.

The picture was bad, as DMV photos tend to be. Dark, curly hair that fell down to his chin line. A dark pencil thin mustache under his nose. That was where the resemblance to Marty Jenkins ended. Even with the grainy shot, she could tell the guy was good-looking, as Crystal had claimed. And this dude was muscular. Big shouldered bodybuilding type, she'd say. Kept himself in shape.

She scanned the rest of the information. Birth date put him in his early thirties.

Once more she squinted at the photo. There was something vaguely familiar about it, but she couldn't put her finger on exactly what it was.

Keeping the papers she closed up everything, went around to the back, and checked the trunk. Nothing in it but a spare tire and a jack.

Staring down at the empty compartment her stomach jolted with a queasy, jittery sensation. If Thomas Anthony Drew's car was here and clean, what had happened to Hannah's car? Did he take her away in it? If so, she needed to find it. Fast.

Under her breath she cursed her slow GPS tracker.

Santiago must have read her mind. He turned around, craned his neck to take a look at the license still in her hand. A rumble came from deep in his chest. It didn't take much to see Hannah Kaye aka Nitro could be in a world of trouble.

His eyes glowing darkly Santiago put a finger in her face, "Find my dancer, Miranda Steele," he demanded.

Somehow she had to do just that.

At least she had a better chance of fulfilling Santiago's command than she'd had before. Hurrying home with the new information, Miranda sat down at her card table and checked the GPS tracker she'd left running on her laptop.

Seventy-two percent.

Damn. At this rate, by the time she found Hannah Kaye's car, she'd be ready for retirement.

Resisting the urge to write an angry email to the application's creators, she opened a new window and began searching for more information on Thomas Anthony Drew.

This time she got speedier results. After only a minute she had several pages of data. She scanned the details on the first screen.

No rap sheet. No arrests at all. Drew had lived at the same address in a high-rise apartment on Ponce de Leon for the past three years. He worked for Phelps Supply Company in Decatur as a truck driver.

Really? What was he doing off the road and going to a strip club every night for the past two weeks? Had he lost his job? Maybe he was a local driver.

She scrolled to the next page. No record of a marriage. No record of a family of any kind. And then…? Nothing. She pressed the down arrow several times, but the rest of the page was blank.

Maybe this app wasn't as good as she'd thought.

She opened another one that she hadn't used yet. This one was really pricey, so it had better give her something good. She had to get the ID numbers from the other screen. And she had to consult the Help file several times. But after twenty minutes of electronic finagling she found a single account for Thomas Anthony Drew. A small sum in a local bank that hadn't been touched in three years.

What the heck? What did he live off of?

She sat back and rubbed her eyes. Was she seeing things? Before three years ago, it looked like Thomas Anthony Drew…didn't exist.

A frosty shiver went through her.

She recalled sitting in a chair in the manager's office at a nursing home in Evanston, Illinois a few weeks ago. She and her police detective partner had been searching for the suspect in the Lydia Sutherland case.

They thought they had found him, but the records of the man in the nursing home had been doctored. It had turned out to be a ninety-one-year-old man.

She bent down and took off the bracelet she'd clasped around her ankle the other night. The light caught the dull sheen on the heart-shaped pendant. Miranda stared at the initials.

A.T. Adam Tannenburg. Lydia Sutherland's lover.

Tannenburg, the man she'd been searching for, had transferred his identity to the man in the nursing home and disappeared. Had someone likewise borrowed Thomas Anthony Drew's identity?

The idea made the hair on the back of her neck stand up. Feeling suddenly chilly, she rubbed her arms and tried to shake off the sensation.

At least she had data now. She had a place of employment, and a residence. She'd track them both down in the morning. Whoever Thomas Anthony Drew was, she'd find him.

She put the bracelet around her wrist, printed out her research, and shutdown her laptop. She gathered up all her papers, put them in her briefcase for the morning and moved into the bedroom. Her hopes started to rise.

Disregarding the missing information from three years prior, there was nothing in anything she'd found on Thomas Anthony Drew to indicate he was a weirdo. Maybe he had really fallen in love with the explosive Nitro. There was probably a reasonable explanation for the lapse in his records. Probably issues with her applications. And maybe Hannah Kaye had gone off with Drew for a fling, as Crystal had said back at the club. Maybe they had flown to Vegas to get hitched and were on their honeymoon right now. That was what Yolanda had hoped for.

It could have happened.

Everything could turn out just fine. And with luck, she'd find Hannah Kaye and have her back in class tomorrow. Or at least know where she was and where she'd been all this time.

She pulled down her covers, got into bed and switched off the light.

Yes, everything would be all right. If there had been a glitch in that data. If her optimistic interpretation was right. If the stubborn nagging in her gut was wrong.

And if the dancer was still alive.

CHAPTER TWENTY-FOUR

Parker sat back in the creaky chair at Dave Becker's desk in the Agency lab and rubbed his tired eyes with both hands. The muscles in the back of his neck ached. He felt as stiff as cement.

He and Dave had searched through hours of disk recordings from the surveillance cameras planted in the office. Now displayed on Dave's large flat screen monitor was the section of the cube bank near Miranda's desk. Parker had watched it until the pale blue tones of the office décor had melted into a grayish blob. They had both grown numb listening to the steady hum of office noise.

But they had seen little activity.

Occasionally a worker would pass by, stop to chat, continue on. An hour later another would stroll past on his way to the restroom. A few minutes later, he would return. At lunchtime there would be a flurry of commotion. Then the screen would return to its static image.

It was the dullest of deadly dull work.

So far only Agency employees had appeared on the recording. No one Parker didn't know personally to some extent. No one he didn't trust. No one who made any suspicious moves.

He feared they had reached another dead end.

Parker glanced at the time in the corner of the screen. Past eleven. He was working his employees to death. And for what?

"Did you get something to eat?" he asked Dave.

Dave's body jolted out of his concentration at the question. He gave Parker a shy look and shrugged. "Yes, sir. I got something across the street while you were...out."

Parker's dinner date with Wilhelmina Todd had already faded into a distant memory, but he could see Dave was longing to ask about it. He was glad his employee was discreet enough to contain his curiosity.

Parker rose to stretch, then reached for the jacket and tie he'd laid across the back of a nearby chair. "Perhaps it's time to call it a night."

Dave sat back, watching an image on the screen move slowly through the cubes. "I'm wondering something, sir."

"What's that?"

"Maybe we're looking at the wrong timeframe."

They had agreed to focus on normal business hours. The time when clients stopped by for appointments. They had hoped to find someone lurking around Miranda's desk—at some point during the day.

They had started with the recordings from nearly a year ago, early October of last year when Miranda had gone to Lake Placid, and worked from there. Her desk had been empty most of the ensuing months. She had been convalescing from the dire injuries she'd received in the northeast.

"This is the timeframe with the best opportunity to access Miranda's phone," Parker reminded Dave.

She had come into the office in January of that year for half a day's work, which had proven too much for her. She'd left her phone at her desk by mistake. Wanting her to stay home and not think about work, Parker hadn't brought it to her. It had remained in her desk drawer for two weeks.

Frowning Dave nodded. "Yeah, you're right."

Parker draped his coat and tie over his arm. "Let's stop for tonight. Don't come in before eleven tomorrow. I want you fresh."

"Okay, sir." But there was a far away tone in Dave's voice. He was at his keyboard again.

Wearily Parker scowled. "What are you doing?"

"Just trying something."

Parker was considering ordering him to stop when there was a knock on the door.

"Anybody in here?"

"Of course, he is. Becker lives in here." Janelle Wesson made a long-legged march into the room, followed by Curt Holloway.

She blinked when she saw Parker standing beside Dave's desk. "Oh, hello, sir. I thought you had left."

"I did. I came back."

Wesson folded her arms self-consciously, still in her robin's egg blue suit. Holloway was still in his sport coat and tie.

Standing next to him was Sybil, his receptionist. She'd changed from her usual silky and fashionable attire she wore at the front desk to jeans and a form-fitting T-shirt with an artistic painting of a blue horse on the front. Her brown-and-auburn hair was pulled back with a matching artificial flower. She smelled as if she'd just refreshed the expensive perfume she liked to wear.

Despite their attire, all three of them looked rumpled and weary, dark circles growing under their eyes.

He should give them all the day off tomorrow and let them return to their normal tasks the next day. This had been an exercise in utter futility. From now on he would work on this case alone. If he wanted to waste time, he would waste only his own.

"Why are you all still here?" he grunted at them.

Holloway pointed a thumb at the receptionist. "Sybil's been helping us go through the logs, sir."

"Have you found anything?"

"No, sir. No odd calls. No strange visitors. That's what we came to tell you." Holloway's shoulders slumped.

"I'm sorry, sir," Wesson said.

"Really sorry," Sybil echoed.

Dear Lord, it wasn't her fault. It wasn't anyone's fault. If the person they were looking for wasn't in the logs, he wasn't in the logs.

"Let's all go home," Parker said longing for his bed and changing his mind about that strong drink before lying down.

"Wait. I think I might have something here."

Holloway turned to Dave. "What, Becker?"

Wesson moved over behind Dave's chair and peered at the screen. "Is that from those surveillance cameras?"

"What is that?" Parker wanted to know.

But he could see it for himself. The area around Miranda's desk was on the screen. The same recording they'd been viewing for hours. But the lighting was different this time.

"We've been looking at regular office hours." Dave said, his voice filling with childlike excitement. "But I thought we'd try a little later in the evening. This is from eight at night."

Parker squinted at the screen feeling as if his eyes were playing tricks on him.

A grayish figure stood in the opening to Miranda's cube. He wore some sort of uniform. He looked as if he were studying her name tag. After several moments he stepped right into the workspace. The camera angle was sharp, a lot was hidden behind the cube wall, but it was plain what the man was doing. Rummaging through Miranda's desk drawers.

When he found what he was looking for, the grin on his face was as clear as the noonday sun on Mercury.

As was what he had in his hand—Miranda's cell phone.

He did something with the device, then bent down so he couldn't be seen. A moment later he stepped out of her cube and disappeared around the far corner.

He had taken Miranda's phone number.

He was the one. Dave had found him.

Holloway clapped his colleague on the back. "Way to go!"

"Good work, Becker," Wesson chimed in gleefully.

But Sybil put a hand to her mouth and let out a squeal as she stared wide-eyed at the screen. "I know him. That's Gabriel."

"Who?" Parker asked.

"Gabriel, sir. I don't know his last name. He's on the cleaning staff."

"Cleaning staff?"

"They come in at night. They dust, empty the trash, water the plants, that sort of thing."

Of course. Parker thought a moment. "With the building management."

"Yes, sir. I have to admit I always thought he was kind of weird."

"What do you mean, Sybil?"

"I don't know. I didn't see him very often unless I was working late. But when I did see him…I just didn't like the way he looked at me."

Parker nodded. At the moment he didn't like anything about the man. He had to find out more about him. Parker had leased this floor from Gypsum Management for years and he had a good relationship with the director, but their offices would be closed at this hour.

"I'll follow up on this tomorrow," he said. "Dave, can you enlarge the image of that man?"

Dave's fingers flew over his keyboard, clicking away. He reversed the recording, paused it just before the man entered Miranda's cube. He pressed more keys and the man's face and shoulders filled the screen. But the image was grainy.

"Can you make that clearer?"

Dave attempted more keyboard magic but the image remained the same. He shook his head. "Not at this resolution, sir."

He should have invested more in the equipment. This would have to do. "Print a copy of that for me."

"Aye, aye, sir." Grainy or not, Dave was obviously thrilled with his find.

Parker reminded himself to commend his employee. "This is excellent work, Detective. Excellent work."

The poor man's cheeks glowed red as a stop sign. "Thank you, sir. Just doing my job."

"More than your job. As all of you have done tonight. And now that we've made some progress, let's go home."

"Good idea," Holloway chuckled. "C'mon, Becker. Let's all get a beer to celebrate."

Turning off his computer Dave shook his head. "I'd better pass or Joanie will have my hide."

"Chicken," Holloway teased. He turned to Parker. "Would you like to go, sir?"

"No, thank you, Curt. I need to get home." And though there was no one at home to chide him for staying out so late, and his bed would be empty, he nonetheless longed for it.

He was going to have a busy day tomorrow. If he could track down this maintenance man, he just might have the answers he'd been looking for for weeks.

As his employees filed out, Parker went to the printer and pulled the photo of the man named Gabriel and studied it a moment.

He was a good-looking man. Broad shouldered, seemed to be in his early thirties. A crop of shaggy, dirty blond hair stuck out from under his ball cap.

The image reminded him of someone. But Parker couldn't think who. He wasn't familiar with the cleaning staff.

He pulled on his coat, folded the paper and put it in his pocket. Draping his tie around his neck he headed for the rear exit.

He'd skip the drink for tonight, he decided. He didn't need it now. Amazing how a bit of progress on a case could lift one's spirits.

But as he reached the stairwell, his memory kicked in.

The image of the cleaning man who had taken Miranda's cell number matched the image in his mind of the suspect on their last case. Or rather, Miranda's case. The cold case she'd worked in Chicago.

He'd never seen a photo of the man, try as they might to find one. But the description was the same. Good-looking. A muscular build. Longish shaggy blond hair. He would be in his early thirties by now. He'd been the love interest of the victim in the case, a twenty-year-old art student named Lydia Sutherland. The police had questioned him in her death.

Miranda had tried to track the suspect down but to no avail. After the death of his mother in a fire that had destroyed the family estate, the young man had completely disappeared.

And Parker knew why.

But he didn't know where the man was now or what he had to do with a cleaning man working for Gypsum Management. It was probably just a coincidence.

In all probability this man named Gabriel had nothing to do with Adam Foster Tannenburg.

And yet the likeness in his mind lingered. And as he reached the parking lot and climbed into his car, Parker couldn't help but feel unnerved by the image.

CHAPTER TWENTY-FIVE

Finished for the night, he climbed the creaky steps to the main area of the forty-year-old house he'd found in the woods, pleased with what he had accomplished.

The hour was late, but he wasn't hungry.

He went into the kitchen and washed the blood off his hands. Then he poured himself a glass of wine, took a bag of ice from the freezer. Carrying them both into the small living room, he switched on the MP3 player on the sparse mantelpiece and smiled at the lovely sound it emitted.

Mozart. The clarinet concerto in A. One of his favorites.

He settled into the old musty recliner near the fireplace and took a sip from the wine glass. He let the liquid play over his tongue, its sharp citrus flavor pleasing him. He'd chosen well. A white rioja from Spain, its lineage going back to the Phoenicians. In his choice of libation he was a purist.

As he was with his projects.

He inhaled deeply, but the air in this place was foul. He scowled at the mold growing along the baseboards. It was only a temporary dwelling, he reminded himself. He would move on soon.

This project was almost over.

He placed the ice pack against his sore jaw. The tender place where she'd kicked him with those long strong legs. He'd made her pay for that affront. Dearly. And her blood curdling cries in response were as lovely to his ears as the strains of this Mozart symphony.

Intensely satisfying.

He laid his head back and closed his eyes as the happy allegro notes of the first movement washed over him. He conducted with his hand a moment until the deep, rich tones of the clarinet began. One of Mother's best pieces. She'd made him learn it, too.

They were so like playing the clarinet, his projects.

You had to know just how the joints went together, how to twist them, how to place the fingers, the tongue to get the right tone and pitch and timbre.

He could play their bodies as well as he once did his own instrument. He could take their shrieks and wails through all the registers at will.

The low chalumeau, the shrill clarion, the high altissimo, his favorite. And the quality was always filled to the brim with helpless terror.

He chuckled to himself. He was quite an expert now.

But as he readjusted the icepack against his sore jaw, the anger simmered again inside him. How dare she kick him?

Yes, he had made her pay. She wasn't kicking now. She had passed out from the pain of her punishment. But it didn't take away the memories.

The way he used to pass out when Mother punished him.

Along his back he could still feel the tufts of the bedcover where she'd make him lie naked. Feel the tears in his throat he swallowed down, knowing it would only be worse if he made a noise. Smell the sickening scent of the strawberry oil she always wore as she neared the bed.

She would start with the clarinet. Caressing, teasing his member until he burned with shame.

He remembered her crooked smile, the delight in her eyes at the unnatural act. The excruciating pain rippling through his body when she grabbed him between his legs and squeezed and squeezed and squeezed.

He would cry out, of course. He could hold back no longer. What child could?

That had always made her so angry. So very angry.

The anger brought on the beatings. Merciless. Unrelenting. Over and over she would strike and poke him with her conductor's baton. She would raise stinging welts, break skin, make him bleed. He would end up crying himself to sleep in the dark closet where she'd lock him after she'd finished with him.

But none of that mattered now, did it? Of course not.

He'd paid her back, too.

And he continued to pay her back with every whore he found who took her place. They were all like Mother. Blond and lovely and seductive.

And they were all dead.

He had done to them what she had done to him. And worse. Much worse. And then he'd finished them off.

And this one? The one in the basement of this foul house?

She had no more than a day left in her. He was sure of that. He could estimate time of death rather precisely after so many years of practice.

He knew how to dispose of a body. *He* had taught him that. But he'd found that wasn't always necessary if one was careful. And he was always careful. Meticulously careful. As thorough and detailed as he was in the crafting of his punishment for these whores.

Whores. That was what they were. *He* had taught him that, too. He could still hear his harsh voice croaking out the words that night he watched him fuck and kill the one who was supposed to have been his.

He'd told her what she was that night.

Whore. Whore. Whore.

The words clanging in his head he groaned and pushed the memory back into the past where it belonged. The wine made his thoughts drift. Not so far back now. Only a year ago.

To last October.

He'd just finished a project and was in the living room of the house he'd selected, much like this one. He'd been settling down in front of the television with caviar and a claret to celebrate the completion of another job well done.

And then the news had come on.

Lake Placid. A skating competition. A shooting. A dreadful disaster. People were dead.

And then the screen flashed a photo of one of the victims, a man in a policeman's uniform, taken years ago.

His chest had spasmed with shock.

It was *him*. *Him*.

In his uniform. Just the way he remembered him. He was dead.

Then they showed someone being carried out of the stadium on a stretcher. He had stared at the image dumbfounded. His heart began to burn and pound with painful, violent memory.

It was her. She had killed him.

He'd never expected to see her again. Never thought he would find her. Never intended to. That wasn't his plan.

Or was it?

He couldn't ignore it. It was as if fate had handed her to him, delivered her right into his hands. He listened carefully to the details of the broadcast. They said she worked for a private detective agency in Atlanta, Georgia. And that she might not live.

Immediately he'd travelled to Lake Placid. He'd gone to the hospital, tried to get in to see her, but there were too many people.

Instead he'd waited and watched.

And after a time she recovered and went home. And when she did, he followed her. And watched some more. She went into rehabilitation and eventually returned to her place of employment.

He learned all about her. Where she lived. Who she was married to. Her friends. Her colleagues. Her routines.

Months passed and she started to travel with her husband. Again he watched her on television, all the while a plan forming in his mind.

He thought of her image on the screen during her press conference in Las Vegas. Her dark, unruly hair, the blue of her eyes, the form of her body beneath her professional suit, her confident stance.

She'd grown strong, bold.

But the strong could be made weak. And no one could weaken a whore like he could. He could hear her cries now. Feel her shudder with electrifying pain. See the shape of her lips as she begged him to stop. Soon. Soon.

Now after so much waiting, after so much watching, his plan for her was about to come to fruition at last.

Of course, her separation from her husband had thrown a wrench in his plan. But it had only caused him to come up with a better one. One that would destroy them both with its agony.

He chuckled to himself and reached for his wineglass. She was a delight to chase, would be more of a delight to capture. She kept him on his toes. It would almost be a shame to end her. But not quite.

The pain in his jaw was subsiding, soothed by the knowledge she would soon be in his hands. He inhaled deeply in anticipation of the things he would do to her. This would be his greatest project of all.

His finale. The last movement.

At last he would have her. And when he was done with her, he'd be done for good.

CHAPTER TWENTY-SIX

Footsteps followed her.

Noiseless footsteps she could feel in her nerves rather than hear. They were behind her now. Growing closer, closer.

She clamored down the stairwell. Flight after flight after flight. Her heart pounded in her ears like a hammer breaking bone.

Down, down she went. As if she were descending into the center of the earth. But then the stairs were gone. Tall neatly trimmed hedges surrounded her. A shadowy dark green path lay before her.

Only one way to go. The footsteps were close behind.

She ran.

Her bare feet slapped on the dewy grass. She pushed herself faster, faster, faster. Rounding a turn she thought she might slip on the moisture. Somehow she managed to keep her balance and go on.

The footsteps were getting nearer.

She had to get away. And yet she wasn't just running from him. She was running toward someone.

Someone she had to save.

But she was growing tired and there was only one path after another and another. No end to it. She was caught in a maze.

Trapped.

She gasped for breath, her lungs burning. Her chest felt as if it might explode. She needed to stop. Just for a minute.

But it was too late.

Rough hands reached around her, snatched at her throat. She lost her balance and went down hard. Pain rippled through her body. She wasn't on the soft grass now. She was on the icy pavement.

In an alley. On a cold February night.

The hands kept grasping for her tearing at her face, her clothes.

"Stop," she cried. "Leave me alone."

She struggled, punched, scratched, struck out. It did no good.

The hands turned her over as if she were a rag doll. He hovered above her. She strained to see his face, but it was covered with a dark ski mask. Her vision blurred with her tears, but she could see him reach for his pants, hear the clang of his belt buckle and the unzipping as he pulled them down. She felt the hands tearing at her underwear.

She closed her eyes, braced herself for the pain, the helpless desperate pain. And all the despair that went with it. All she could sense now was the nauseating smell of cheap cologne. And the sound of his raspy voice whispering against her ear.

Whore, whore, whore.

Miranda's eyes jolted open and her mouth parted in a loud cry.

She turned her head, felt the sheet beneath her damp with her own sweat. She squinted at the light coming through her window. Daylight. It was morning. She was in her own bed.

Her heart still racing, she sat up and rubbed her face.

A nightmare. Another one.

When were they going to end? She thought they had once. But they'd come back. They'd started up again in Las Vegas. She'd had them during her last case in Chicago. She remembered those. Leon chasing her down, striking her, raping her.

She shuddered and wrapped her arms around herself for comfort.

It was stupid. These dreams weren't real. Leon was dead.

And then she remembered Parker's real life arms slipping around her after a bad dream, holding her close, soothing her pain away.

Parker.

He was the real tragedy of her life, she thought, as the horror of the nightmare subsided into the ache she was living with day-to-day because of that man. If only he had listened to her. If only she could have made him understand. If only they could have worked something out. But no.

He was too stubborn to even discuss their differences. He was a my-way-or-the-highway kind of man. At least when it came to what she did for a living.

With an irritated grunt she shoved the sheets aside and got up. She didn't have time for psychological nonsense. She had to go to work.

She got a shower and dressed. In the kitchen she grabbed her briefcase, a protein bar, a cup of coffee, and headed out the door.

First stop, Phelps Supply Company. Thomas Anthony Drew's place of employment. By the end of the day she intended to find out everything there was to know about the owner of that light gray Hyundai—including the whereabouts of Hannah Kaye.

But before she had reached the decorative dumpster that sat beneath her window, her cell rang.

She reached for her phone and grunted when she saw the number. Chambers. What the hell did he want?

"Steele Investigations," she answered professionally as she balanced the cell under her chin and the rest of her things in her arms while she unlocked her car.

"You know anything about an abandoned car near club *Exótico*, Steele?"

Uh oh. She pulled the door open set her cup in the holder, tossed her briefcase on the seat. "Good morning to you, too, Chambers. Why would I know anything about that?"

"Someone in a nearby apartment called it in last night. Seems it had been sitting there a few days and he thought the owner would come get it eventually. But around nine o'clock last evening a gang of thugs showed up and broke into it."

Good grief. She hadn't been thinking about nosey neighbors last night. She climbed inside and started the car.

"When we got there everything seemed to be intact except the glove compartment had been cleaned out."

Play dumb, she decided as she turned onto Juniper Street and headed east. "Once again, why should I know anything about that?"

"Because the good neighbor described the person who broke into said vehicle. It was a woman. And she looked just like you."

Jeez. Chambers sure knew how to ruin a morning. She laughed breezily. "What a coincidence."

"Isn't it though? So if you do happen to know anything about the contents of that glove compartment, perhaps you'd be good enough to swing by the station and turn it in?"

"Sorry, Chambers. I've got appointments this morning. Maybe later this afternoon."

"Gee, Steele. I'd hate to have a judge issue a bench warrant for you."

She glowered into the phone. "I'll be there as soon as I can. Hey, have you gotten anywhere with the search for Hannah Kaye's car?"

Her app had been stuck on eighty-three percent when she'd checked it this morning. Surely Chambers could do better.

But all she heard now was a lot of throat clearing. "Haven't run it yet," Chambers said finally. "Had a double shooting come in last night."

And yet he had time to worry about some papers taken from an abandoned car. But that was okay. She didn't want him involved in this case anyway. "Never mind," she told him.

"Don't you worry, Steele. I'll get to it soon."

Sure, sure, she wanted to say, but decided not to challenge him. Chambers had too much male ego not to brag if he got a lead. If that got back to Santiago, she'd be in a world of hurt.

"Just be sure you bring those papers in today."

Rolling her eyes, she gave him her best imitation of a mocking little girl voice. "Whatever you say, Officer."

And she hung up.

CHAPTER TWENTY-SEVEN

Phelps Supply Company in Decatur turned out to be a warehouse on Church Street next to a strip mall and across from a burger place.

After a forty-five minute drive that would have taken fifteen without traffic, Miranda parked her Acura near the loading bays and sat watching two big dudes in tan uniforms struggling to get a pallet of heavy-looking boxes into the back of a truck.

Good place to start.

She got out and made her way over the gravel, noting the sky was turning gray and there was a welcome cool breeze in the air.

"Hey, there," she called out, pretending to be a friendly local.

The men ignored her as they continued to grunt under their load. Both their faces were shiny with sweat as their muscles strained.

Before she reached the dock a voice rang out behind the men.

"Jones! Connelly! What in tarnation are you two knuckleheads doing?"

A small bald man in a blue short sleeved shirt and a cherry red bowtie marched up behind them. He carried a clipboard in one hand. Must be the manager.

One of the big dudes set his end of the package down and straightened. "Trying to load this delivery, Mr. Phelps."

The little guy, who Miranda took to be Mr. Phelps, waved both hands in the air. "Use the forklift."

"It's got a flat tire."

Phelps gestured inside the darkened space of the warehouse. "Well, fix it then."

"No time. We're behind."

The little guy glared at his watch, put his hands on his hips. "Where's Montgomery?"

The second big dude, who'd also put his end of the package down by now shrugged, palms up. "Didn't come in today."

That brought on a string of cussing from Phelps that would have made a lesser woman blush. But Miranda had heard similar diatribes before from construction bosses she'd worked for.

Phelps' entire bald head turned as red as his bowtie.

Better be careful. Might drop over of a heart attack with a temper like that in the Georgia heat. Well, it was a few degrees cooler today.

"Fix the damn tire now," Phelps yelled. "You're going to hurt yourselves and give me a workers' comp claim. I'll call the client and tell them you'll be late."

"Yes, sir." The big dudes said together. Then the two of them disappeared into the warehouse.

"Excuse me," Miranda called out before the boss man got away.

Phelps peered down at her as if she were a mutant from outer space. "Yes?"

Miranda peered at the angry little man. "You the owner?"

He flapped his arms in a what-now? gesture. "What if I am? Are you a lawyer or something?"

"Private investigator."

His head jerked back in surprise. "Is one of my guys in trouble?"

"Not that I know of." Yet. "I just need a few minutes of your time, if you can spare it."

Taking out his cell phone, Phelps shook his head. "We're pretty booked up this morning, as you must have overheard."

Miranda smiled up at him. "Okay. I'll go talk to the local police instead. I saw a station right up the road." She hadn't really but there was probably one nearby.

She took a half step toward her car, watched him fume, his head turning from that cherry color to pink to cherry again.

Finally he gave her a come-ahead wave. "Five minutes. Let's go to my office."

While Phelps made his call to the client who was going to get his order late, Miranda climbed the cement steps to the ramp and followed the little guy through the warehouse.

They passed a dozen aisles of tall shelving units all filled with cardboard boxes of various sizes and finally slipped through a door at the far end. Here they crossed a space that looked like a waiting room with cheap chairs and cheap linoleum on the floor. One wall was covered in cheap paneling.

Phelps' office was at the end of it. He ushered her inside and offered a chair with a cracked seat cushion.

The office was small, messy, and smelled of the cheese-and-egg breakfast sandwich lying half eaten on the desk.

Made her new place look like a showcase, Miranda thought as she gingerly sat, hoping the chair didn't pinch her butt.

Phelps settled down behind the desk in an office chair that looked like it came from the fifties. "How can I help you?"

She took out a business card and handed it to him. "My name is Miranda Steele and I'm working on a missing persons case. One of your employees may have been involved."

He took the card, glanced at it, shook his head. "All my guys are aboveboard. All bonded. I check everyone out myself before I hire them."

She smiled again. "I'm sure you do, Mr. Phelps. However, I'm looking for someone in particular."

His chair creaked as he sat back and folded his arms over his skinny stomach.

Miranda reached into her briefcase and took out the driver's license she'd pilfered last night. "His name's Thomas Anthony Drew."

Phelps took the card and studied it, irritation playing over his face. "Yeah, he worked for us. I remember him."

Didn't look like the memory was a fond one. "He doesn't work for you now?"

"He quit two months ago. First week of June. I remember because we had a big order and I needed every driver I could get. Monday morning comes and he's a no show." He uttered a few more curse words under his breath.

Two months ago. Miranda scanned her memory banks. That was about the time she and Parker were heading out to Las Vegas. "So Drew was a driver here?"

Phelps nodded. "Did a lot of the local runs. He started in February, I recall. That's the time of year I take on new drivers."

"What exactly do you do here, Mr. Phelps?"

"We deliver medical supplies."

"What sort of supplies?"

"You name it. Stretchers, incubators, operating tables. X-ray machines, ECGs, defibrillators."

Drew must have been strong to handle loads like that, though he'd probably used the forklift.

"We do small stuff, too," Phelps said, a tinge of pride surfacing. "Syringes, cold packs, foam cushions. Right down to band aids." He smirked as he handed the license back to her. "Drew had the deliveries for Saint Benedictine Hospital, one of our biggest clients. We almost lost them because of him."

Saint Benedictine Hospital? That was where she'd done her rehab after her injuries in Lake Placid. "Have you been in contact with him since he quit?"

Phelps shook his head. "Nope. I docked him for part of the loss. Expected him to fight me on it, but he never even picked up his last paycheck."

That was odd. Miranda had quit a bunch of jobs she'd gotten fed up with over the years but she'd never left money on the boss's table. So where did Drew go? He was obviously still in the area. Had to be working someplace.

"Did he ever contact anyone here for a reference for his next job?" she asked.

Phelps bared a set of yellow teeth. "Nobody would give him a good reference after the stunt he pulled."

Good point. She needed to know more about the guy. "Before the day he didn't show up was Drew a good worker?"

Phelps jiggled his hand in the air. "He was okay. Strong as an ox. But a little…what would you call it? Distracted."

"Distracted?" Not a good quality for a truck driver.

"A dreamer. I think he played music or something. Had an eye for the ladies though."

That remark set off Miranda's sensors. "Why do you say that?"

"My bookkeeper told me he was always hanging around her office. Said it gave her the creeps."

Now they were getting somewhere. "Can I talk to her?"

"She's off today."

Miranda considered her options. It would be nice to talk to some of Drew's coworkers and get their perspectives on the guy, but this lead promised more relevant information. And if Thomas Anthony Drew had Hannah Kaye somewhere, she needed to cut to the chase.

"Is there any way I can talk to your bookkeeper, Mr. Phelps?"

He shook his head. "I don't give out my employees' personal information."

"Can you make an exception? A young woman's life may be at stake."

It was if Phelps just put together what she'd said about the missing persons case. His jaw went back and forth as he considered the implications.

Finally he picked up his phone. "I'll call her and see what she says."

CHAPTER TWENTY-EIGHT

The bookkeeper, whose name was Peggy Kinley, turned out to be a lot friendlier than her boss. She said the investigator could come right over and speak to her. Phelps had no choice but to hand over her address.

The woman lived in a nice second-story apartment off Buford Highway in Duluth. Half an hour later, Miranda was sitting on a creamy sky blue couch in her eggshell painted living room, sipping coffee.

"I appreciate your seeing me so quickly," Miranda told her.

"Oh, no problem," the woman said with a thick southern accent that sounded like she'd come from a deeper part of the state. "When Mr. Phelps said you were looking for a missing woman, I just had to help."

She seemed to be around Miranda's age and was a pretty, tan woman with a lot of blond hair and a lot of freckles. Must like the sun.

"Still, thank you for letting me come over on your day off."

Making a puffing sound with her lips, Peggy Kinley settled onto the other end of the couch. "Day off. That asshole cut back my hours." She opened a packet of artificial sugar and daintily sprinkled it into her coffee cup, shrugging in resignation. "At least I have some time to get errands done so I can be with my kids more. They're in school now."

Miranda cast a glance at the photos along the white fireplace in the corner. A young boy and girl were featured in most of them, but there was a man in them, too."

"Are you married?"

"Oh, yes. Going on nine years. Ken's a firefighter. He's at the station now. They go in twenty-four hour shifts, so I'm on my own today."

"I see."

Miranda sipped her coffee—hers was black, of course—and took in Peggy Kinley's long blond hair and trim tan body. She smelled of an orangey body mist and had on tight white shorts and a pink top that didn't hide the fact she was well-endowed. She had a lot of similarities with Hannah Kaye. Friendly, talkative, trusting. Too trusting maybe.

"So tell me what you know about this man." Once again Miranda took out Drew's license and showed it to Mrs. Kinley.

She watched the woman's face.

A crease formed between her large brown eyes and the ends of her lips twisted a bit.

"Why, that's Tommy Drew. Mr. Phelps didn't mention he had anything to do with your case."

"How do you remember him, Mrs. Kinley?"

"Oh, call me Peg. Everybody does. How do I remember him?" She grimaced a little more as she studied the photo. "He was a nice enough guy when he started, I suppose."

"Do you remember when that was?"

She tilted her head. "Had to be back in February. That's when Mr. Phelps always brings on new truckers to train for the year."

So Drew hadn't been with the company long.

"Anything in particular you remember about Drew?"

"About Tommy?" she fiddled with her coffee cup. "I don't really have much to do with the warehouse workers. Except on payday."

Didn't want to talk about it. Miranda was familiar with the avoidance techniques. "Phelps mentioned Drew didn't pick up his last check."

"Oh, yes. That's right. He didn't come in to work one day. And he never picked it up after that. I mailed it to his address but it came back."

That was a disturbing thought. "Did you mail it to the address on that license?"

Peg studied the data on the card and seemed relieved not to be looking at the photo any longer. "I'm pretty sure that's it. I'd have to look at his old file to be sure."

"That's okay," Miranda said.

A new address would have popped on the background check she'd run last night. She'd find out what the deal with the address was when she visited Drew herself in the next little while.

With an awkward smile Peg handed the card back to her as if it were a dirty rag.

Miranda fixed the woman with her gaze. She didn't want to miss any telltale signs, though she'd already seen plenty. "Is there anything else you remember about Drew, Peg?"

"Well…"

"It would really help my investigation."

She gave a quick nod and took in a breath. "Tommy could be awfully…friendly at times."

"Friendly how?" Miranda asked trying not to sound like a bulldog.

Her hands folded on her lap, Peg shifted her weight. "He'd hang around my office a lot, linger in my doorway. He used to bring me coffee, too." Now Peg's eyes showed real apprehension. "He knew just how I took it. A little cream and one packet of artificial sugar. I hadn't told him that. It seemed a little…"

"Creepy?"

She nodded.

The bastard had stalked her. Right where she worked. Miranda felt her stomach go hard. But there was more. "What else?"

"Well, for a while, he kept doing that. I kept dropping hints to go away. Telling him I had payroll to get out. Reminding him he had a delivery. Talking about Ken."

"How did he react?"

"He just kept standing there, staring at me. Well, eventually he'd go in the back and do his work, but the next day he'd be back in my door."

Looked like Tommy Drew was more than a creep. "Did you ever tell your husband about it?"

Peg's eyes grew wide. "Oh, no. Ken would have beaten the crap out of him."

Couldn't have that. "What did you do?"

"Nothing at first. But Tommy just kept on. So after a while, I told Mr. Phelps about it."

"What happened?"

"He told me Tommy wouldn't be bothering me again. I think he took him in his office and read him the riot act. I heard yelling coming through his wall when I passed by that day. Not that that's unusual."

"Did Drew stop bothering you then?"

She nodded. "Yes, but…"

Peg was rubbing her hands now. Had to be a disturbing experience and it didn't look like she was quite over it.

Miranda waited for her to say more.

Finally, she took a deep breath. "The day before I talked to Mr. Phelps he…" She stared down at the coffee table. "I was concentrating hard, working on my computer like usual. And when I looked up, he was right there, leaning over my shoulder."

Miranda felt a shiver go down her own spine. She wanted to teach this lady some self defense moves.

"He said I smelled of strawberries. I stopped wearing that scent."

Funny how mentally invasive a predator can be. She knew only too well.

Miranda decided she'd distressed the woman enough. She started to rise. "Thank you for your time, Peg. I'm sorry to bring back bad memories."

"No, I want to help." She reached out for Miranda's hand. Her voice had a desperate tone.

Miranda sat again. "Is there anything else you want to tell me? Anything that would help my investigation?"

Peg let her go and rubbed her arms. Then she took a sip of coffee to fortify herself. "It's just that…"

"What?"

"Maybe it was my imagination. But that day Tommy came into my office and got so close to me?"

"Yes?"

"Well, I had thought he had some kind of crush on me, but that time..." She shook her head.

Miranda waited.

"That time? The look in his eyes?"

"What about it?"

"He looked like he wanted to kill me."

CHAPTER TWENTY-NINE

It wasn't looking good for Hannah Kaye, Miranda thought as she turned onto North Decatur and headed back to Ponce.

She could still feel the disgust and fear she'd picked up from Peggy Kinley. The poor woman. Though Phelps had to be a jerk to work for, at least he'd stuck up for her. The bookkeeper could have been attacked on her way out to the parking lot. If the timing had been a little different, she could have been looking for Peggy Kinley now as well as Hannah Kaye.

A hard core of resolve balled up like a fist in her gut.

The one she always felt when she knew someone was in trouble. When someone else needed to pay for what he'd done to others. This was why she did this work. This was why she'd give up everything to keep doing it. Why she had given up everything, even the man she loved.

No need to think about that now. She had to stay focused.

So Tommy Drew liked blondes. Leggy blondes. Tan or pale skinned blondes with good figures who liked to show them off, maybe a little too much. She thought back to her training and her knowledge of serial killers. The mission oriented ones who focused on ridding the world of a certain type. Usually prostitutes. Or women they imagined were prostitutes.

Was that what she was dealing with?

She hoped not.

Still as she cruised through the shady tree-lined neighborhood on her way to the high-rise, she felt for her Berretta in the shoulder holster she'd slipped under her jacket this morning.

It was loaded, she'd already checked. But she'd make sure to check it again before she faced Tommy Drew.

Rising up from a cluster of sprawling trees with thick feathery leaves, Thomas Anthony Drew's apartment building was the tallest of its neighbors in this area of Midtown.

Nestled among shops and restaurants that strove to provide an eclectic experience to their clientele, it seemed too pricey for a truck driver. Especially an out-of-work one. But she didn't know the whole story on that yet, Miranda reminded herself, as she found a parking spot along a side street and climbed out of her car.

The smell of rain was in the air and the temperature was dropping lower. Might be down to seventy-eight. As much as she welcomed the relief from the heat she hoped she wouldn't get soaked before she could talk to Tommy Drew. Wouldn't be too intimidating.

But on the bright side, this place wasn't too far from her own. Maybe she'd find Hannah Kaye, wrap up this case, and be back home in time for a late lunch.

Somehow she didn't think she'd get that lucky.

She had to hoof it around the block but the entrance to the place was easy to find, and she smoothly followed a resident inside and rode the elevator up to the ninth floor.

So far, so good.

On the ninth floor she made her way through a light colored quadrangle of halls until she reached apartment nine-twenty-nine. This was the place. The address on the driver's license. The one where Peggy Kinley had sent Drew's last paycheck.

Taking a deep breath, Miranda made sure her Berretta was in easy reach and knocked.

No answer.

Okay, maybe he was taking a bath. She knocked again. And waited a little longer.

Still no answer.

This didn't bode well. Maybe he and Hannah had had a big night and they were deep sleepers. Sure, that was it.

She knocked again, this time harder. Again she waited.

Nothing.

Tapping her foot, she stared at the peephole. The creepy dude could be on the other side staring back at her. Maybe she should get the manager to let her in. Then she thought of what Parker would do in a situation like this. What she'd seen him do any number of times.

She looked up the hall, down it. Nobody there. She hadn't seen a soul since she got off the elevator. That could be good or bad. But instead of weighing the pros and cons she reached into her pocket and took out her trusty picks.

The sharp thin one would work for this. She stuck it between the jamb and the latch and presto—the door opened for her.

She pushed it open a little farther and peeked inside. There was a short alcove with a cutout space holding a vase of flowers on one side, a partial view of living room on the other.

"Mr. Drew?" she called out.

No reply.

Leaving the door ajar she took a step onto the polished walnut floor and listened hard. All she heard was the hum of the A/C.

As she took another tentative step, she reached for her Beretta and held it at her side. Better safe than sorry.

"Mr. Drew," she called again.

Still no answer.

She tiptoed around the corner and stepped into the living room. Empty.

The place was on the tiny side but still fancy. Hardwood floors throughout. Open kitchen along the side with granite counters, stainless steel fridge and dishwasher. Lime and tangerine tones accented the generic eggshell of the walls. She'd painted a number of apartments with that bland color in her day.

Lots of generic pictures on the walls to match the generic furniture. Big screen TV opposite the doors leading to the balcony.

She crossed the room to a small hallway and found the bath, the single bedroom with the single bed. It had been carefully made with a spread matching the décor and throw pillows arranged just so.

No dead bodies. Or live ones either. The place was vacant.

Everything was neat and tidy. Not a book or a knickknack out of place. And this was supposed to be a bachelor pad?

It didn't look very lived in at all. In fact, it looked…staged.

Then it hit her. It was staged. This wasn't somebody's apartment. This was a model.

She crossed back to the outer door, closed it as she left and headed back to the elevators. She was going to hunt up the apartment manager and find out where Thomas Anthony Drew had moved.

CHAPTER THIRTY

Parker felt the familiar stab of irritation in his gut as he rode down the elevator of the Imperial Building.

He'd had another restless night after his date with Wilhelmina Todd and what Dave Becker had discovered on the surveillance recording last night. He'd managed to stay away from the whiskey bottle but he'd tossed and turned all night, hungry for pursuit.

And now he was behind on following up this new lead.

Just as he had arrived at the office Gen had called to remind him of his meeting with Don Peregrin this morning. The client had been so pleased with the work Dave Becker had done, he wanted to expand security arrangements to all his dealerships throughout the state. It was a big job and the meeting had dragged on. There had been a good bit of planning and discussion over the breakfast of coffee and Danishes Gen had had brought in. And after Peregrin had left, Parker had met with Gen and Judd to discuss the need to hire more technical personnel—a commodity always in demand in Atlanta. Prospective employees would need a forensics background and be willing to go through the training the Agency provided. They had decided to put out ads and start scheduling interviews.

Another time commitment.

Not that any of this was bad. It was wonderful that the company he'd built from the ground up was prospering more than he'd ever imagined it would.

But this morning all Parker wanted to do was learn more about the man on the surveillance recording he'd seen last night. The man named Gabriel. The man who had tampered with Miranda's cell phone.

He reached the ground floor and made his way through the lobby to the glass doors with the etched phoenix of Gypsum Management. He'd never quite understood the connection of a phoenix with gypsum or with office building maintenance, but logo design wasn't what he had come here to discuss.

A well-groomed male receptionist greeted him at the counter with a clean white smile. "Mr. Parker. How good to see you this morning. Ms. Westbrook is expecting you. Please step this way."

Parker had called as soon as the office opened that morning and had made an appointment with Diana Westbrook—which he'd had to change after Gen's reminder.

The receptionist gestured through a door and Parker stepped onto the forest green carpet and took in the mauve walls and paintings of the sedate office.

Diana rose from her desk and extended a hand. "Good morning, Wade. It's good to see you."

She was a handsome woman. Dressed in a black and summer yellow business suit that few women could wear, her short dark red hair was demurely styled and her bright green eyes were as welcoming as he remembered them.

She was a few years younger than himself. She'd managed this building ever since he'd moved in, and they'd had a good business relationship and a casual social one for years.

She did her job efficiently, quietly and he'd never had an occasion to complain. His rare visits to her office were purely formality.

He felt a bit awkward bringing up the matter he'd come to discuss.

"And you, Diana." Parker shook her hand and waited for her to sit before he took the guest chair. "How are your sons doing?"

"Well, thank you for asking. Roger is in law school and James is out in California documenting surfers. I never thought he'd make a go of a surfing blog but a parent can't argue with success."

"No, we can't."

"Gen's doing well, I presume?"

"Yes. She's fine." His heart softened at the mention of his daughter. He suddenly realized how much Gen's stubborn strength had been holding him up these past weeks.

"The fall fundraiser is coming up soon. Is that what you've stopped by about?"

"Actually, no." He usually had no problem making requests for information but this time… "I'm not sure how to say this, Diana."

She blinked at him, her warm smile disappearing. "Is something wrong? Is there a problem with the building? I'm sure it's nothing that can't be fixed."

It was the response of a manager not wanting to lose a steady customer.

Parker shook his head. "Nothing with the building. But there seems to be an issue with personnel."

"Personnel?"

"The cleaning staff in particular."

"Are they not doing their job? Neglecting your break room? Leaving unemptied trash cans? Gloria's in charge of that department. I can call her in." She picked up her phone.

Parker gestured for her to put down her cell. "It isn't that."

"What is it then, Wade?"

"One of our employees has experienced a security breech."

Her expressive brows drew together in confusion. "What do you mean?"

"As you may recall, I had surveillance cameras installed some years ago." Though notice wasn't required, he had informed Diana of his decision at the time out of respect.

"I remember that. But the issue was resolved."

"Yes. However, one of my technicians and I were going over the recordings last night and found something disturbing involving one of your cleaning people."

"What did you find?"

"It seems this employee tampered with someone's cell phone. Since then, my employee has received several threatening texts."

Her eyes went wide. "And you think my employee is sending them?"

"Possibly. My receptionist was also working late last night and recognized him on the recording. She said his name was Gabriel."

She shook her head. "I'm not familiar with that name. We do get a good bit of turnover on our cleaning staff."

"I understand. The recording is dated the last week of January." He reached for his cell. "In fact, I have a clip of it here to show you." He had asked Dave to put it on his phone this morning.

Parker scrolled to the video and tapped the Play button. He turned the phone toward Diana and watched her face go hard with shock as the man in the recording bolted into Miranda's cube. When he began to examine Miranda's phone, she let out a gasp.

"My word, Wade. This is outrageous. I'll call Gloria right away."

Again he stopped her. "What I need from you, Diana," he said in his cool investigator's tone, "is information on this man. I'd like to handle the matter myself."

She stared at him, the meaning of who he was and what he meant sinking in. Slowly she nodded her head. "I can access the employee records. Give me just a moment. I'll be discreet."

She rose and left the room. For an excruciatingly long time, in Parker's opinion. Though he knew it was only a few moments.

When she returned she had papers in her hand.

"I found him. Fortunately we keep photo IDs on file and cross reference by first and last name. The person on your video seems to be Gabriel Anthony Pierson."

She laid the papers on the desk and turned them around for Parker to see.

He took in the photo. The shaggy, dirty blond hair, the muscular build. It was the man on his recording all right. He had his head down as if he hadn't wanted to be photographed. And there was something in his eyes. Something most observers would miss.

A distance, a detachment, a desire to be elsewhere. And a tiny spark of hate. Parker had seen the look before in the eyes of hardened criminals. That thought was disturbing.

"He worked for us from November of last year through January," Diana said.

Parker scanned the data on the paper. "Yes, I see that. Left without notice."

"Too many do that, I'm afraid. But Gloria worked a few extra shifts herself until Pierson could be replaced."

"I appreciate that," Parker said. Though his attention was on the man's address. A high-rise on Ponce de Leon. He hoped that was still his residence.

He tapped the paper. "May I have a copy of this?"

"This one's yours, Wade," Diana said.

"Thank you." Parker rose. He folded the paper and slipped it into his suit pocket.

Dianna got to her feet as well. "I'm sorry I couldn't be of more help. If there's anything else I can do to rectify the situation, please let me know."

Parker patted his jacket. "This is enough. Again thank you, Diana. I can see myself out." He started for the door.

"Wade, what do you intend to do with that information?"

He turned back, his expression purposely bland. "That remains to be seen."

As he hurried back up the elevator, Parker felt like a hound on the hunt. At last he had a scent now and he was hell-bent to follow it. A quick check of this Gabriel Pierson's background and he would be out the door and on his way to midtown.

But as soon as he stepped through the office entrance he was met by Gen.

"Did you forget the meeting?"

He scowled. "Which meeting?"

"Reviews. Judd and Tan are already in the board room. I've got lunch coming. You didn't see the delivery man, did you?"

Gen was in full business mode. A slate gray suit with an elegant sheen over her slim body, a string of gold at her neck, modest pumps on her feet, eyes eager, body poised and ready to take charge of the world.

Quarterly reviews. How could he have forgotten? They were due by the end of next month and he always insisted on turning all the paperwork in early.

With a heavy sigh, he acquiesced. "Very well, Gen. I'll be there in a moment. I just need to drop something off in my office first."

"Don't be late, Dad."

Despite his frustration Parker smiled at her tenderly. His talented daughter would do well managing the business side of this agency.

"No intention of it," he said resisting the urge to kiss her on the cheek.

And he hurried off.

CHAPTER THIRTY-ONE

It was quarter past two, almost two hours later, when Parker finally made it out the front door and into the parking lot.

With the fervor of a lion prowling for prey he climbed into his Mazda and spun out of the lot heading for midtown and Gabriel Anthony Pierson's apartment. The background check he was running on the man hadn't finished but he hadn't bothered to wait for it. An in person visit was what the situation called for.

What would he say to the man once he found him? Split his lip in two was his first inclination.

Not the best way to get the proof he needed. Or a conviction for harassment.

No, he would be reasonable. Ask questions, ascertain details, determine motives. And he would record the conversation on his phone.

But forty minutes later, after he had knocked, gotten no response, and picked the lock to apartment nine-twenty-nine of the high rise, all Parker could do was stare at the silent living room he stood in.

Everything from the perfectly placed cushions on the light green couch, to the lack of dust on the artificial flowers, to the empty refrigerator in the spotless kitchen told him this was a model. Besides a cleaning man could never afford an apartment like this. Not without several roommates to share the cost. Or a benefactor.

Gabriel Anthony Pierson had given his former employer a false address.

But to be thorough, Parker would make certain of that by checking with the landlord.

He found the landlord's office on the first floor. It was actually a small rental unit turned into a workspace and stuffed with glossy oak veneer filing cabinets and a matching pressboard desk which was cluttered with pamphlets and other sales paraphernalia. The desk had been pushed up against a set of balcony doors and a young man sat behind it.

Parker waited for him to get off the phone.

"Mr. Hunter?" Parker said as soon as he did, eyeing the name plate on the desk.

"Yes, how can I help you today?" The young man sat straight up with a bright salesman's smile.

He seemed to be in his early twenties, perhaps newly graduated from college. He had a clean cut appearance. The stream of light from the doors cast a sheen on the styling gel of his short brown hair. His nails were neatly trimmed and he wore a nicely pressed suit and a crimson tie.

"My name is Wade Parker."

Hunter extended a hand along with a wide, toothy grin. "It's your lucky day, Mr. Parker. We're offering a move-in special with the first month free."

Parker smiled at him patiently. "I'm not in the market." He reached into his jacket for a card and handed it to Hunter. "I'm a private investigator."

"Oh?" The young man dropped the false smile. "Is something wrong?"

"I'm looking for someone who claims to have rented from you. It was in November of last year." The time Gabriel Pierson filled out his employee records for Gypsum Management would be a good guess. "I'm wondering if you can confirm that for me."

Hunter's thin brows rose. "You mean look up the rental records?"

"That's exactly what I mean."

Eyes wide Hunter adjusted his seat, then his tie, then he glanced around the office. He was the only one here. "I think I'd need to get some sort of clearance before I did that."

Again Parker smiled. "I'm simply looking for information, Mr. Hunter. Your boss doesn't need to know."

The young man's lips twisted back and forth. He uttered a nervous laugh. "Now that wouldn't be very ethical of me, would it? But I can take down the information, check with my boss and get back to you. What's the name of the party?" He reached for a sticky pad and a pen from a holder with the apartment's name etched on it.

"Gabriel Anthony Pierson," Parker said smoothly. "My information states he resides in unit nine-twenty-nine, but there doesn't seem to be anyone at home."

Hunter sat back and tossed the pen on his desk. "Nine-twenty-nine is our model."

Parker feigned surprise. "Is it?"

Looking dazed Hunter stared out the window a long moment then suddenly he turned to his keyboard and began to type. "P-i-e-r-s-o-n?"

"Yes, that's correct." Parker wondered what had changed the young man's mind.

After a moment Hunter stopped typing and stared at his screen.

"What is it?"

Hunter licked his lips and twisted nervously in his chair before shaking his head. "I'm sorry, sir. There's no record of a Gabriel Anthony Pierson renting any of our units in the past year."

"Did you check under the last name alone?"

He nodded. "Pierson. Gabriel Pierson. G.A. Pierson. There was no one by that name."

Parker had been afraid of that. It only added to the incriminating image he'd seen on the surveillance recording last night. He needed to get back to the office and examine that background check.

"Thank you for your time, Mr. Hunter. I appreciate your efforts." He turned to go.

"It's really funny. A weird coincidence, I guess." Hunter's voice had a strange tone.

With a frown Parker turned back. "What is?"

"You're the second person today to ask about that unit."

"The model?"

He nodded. "Yes. A woman was in here earlier asking who rented nine-twenty-nine."

Parker's chest tightened. "A woman?"

"Yes, sir. Dark haired, pretty, well dressed. Very insistent."

Parker blinked at the man, hoping he'd misunderstood him. "May I ask her name?"

Hunter hesitated a moment, then shrugged. "She left a card. Let's see. Where did I put it?" He scanned his desk and found it under a paperweight. "Here is it. Miranda Steele. She's a private investigator, too."

Hunter handed him the card.

Reaching for it Parker felt as if the young man had stabbed him in the chest. Stunned he ran a thumb over the embossed lettering as he studied the card a moment.

A plain white background with no logo. Her name, new address and phone number were printed in a simple font. The sensation in his chest grew tighter. Confusion peppering his brain.

How could Miranda be looking for Gabriel Pierson?

He turned the card over. There was handwriting on the back. "What's this?"

"Oh," Hunter said, "that's the person she was looking for. I wrote it down there. Who was it again?"

Parker read the writing on the back. "Thomas Anthony Drew." Same middle name.

"Yes, that was it. Thomas Anthony Drew."

There had to be some sort of mistake. "Are you sure Ms. Steele was asking about unit nine-twenty-nine?"

"Yes. Very sure," Hunter said. "It was only a few hours ago. I was just about to close for lunch when she came in."

Parker drew in a slow breath, a barrage of questions churning inside him. He'd run a background check on this Thomas Anthony Drew when he returned to the office.

He handed the card back to Hunter. "Thank you again for your time."

The young man turned the card over, the dazed look in his eyes returning. "Weird coincidence…" he said again

"What is?"

"That guy never rented from us either."

CHAPTER THIRTY-TWO

After her visit to the landlord, Miranda hadn't had time to think about what to do next.

On her way back to her car from the apartment building where Thomas Anthony Drew *didn't* live, she'd gotten another call from Chambers, whining about the things she'd taken from Drew's Hyundai last night.

She rolled her eyes. He had the VIN number. He could get anything he wanted from that. Realizing that fact, she peppered him for information. But he knew less about Drew than she did.

Only because she wanted to stay on the police detective's good side, whatever that was, she drove back to her office and started making photocopies of everything on the used copy machine she'd bought when she'd purchased the furniture and office doodads at the thrift store.

As they say, you get what you pay for. The thing broke on the first try.

Actually, the long lines of black smudge on the paper told her she probably needed toner. Too irritated to mess with it, she decided to use some of Santiago's cash and headed to a copy shop instead.

She was a mile away from the shop with a nice folder of clean clear copies when her notorious client called. He wanted an update, of course.

"I'm working on it, Carlos," she told him trying not to let her annoyance show.

"I want copies of the ID photo of that *sucio bastardo*."

More copies? "Why?"

"I want to circulate it. Some people in the club are remembering him."

It was grasping at straws to hope anyone at the club could remember a detail that would tell her where Tommy Drew was now, but just in case, she turned the car around and headed back to the copy shop.

She made twenty copies, drove out to the club and gave them to Santiago to distribute. One of the bouncers told her he now remembered Drew and gave her a height and weight description that matched the information on the driver's license. But that didn't tell her where Drew was.

This guy was good, she thought, as she sat in traffic on Piedmont. He knew how to cover his tracks.

So what was the next step?

She could hand over the papers to Chambers and bring him up to speed. He'd want to notify Hannah Kaye's parents. Probably put them on TV and blast the media with photos of the missing college student.

The case would be out of her hands then.

And the media coverage would drive Thomas Anthony Drew deeper underground.

The troubling thought pressing in on her, she switched on her windshield wipers. The rain she'd smelled earlier had started up. The light turned green. Two cars in front of her got through and she had to stop again.

She let out a groan.

She didn't want to drive out to the police station. She wasn't ready to turn things over to Chambers. But she had only one ace in her hand left. The GPS tracker on Hannah Kaye's car. If it hadn't crashed by now.

Only one way to find out. Turning out of the traffic and onto a side street, she decided to head home.

Chambers could wait.

CHAPTER THIRTY-THREE

It took Miranda another twenty minutes to get back to her apartment, but at least the rain had decided to stop and the sun was shining again.

Her stomach, on the other hand, was rumbling like a semi with a bad muffler. She'd only had a protein bar all day and it was almost four o'clock.

She went into her kitchen and reached for her trusty bag of corn chips. She had just jammed a fistful into her mouth when her cell rang.

It was Chambers again.

Didn't that guy have a life?

Slowly she finished chewing and decided to let it go to voice mail. She got herself a cold bottle of water from the fridge, washed down another couple of handfuls of chips. But before she could get out the salsa, he called again.

"What?" she barked into the phone.

"Where are my papers?"

"Your papers?"

"The papers you were bringing to me two hours ago?"

"I got tied up. I've got a business to run, you know."

"Look Steele. I've got to run fingerprints on everything from that car."

She suppressed a groan. "Why? You've got all the available intel on the guy."

"Because it's protocol."

Stuffy old bureaucrat. From what she remembered Chambers had always been a rule follower.

"Okay, okay. I'll be there in a little bit." She came around her card table to see what percentage her GPS tracker was stuck at. "Just let me—"

She froze and stared at the screen.

Chambers voice registered in her ear. "Steele? You still there?"

She barely heard him.

All she could hear was the low beeping noise. The beeping that matched the flashing circle on a map. The tracker had worked.

"Steele! What's wrong, dammit?"

She found her voice. "I found it."

"Found what?"

"What do you think? Hannah Kaye's car."

"I was supposed to—never mind. Where is it?"

She grabbed her mouse and clicked at the map. It was west about thirty miles from here. She gave him the general area. It would take her a while to get there. She didn't have a minute to spare.

"Sorry, Chambers," she told him, excitement in her voice. "I gotta go."

"Don't go out there alone, Steele."

"Don't have time to wait for an escort, Chambers."

"You had better if you want to stay alive."

He was assuming the worst. She was sick of the big boys trying to protect the little girl. "I can take care of myself. If you're concerned, meet me out there."

She knew he would. And it would be good to have backup. But she wanted to get there first.

She hung up.

She raced into her bedroom, grabbed a spare clip for her Berretta from the drawer, packed up her laptop, and shot out the door as fast as she could go.

With any luck, Hannah Kaye might still be alive.

CHAPTER THIRTY-FOUR

Parker sat in his office staring at his computer screen, a contemplative finger under his chin.

He didn't want to acknowledge the disturbing emotions rumbling in his chest. He didn't want to admit what he'd discovered. He didn't want to admit this task was going to be a lot more difficult than he'd first thought.

But there it was, right on his screen.

The cleaning man, Gabriel Anthony Pierson, had a spotless record. No arrests, no warrants, no judgments of any kind. He also had no wife, no children, and no siblings. And interestingly enough, no history before the past three years.

Parker knew identity theft when he saw it. And so he'd spent the afternoon doing some deeper digging. And he'd discovered exactly what he'd expected to find.

The real Gabriel Anthony Pierson.

He was a carpenter who'd lived and worked in Macon, Georgia all his life. He'd attended the First Baptist Church there. He had a wife, three children, eight grandchildren, and six great grandchildren.

And he'd died three years ago at the age of eighty five.

And so the man in the video who had tampered with Miranda's phone was just as unknown to Parker as when he'd started this quest.

He rubbed his eyes considering what to do next. Before he could decide Gen knocked on his door.

He smiled up at her. "What is it, dear?"

She gave him a don't-call-me-dear-at-the-office look, stepped inside and sat down. Her face, her makeup, and her slate gray suit were just as fresh and crisp as they had been that morning. At times, she amazed him.

"Don Peregrin signed the contract," she said.

That made his smile wider. "Excellent work."

"You're the one who did all the persuading."

"I couldn't have done it without your facilitating skills."

"Just doing my job, Dad." She put her hands in her lap and gave him the look she used to as a child when she wanted him to buy her something special. "So, I say it's time to leave work early and celebrate."

His brow rose in suspicion. "What do you have in mind?"

"Coco's got a new set she's performing tonight at the Gecko Club. She and Antonio want us to come."

He studied her a moment. "Is that all?"

"Why should there be anything else?"

"I'm afraid I'm exhausted, dear. I'd like a quiet evening at home."

Her glare told him she thought he'd had too many quiet evenings at home lately. "C'mon, Dad. It'll do you good. And you never know who you might run into."

He eyed her cautiously. "You don't have another surprise date set up for me, do you?"

She raised her slender shoulders. "What if I do? Can't a daughter take an interest in her father's love life?"

He shook his head at her. "Really, Gen. I'm not ready for a relationship."

Her face turned solemn. "You've got to get over her, Dad."

"I am. I'm managing."

"She wasn't good for you. I always knew that."

"You did," he said.

But his heart told him it had been true when he'd set it on Miranda Steele. They were good together. She'd delighted and amazed and annoyed him like no other woman ever had. Including Gen's mother.

And he missed her.

He missed her laughter and her silly jokes. Her quick mind and her tenacious spirit. And the way she could always arouse every nerve in his body. She had filled his life with joy when he'd thought there was no more joy to be had. She had filled his heart with love.

But it wasn't meant to last.

There was too much fire and sizzle in Miranda for him to contend with. Perhaps he was too old for her.

Gen rose and took his hand. "Come with me to the Gecko Club tonight, Dad. Coco and Antonio will be so disappointed if you don't."

He sighed deeply. He was at a standstill with the data on his screen. Perhaps a diversion would shake an idea out of his brain.

What a man did for his children. "Very well, Gen."

As he got to his feet she reached up and kissed his cheek, warming his heart so that it nearly came to life again. He loved her dearly for that. For everything she meant to him.

"I promise," she smiled. "You won't be disappointed."

CHAPTER THIRTY-FIVE

The clouds hovering over the distant tree line were growing darker. As she raced down I-20 heading west, Miranda prayed it wouldn't rain again.

In the rain it would be harder to deal with whatever she was going to find when she got to Hannah Kaye's car. Rain would slow her down. And it had already taken too long to get out here.

She'd stopped to fill up the Acura's tank and had fought the traffic nearly all the way to Six Flags.

She'd transferred the GPS tracker to her phone, and it had taken her into Paulding County, past Mableton and Austell and Lithia Springs. Following its directions after several more miles she turned off the main highway.

Here the road became a two-lane. She passed apartment buildings and gas stations and strip malls for a while, then the road turned totally rural. Long and nearly clear of traffic, it stretched before her broken only by the occasional church or convenience store. Every once in a while a narrow side street shot off into heavy tree cover. Her tracker told her to keep going straight. She did.

Mile after mile after mile.

When it beeped she jolted at the noise. It was telling her to turn right onto one of those side roads. Stomach tensing she did, though she felt as if she were heading into hell, risking getting stranded on a deserted road in the woods.

Here the pavement grew narrower. The road markings faded. A weathered sign told her the speed limit was thirty-five. She ignored it and sped on.

Some of the tall treetops had been cut away for telephone lines. A sign of life? She hoped so. There were more trees up ahead. In Atlanta there were always more trees. An endless tunnel of thirty kinds of oaks and fifty kinds of pines, often covered with thick leafy kudzu, tall and green and silently ominous. Above her they swayed gently in the wind that was kicking up.

Up ahead rose a bit of civilization. She zoomed past a row of modest country houses spread out with at least an acre between them. As she went on, the space became two and three acres. And then the homes disappeared.

There was nothing around her but thick, deep forest.

She glanced at the tracker. It was still flashing the way but, she reminded herself, she hadn't used it before. Was it taking her on a wild goose chase?

Just then it beeped again.

She startled in her seat and cursed the thing. But all it responded with was a command to turn left.

She peered out the windshield. At first she didn't see where she could turn. Then she spotted the narrow dirt road, its red Georgia clay nearly glowing under a patch of sunlight among the clouds. Something about the look of it made her heartbeat mount. But if this was where Hannah Kaye was, this was where she had to go.

Hair rising on the back of her neck she turned the steering wheel. And as she did the sky turned dark and lightning flashed in the distance like a bad omen.

She pressed on.

The road was bumpy, littered with holes from past rainstorms. Several times she feared she might bust an axle.

"If you damage my car," she muttered to the tracker, "I'm suing your creator's ass."

But she wouldn't have to bother.

As she came around another rough curve, she saw what she was here for in the distance through the pines.

Hannah Kaye's cranberry red Corolla.

She had to drive a few more yards before she could get a better view. Beyond the car stood a murky, tan colored house with a charcoal roof. The place looked like it had seen better days.

It was a sort of split level with siding that needed painting and a rotting old roof that needed replacing. A window on the upper floor was boarded up. Dingy gray encased a lower level that might have once been used as a garage. A pair of sliding patio doors in its side were also boarded up.

As Miranda inched closer in her Acura she saw no movement at all in the windows. But she noticed there was only a single set of tracks in the dried mud lane. They led straight to the Corolla's rear tires.

She turned her car around—in case she needed to make a quick getaway—and parked as close to the front door as she dared.

It occurred to her she might need a flashlight. Opening her glove compartment she took out the police issue maglite she'd stored there. Once more she checked her Beretta. As she did another bolt of lightning flashed across the sky.

She got out, closed the door noiselessly, and picked her way across the neglected yard to the porch, the wind tossing her hair.

The porch boards were slick and black and she didn't think they'd hold her. But taking a deep breath, she put her foot on the first step. It didn't cave so she hurried up the rest and stopped at the screen door.

Knock or just go in?

Better not to give your presence away, she decided and put her hand on the knob. It was probably locked. But as she gave it a turn, it opened easily. The solid door was already ajar.

Trusting owner? She doubted it.

For an instant she thought of Chambers' warning. Maybe she should wait for him. But what if Hannah Kaye was dying in there? What if he got here seconds too late to save her life?

She had to go in.

Slowly she reached for her Beretta. After a quick glance behind her that revealed nothing, she gave the exterior door a push and it creaked open.

Heart banging in her chest Miranda stepped inside the house.

CHAPTER THIRTY-SIX

The first room was a grimy living room.

A cutout divider across the room revealed a dingy kitchen. In the far corner of the first room sat a ratty looking recliner with a small end table and a lamp. Along the opposite wall stood an old-fashioned fireplace that had been painted over. The air was hot and dank and musty. Might be some rotting food in the kitchen. And the baseboards had a nice crop of black mold growing along their edges.

For a fleeting moment Miranda wondered why the place hadn't been condemned.

She switched on her maglite and ran it over the stained walls. No signs of life. To her right was a staircase leading to the upper floor. Beside it was a closed door, its paint just as stained as the walls. Had to be another staircase behind it to get to the lower level she'd seen from the outside.

So would it be up or down?

Up, she decided. Maybe the occupants were asleep.

Silently she crossed the room and put her foot on the first step. As she shifted her weight the stair moaned.

Miranda held her breath. Didn't want to wake them.

Why was she thinking in the plural? She was assuming Hannah Kaye was still alive and that she'd find her and Tommy Drew together in a bed upstairs.

That would be the best case scenario.

She took another step. This stair was quieter. Creeping along she tiptoed all the way up. On the landing she found three doors, all of them ajar. She took them counterclockwise.

The first was a bathroom with a sink that needed cleaning. No towels. No toiletries. No cabinet behind the cracked mirror. No curtain on the tub. No one in the tub.

She moved to the next room.

This one looked like it might have been used as a bedroom but it contained no furniture. It had been painted a pale pink but that had to have been years ago. Black mold speckled the walls and baseboards from the moisture seeping through the ceiling and the unsealed window. An air vent in the corner was dark with grime.

Oh for two.

They had to be in the last room. Miranda moved silently down the hall and nudged the door open with her Beretta.

"Tommy Drew?" she said softly.

No answer.

This room was in a little better shape but it wouldn't win a Good Housekeeping prize. Here also there was no furniture except for a single mattress in the corner with a rumpled sheet on it.

Miranda tiptoed over to it.

Could be some nice DNA on that sheet. She didn't have the resources to process it. She'd let Chambers handle that. A small closet with a folding door stood open. If anyone had hung any clothes in there they were gone. All that remained was a single hanger.

As she stood staring at it she heard the rumble of thunder outside. Rain began to pelt the roof. She felt a slight relief from the too-warm, too-moist air. The temperature must be dropping.

But it didn't do anything for the anxious feeling in her gut.

Giving up on this floor she went back down to the living room.

As she reached the last step she realized how bad the room smelled. She'd thought it was a kitchen odor. She should have known better.

Only one more place to check.

As she eyed the door to the lower level her heartbeat kicked up. Her nerves began to dance wildly. Suddenly she felt like ants were crawling up her neck.

Mustering her courage she strode to the door and flung it open.

The foul air stung her eyes. Dear God, she should have known.

Beretta still drawn, holding her maglite under the grip, she plunged into the stench and down the stairs, ignoring their creaking.

As she reached the last step Miranda's heart nearly stopped. Her stomach roiled and she had to fight the gag reflex hard.

She'd seen some pretty frightening scenes in her time, but nothing like this. It was much worse than she'd imagined. Worse than anything in her most terrible nightmare.

Instead of the familiar mold these walls were hung with acoustical foam, as if someone wanted to block in the noise. The patio doors were boarded up on this floor so there was no outside light. In the far corner stood an empty cage. About three foot by three and six feet long. A faded blue blanket lay on the floor next to it stained with blood.

A disturbing enough sight but that wasn't what caught her attention.

Overhead some sort of pulley system had been strung up over the reinforced beams. Thick ropes had been anchored to the wall. The ropes had been strung through the pulley and used to heave the victim up by her bound wrists.

And there before her, hanging from those ropes was the naked body of Hannah Kaye.

For an eternity all Miranda could do was stare up at her, the foul stench in her throat.

It was a grisly sight.

Grotesque bruises and welts and cuts covered her torso, her arms, her legs. Flies and gnats buzzed around streams of dried blood caked on her skin where it had oozed from the gaping wounds in her thighs, her sides, her breasts, between her legs. Of the eight to ten pints in the human body, at least half had pooled on the floor below her.

The blood meant he'd done all that to her while she was still alive.

She must have died in incredible pain.

The angle of the cuts indicated she'd been hanging up there while he'd worked on her. It was as if he'd used her as a human piñata. How had he done it? With a long knife? A sharp poker of some sort? He'd cut her just enough to cause pain without killing her. Until he was ready for her to die.

She could imagine the sick, sadistic bastard digging into her flesh. Over and over and over. Watching her suffer. Enjoying it.

Her long blond hair hung over one shoulder, matted with blood. Her tongue was extended down her chin in total resignation.

But most disturbing of all were the big cloudy blue eyes. Wide open, bulging, peering down at Miranda and asking "Why? Why did you let this happen to me?"

If only she could have gotten here sooner.

As she stared up at the woman whose life had been cut so short Miranda felt her whole body shiver. She began to quake from head to foot. A feeling of helplessness overwhelmed her. If she didn't get out here, she was going to lose her mind.

Turning she ran up the stairs and out the front door.

As she reached the porch a loud thunderclap exploded overhead. It seemed to shake the whole earth. Rain began pouring down in sheets.

Not caring if she got wet, Miranda ran into the yard getting doused to the bone. She ran for her car, fumbled with the handle, climbed inside.

She sat there hugging herself, still shivering, numb with shock.

Water dripped from her hair, her clothes onto the floorboards. She turned her head and saw her Beretta and the maglite lying in the passenger seat, both wet. She couldn't remember putting them there.

Could barely make out what was around her. All she could see was the image of that poor, poor girl. The student, the dancer she had been too late to save.

Her brain starting to rouse, she dug in her pocket for her cell phone. With shaky fingers she dialed the number.

He answered after the first ring.

"Steele?" There was concern in his voice.

"I found her," she breathed. "I found her, Chambers."

"Is she—?"

"She's gone. Get out here fast and bring your CSIs."

Before he could answer she hung up. For several long moments she sat, rocking, hugging herself, trying to get the image of that mutilated body out of her head.

And then as another bolt of lightning split the sky, she burst into tears.

CHAPTER THIRTY-SEVEN

The rain had subsided to a drizzle by the time Chambers arrived with his entourage of squad cars with their sirens and flashing lights.

They parked around the muddy yard and surrounded the house, weapons drawn, their brouhaha announcing their presence to no one. Guess the word of a lowly PI that nobody was in the house but a dead woman wasn't good enough.

She stayed in the car and let Chambers come to her to take a statement. She gave it to him, retracing her steps and describing what she'd seen in a dull monotone.

She watched his face go pale as he made notes on his clipboard.

Finally he drew in a breath. "Sorry you had to go through that, Steele. Wish you had waited for me."

Yeah right. So he could what? Get the glory? Take over? Protect her? But she guessed he was just doing his job. And so was she.

Santiago's black BMW rolled up into the yard jogging a vague memory that she'd called him while she'd waited for Chambers to arrive.

The gangster got out of the backseat of his vehicle, heedless of the barrage of law enforcement officers or if the misty rain ruined his silky white shirt. He shot a rueful look at her huddled in her Acura, then marched over to one of the cops.

One of the drug lord's men dressed in bodyguard black emerged from the driver's side of the BMW and stood near the hood, his big arms crossed over his hulky chest.

Arms flailing Santiago screamed at the officer. She could hear it through her closed windows. A moment later Chambers came out of the house, took in the scene and motioned for Santiago to come inside.

The bodyguard remained rock solid at the car. Must have had his orders.

Francisco, she thought, surprised she'd remembered his name. She'd borrowed his hog the night she'd raced Santiago down Peachtree. The night they'd met.

She'd taken a big risk then, just as she had coming out to this remote house. Parker was right. She did rush into danger. She could see now why it drove him crazy. No man would put up with that for long. But what choice did she have? It was her duty, her job, her destiny.

Though this time she hadn't had the chance to face down the killer. She'd been too late to save a life.

Santiago came out of the house and strolled over to her car. He rapped on her window with his knuckles.

She rolled it down.

"I'm sorry, Carlos."

He nodded, looking back at the house, his face paler than she'd ever seen it. Even after the violence he must have seen in his life on the streets, the sight of Hannah Kaye's body had shaken him.

"*Hijueputa*," he growled under his breath. Son of a bitch.

Yeah. *Hijueputa*.

He leaned down close to her his black eyes shining with hate. "Miranda Steele," he said in a low rumble. "Find who did this to my dancer."

CHAPTER THIRTY-EIGHT

The police finished up and started to leave. Chambers came over and asked if he could drive her home. Miranda declined and instead offered to drive up to Gainesville with him to inform Hannah's parents.

He shook his head and told her to go home.

So she headed back to the city still numb with shock but recovered enough to drive. She found an oldies station playing hard heavy metal and cranked it up all the way, trying to drive the gory image from her mind.

But it would take more than Led Zeppelin and ZZ Topp to do that.

The rain had stopped by the time she got home and the sun was setting in a blaze of color. The air remained cooler. Fall was coming on. Climbing up the stairs she wondered if she should stay in Atlanta. She didn't have roots here anymore. What was the point?

Inside her apartment, she cleaned her Beretta and put it away in her drawer. Then she opened the bottle of Jack Daniels she'd picked up on the way home. She got a mug from her cabinet—another one of those cat cups. This one had a gray kitten sniffing a blue flower in a garden.

She poured two fingers into it and gulped it down.

The booze burned her throat but after a minute her muscles started to relax. She poured another two fingers and carried the mug and the bottle into her bedroom. She stripped off her damp clothes, took a shower, pulled on a T-shirt and lay down on her bed.

Hannah Kaye. A young woman who had her whole life in front of her. Promising future as an architect building hospitals. A boyfriend who seemed crazy about her with a compatible dream of designing medical machinery. They could have graduated, married, had terrific careers, children, the works.

But no, that wasn't enough. Hannah wanted more. She wanted excitement. Attention. The thrill of men drooling over her, chasing after her.

And she got it. But it wasn't exactly the kind of attention she'd intended. She'd made a mistake. Fallen for the wrong guy. Made a bad choice.

And her last days had ended in excruciating pain and no doubt an agonizing series of if onlys.

If only she hadn't broken up with her boyfriend. If only she hadn't gone off with the customer in booth three. If only she had told somebody about this guy. If only she hadn't taken the job at Santiago's club. If only she'd been just a little smarter, a little more cautious.

But she hadn't been. And she'd paid for it with her life.

Find her killer.

Miranda poured more whiskey into her mug and groaned out loud. Who did Santiago think she was? Superwoman?

The police would have to do that.

When Chambers questioned her at the scene she'd turned over the papers he wanted and filled him in on everything she knew about Thomas Anthony Drew. It was up to the police detective and his cronies at the station to find him now. Chambers had better equipment, more manpower, the power of arrest.

She couldn't do it. She didn't have the will. Not her job.

Miranda stared at the heart shaped pendant on the ankle bracelet around her wrist. A.T. Adam Tannenburg. Just now that case felt like another failure. She took off the bracelet and laid it on her night stand beside her phone.

She picked up her mug. It was empty. She refilled it and chucked down the last mouthful of Jack Daniels. As the alcohol took effect, she fumbled for her light switch and turned it off. She lay her head on the pillow, her brain reeling. Sleep. She needed sleep. A good night's sleep and she'd be able to figure out what to do. She felt as if she could sleep forever.

And as she rolled over in the darkness and drifted off, Miranda realized she wasn't sure anymore what she had the will to do.

CHAPTER THIRTY-NINE

Nine forty-five in the morning. She should be at the office in a meeting but where was she instead? Taking back anniversary gifts for Miranda Steele.

Gen Parker fumed and bristled as she waited for the clerk, who had to discuss the matter with her manager. Yes, Gen knew the item had been purchased over three weeks ago. But it wasn't even her gift. She was doing a favor for a friend.

Then again, maybe it was all her own fault.

Livia Burton, whom she'd invited to the Gecko Club last night as a possible future date for her father, had unloaded the chore of returning the gift she'd bought for his first anniversary.

She'd been busy, Liv had said, and forgotten to return it. She was a real estate agent, Liv had reminded her, as if Gen didn't already know it—Liv used to work for her grandfather—and she had three showings the next day.

Could Gen be a dear and return it for her? At that point Gen had been relieved her father hadn't taken an interest in the woman.

And then there were the two gifts from Wendy Van Aarle and her family that she'd promised to take care of. They'd also been too busy to take them back, what with school starting and Wendy's ice-skating. She should have told Iris no, Gen thought, but she'd been trying to be nice.

That was her problem. She was just too damn nice.

She'd already returned the hand-stitched leather-bound photo album from Livia. And the personalized stationery with a pair of matching his-and-her Italian designer pens from Wendy. Her mother must have helped her pick that out.

Once she'd gotten rid of Iris's gift, she'd be done. And what a gift it was. A bowl made of Swarovski crystal with two lovebirds perched on its rim. Her father would have adored it.

Love birds. That was a joke.

She tapped her tapered fingernails on the glass counter.

What was taking that clerk so long? She had the receipt. The bowl wasn't damaged. Surely they could resell it.

She should have torn that clerk's head off when she made a fuss. Instead she decided to follow her father's example and use kindness. The technique didn't seem to work as well for her.

He was such a sweet man, a good man. He deserved someone so much better than Miranda Steele.

What he'd ever seen in that selfish, hot headed bitch she'd never know.

Sure, she was good at what she did. She'd even saved her life once. Though it had been Miranda's actions that had gotten her in that spot. So she was a great detective. So what? You could get into real trouble mixing your personal and professional life. She ought to know.

Curt Holloway had had the eye for her for weeks now. And though he made her blood race, did she give him the time of day? Not on her life.

Work and love don't mix. That was why there were rules about that in most organizations.

She guessed her father was learning that lesson the hard way. Poor Dad.

At last the clerk returned with a bright smile, an apology, and a hand full of cash.

Finally.

Gen thanked her as sweetly as she could and made her way out of the store.

Free at last.

She hurried over the marble floor, past the fountain and into the parking deck. She'd parked here thinking it would be faster to get back out on the street.

She glanced at the time. Damn, she was late for that meeting. Plus she had those reviews from yesterday to finish up and another potential client coming in just before lunch. She'd better call Sybil and let her know where she was. She'd been in too much of a hurry to even text her earlier.

She stopped in front of a thick concrete pillar to dial. She didn't notice the vehicle parked just behind her. She didn't hear him get out. Or his footsteps as he came up behind her.

But she did feel the rough hand as it slapped over her mouth, clamping it shut. An arm went around her waist pinning her arms against her body. Her cell phone tumbled to the ground.

Heart pounding she screamed into the sweaty flesh, tried to bite. Then she kicked out behind her the way she'd seen some of the investigators do in the gym. Dear God. Dad had taught her self defense skills once. But suddenly she couldn't remember any of it.

Not anything that worked anyway.

The man holding her began dragging her across the pavement. She kicked and screamed into his palm trying to cry out for help. But there was no one around and he was so strong.

Tears stung her eyes. Her chest burned so hot with fear she thought she was going to have a heart attack.

She couldn't get away. She just couldn't get away. From the corner of her eye she caught a glimpse of where he was taking her.

To an ugly dark red truck with a light colored stripe. F-150. Dent in the door. Crew cab. She tried to make out the tag number but she was at the wrong angle. Skin, she thought. DNA.

As they reached the truck, he removed his hand from her mouth an instant to open the passenger door.

She screamed and managed to twist her hands enough to dig her nails into his wrist.

He stifled a yell. For an instant she saw his face. Crooked mouth. His eyes were wild.

Then she realized he was reaching for something in the truck. A rag of some sort. Was he going to gag her? She tried to get another kick in but he'd already jammed the rag onto her nose and mouth. She couldn't breathe.

Was he trying to suffocate her?

No. Too late she realized there was something on the rag. Something to make her go to sleep. Something to knock her out.

She felt her muscles relax. She lost control of her body. He lifted her into the back seat and strapped something around her hands. She was as limp as a ragdoll.

Help, she thought as he arranged her feet on the floorboard and leaned her head back against the mat. He was about to close the door and she knew he would take her far away.

She wanted to cry out, struggle, run away. But she couldn't budge.

And the last thing she saw before he closed the door was a patch of shaggy dark blond hair under a ball cap and a vicious smile of satisfaction.

CHAPTER FORTY

Parker was back at his desk, this time reviewing the data he'd unearthed on Thomas Anthony Drew, the man he'd learned about yesterday at the high-rise on Ponce de Leon.

He'd discovered some interesting bits of information since then.

Drew had worked at a place called Phelps Supply Company in Decatur delivering medical equipment from February to early June. He was unmarried and seemed to have no close living relatives. He had a bank account where he had deposited checks from his employer, but had made no withdrawals.

And he owned a light gray Hyundai that was currently impounded by the police. It had been found abandoned two days ago in the vicinity of *Exótico*, Carlos Santiago's strip club.

Parker brought up the DMV photo of Drew.

A good-looking man in his early thirties with dark, curly chin-length hair and a pencil mustache. Well built, strong looking.

He brought up the employment shot of Gabriel Anthony Pierson and arranged them so they sat side-by-side on his screen.

Pierson was good-looking and well built as well, but there were obvious differences. Drew's dark hair versus Pierson's shaggy blond. Drew's thin dark pencil mustache. Pierson's look was slouched and sullen while Drew's was more alert. The shape of Drew's mouth was different, as was his nose. Still, the two might have been brothers.

And both men had listed the same residence for the past three years on all the documents Parker could find on them.

And they shared the same middle name of Anthony. What did these two men have to do with each other?

Parker wondered if a deeper search would lead him to an eighty plus Thomas Anthony Drew who was deceased. And what that would mean.

Why was Miranda looking for him? She had to believe he had something to do with the missing dancer from Santiago's club she was searching for.

He sat back and considered what to do.

It would be a simple matter to pick up the phone and call her. Ask her directly.

But then she would ask why he wanted to know, and he'd have to tell her he was pursuing the text messages on her phone again. That would be a pleasant conversation.

No, he wouldn't call Miranda. He'd tap a source at the Atlanta Police Department and find out more about Drew's car first.

He reached for his coffee cup and took a sip of his third helping this morning.

He hadn't slept well after his night at the Gecko Club. The memory of the evening made him wince.

He'd arrived at the club around seven and found Gen at the table she'd reserved for them. He'd also found no less than three ladies, social acquaintances he'd sporadically dated after Sylvia died, sitting at nearby tables.

Gen's doing. What part of "not ready" did she not understand?

But he supposed she'd already made the arrangements when he'd told her that. And so, ignoring the ladies, he'd decided to sit back, enjoy himself and listen to Coco's new songs. As usual she sang them beautifully. And Parker could see Antonio was more in love with his pretty blond bride than ever. He was happy for them.

But the performance only reminded him of the song Coco had sung at his wedding to Miranda.

He'd called it an early night and gone home to bed alone.

He switched to his screensaver on his computer and took his coffee with him as he got to his feet and strolled to the window. He gazed out at the tall city buildings in the distance.

What sort of future could he look forward to without Miranda?

Everything he did reminded him of her. He couldn't escape the memories. That dark wild hair. That lovely face. That zest for life. Her keen mind. Her indomitable spirit.

He should go off somewhere. Go on a trip. Get away from the memories. But where would he go? Other places would remind him of her, too. Paris, London, Rome, Hawaii.

Besides, he hadn't yet found the elusive Gabriel Anthony Pierson, the former cleaning man.

And he had a business to run. Which he should be doing now.

He glanced at the time. It was nearly eleven. Wasn't he meeting with a new client this morning? Where was Gen? Shouldn't she be in here filling him in on the details?

She hadn't even stopped by to talk about last night.

He left his office and made the short trip down the hall to his daughter's. He found it empty.

Sunlight cast beams along the shelves filled with neatly placed business and management books. The silver frame holding a picture of her mother sat on her desk in its usual spot. The cream colored sweater she kept at the office hung on the back of her chair.

No coffee cup, no paperwork on the desk. Her laptop hadn't been turned on. Where was she?

Parker reached for his cell phone, dialed her number.

After five rings it went to voice mail.

"Gen, it's your father. The meeting with the representative from Cooper Enterprises is about to start. Is there a problem? Call me." He hung up.

He made his way out to the lobby and the reception desk. "Sybil, has Hans Cooper arrived yet?"

She held up a finger, finished her call, and turned to him. "No, sir. Not yet."

He nodded. "Do you know where Gen is? She hasn't come in yet today."

The young woman thought a moment. "She had some errands to run at the mall. But I thought she'd be in by now."

"Errands?"

"She's, um, returning anniversary gifts for some of your friends."

Parker didn't know what to say to that.

Hiding her embarrassment Sybil cleared her throat. "Have you called her?"

"I got her voice mail," Parker said.

She gave him a gracious smile. "Let me try."

She pressed a speed dial button on her phone and waited. After a moment she frowned. "I got voice mail, too."

Parker stared at her blankly wishing he could will his daughter's whereabouts out of thin air. Then he realized Sybil was speaking to him again. "Excuse me?"

"I said, when did you last see her, sir?"

"Last night at the Gecko Club."

"Oh, that's right. She told me she was taking you there. How was it?"

"It was fine." And the last thing on his mind right now.

"Did she...um...go home with someone?"

Again he gave her a blank stare. "I don't know." He'd left before she had. But Gen wasn't the type for one-night-stands. He turned back to the office. "Let me know when she gets in."

"Yes, sir."

He pushed through the doors and made his way down the hall.

He didn't think Gen would go home with a stranger. She didn't care for spontaneity, but perhaps she had met someone at the club. Perhaps she'd simply stayed out late and overslept. He should try Antonio. Maybe she'd drunk too much and had stayed overnight with him and Coco.

He started to dial Antonio's number then stopped.

It would embarrass her to call and check up on her as if she were still in high-school. She was a grown adult. She was all right. He shouldn't worry so much about her. Perhaps Miranda was right. He could be overly protective at times. It was his raising to protect the women he loved.

He'd just walked through the door of his office to prepare for the Cooper meeting when his cell buzzed.

He let out a breath of relief. There was Gen. She was sending him a text explaining her lateness. Probably embarrassed and apologizing profusely. He resolved not to be hard on her. She was already too much of a perfectionist.

But when he took out his phone again and scrolled to the text, his body went rigid as stone.

The message wasn't from Gen.

It was anonymous. No email address. All too personal. Just like the ones on Miranda's phone.

Its cold words sent a sickening jolt through him, slicing his heart in two.

Good Morning, Wade Parker. You may be interested to know that I have your daughter.

CHAPTER FORTY-ONE

When Miranda opened her eyes the next morning, she thought her head was about to split open on the pillow. Maybe it already had.

Groping around on the pillowcase for her brains and not finding them there, she ran her hands over her face and groaned. She rolled over—gently—and glared up at the sun coming through her window.

She'd slept through the night. If she'd had any bad dreams, she didn't remember them. No need for them now. After yesterday, real life had supplied a big enough dose of horror. She could still see the image of Hannah Kaye's mutilated body in her head. She shook herself trying to get it out.

The rain had stopped. So she had no excuse to stay in bed.

She fumbled for her phone on the nightstand and squinted at it. Quarter to one? Good grief. It wasn't morning. She'd never slept this late. That was the last time she drank half a bottle of Old Number Seven before she went to bed. Or any other time.

Reluctant to get up yet, she scrolled through her messages. There was a text from Wendy. Thank God. Something good to think about. She hoped. Or maybe not.

Hi Miranda. I really miss Mackenzie. Can you talk to her for me?

Miranda's shoulders slumped in defeat. Like she hadn't already tried.

But anything for her kids. *I'll give it a shot*, she thumbed back. *No promises.*

Thx. Wendy replied.

Miranda sighed out loud recalling Mackenzie's visit to her office. She and Wendy were in classes together. She'd thought the ice between them would have thawed by now. How could the two girls she loved most in the world end their friendship over a boy? It was so dumb. Maybe she'd go over to the Chatham place later today and give Mackenzie a talking to.

She scrolled to the next text.

Santiago said he'd be sending his remaining payment to her office that afternoon. That was incentive to get up and get dressed. But she didn't feel she deserved the money. She had so wanted to save Hannah Kaye and she'd failed miserably.

He also wanted to know what she was doing to find the dancer's killer.

Nothing, she thought. But she might as well at least get up.

With all the strength she could muster, she stood and wobbled to the bathroom while pain zigzagged through her head. A hot shower helped with the headache some, but she still felt raw when she pulled on her clothes. She was going into the office in jeans and a T-shirt today. One of the perks of being your own boss. She happened to grab the form-fitting baby blue one Mackenzie had given her for Mother's Day.

On the front it said, *Normal is Boring*. What a sense of humor the kid had.

She went to the nightstand and absently stuffed Adam Tannenburg's ankle bracelet into her pocket. Out of habit she took her Beretta and stuffed it into the back of her jeans under her T-shirt. Then she plodded into the kitchen and scrounged through her cabinets for something for breakfast that wouldn't turn her stomach.

She ended up with a cup of strong coffee and half a peanut butter sandwich on two-day-old rye bread.

What now? she wondered as she ate at her card table.

She wanted to get away. Far away. California maybe. Would she carry on as a PI there? Maybe not. Maybe she wasn't as good at this investigator gig as she'd thought she was. Maybe she'd go back to her old habits and see what struck her fancy when she got out there.

She'd just taken the last bite of her sandwich when her cell rang.

She glanced at the display and her back tensed. Hank Lauderdale. Her first client. The one who'd stiffed her out of her fee after she'd proved his wife had been cheating on him.

She scowled at the screen. Okay, she was in the mood to chew somebody a new one today.

She clicked the button to answer. "Steele Investigations."

His breathless voice came over the phone. "Ms. Steele? It's Hank Lauderdale."

What do you want? she wanted to growl. Instead she forced herself to be civil. Still there was acid in her tone as she replied, "How can I help you, Mr. Lauderdale?"

"Ms. Steele, I am so sorry. I hope you'll let me explain."

"Explain what?" She was going to enjoy listening to him squirm.

"The check I wrote you. It's no good. Have you already tried to deposit it?"

"As a matter of fact, I have. And it was—"

"Oh, my word. I am so sorry. You're never going to believe what happened. You see, when I confronted Luella about those pictures you took of her, she went straight to the bank and withdrew all the money out of our account. She opened another one in her own name and put it all in there."

Miranda stared at the phone. He was right. She didn't believe it. Did this guy think she was born yesterday? "I tried contacting you several times about this matter, Mr. Lauderdale. You never returned my calls."

He made a strange wheezing noise on the other end. "That was Luella, too. She threw my cell phone in the pool."

Really? Now what? Did he want her to do something else for free?

"It's taken me three days to get everything straightened out. But it's all right now. I've got my cell phone back and the bank returned the funds. I've written you a new check and I want to bring it to your office this afternoon."

Miranda didn't know what to say. If he didn't want to pay he wouldn't stop by her office. And he did have a good credit score, she recalled. Was he really going to make good on what he owed her?

"I'm going to add another two hundred onto the check to cover any charges and inconvenience I've caused. I hope you'll take it with my gratitude."

Now this guy was really sounding looney. "Gratitude?"

"Luella and I are back together, Ms. Steele. All because of you."

"Excuse me?"

"After she calmed down, Luella broke into tears. She said she'd started seeing someone else because she thought I wasn't interested in her any more. But since I hired a private investigator to follow her, it proves I really did care. She put her arms around me and we made up! We're going on a second honeymoon to Miami next week. I can't thank you enough."

Miranda was stunned. "I'm...happy for you," she managed to say.

"So please let me make amends and pay you the money I owe you."

He was begging to pay her? That was a new one.

"Okay." It was all she could think of to say.

She made arrangements to meet Lauderdale in her office later and hung up.

Well, she thought. This was new. Money coming in? Grateful clients?

Pondering the meaning of it, she took her plate and cup to the sink and rinsed them. It didn't mean she needed to stick around Atlanta. What it meant was she had enough money to go wherever she wanted and maybe take a little time off to get her head back together. She might even have enough to see her father in Hawaii. That might be the place to move.

She was just drying her hands when the phone rang again.

What did Lauderdale want now?

She answered without checking the number. "Look, Lauderdale. I get it. It was a mix up. You don't have to grovel."

"Miranda?"

The low sophisticated tone rippled through her wrapping her in a blanket of emotion that nearly knocked her over.

"Parker?" she gasped. What could he possibly want?

And then she knew. Divorce papers.

He probably wanted to serve them to her in person. Do something classy like take her out for a nice dinner and discuss terms like two rational adults.

The hell with that. She didn't want anything of his. Hadn't she made that clear when she left? He could send her the papers in the mail.

But before she could tell him so, he spoke again.

"I have a problem." Suddenly she noticed the unsteadiness in his voice.

"What's wrong?"

"Gen's missing."

She leaned back against her counter. "What?"

"My daughter, Gen. She's missing." This time his voice broke.

He sounded so anguished he brought sudden tears to her eyes. "What do you mean she's missing?"

"Someone's kidnapped her."

Kidnapped her? Someone kidnapped Gen? That sounded unlikely. Gen was too mean to kidnap.

"How do you know? Maybe she just went off somewhere."

She heard him take an unsteady breath. "Do you remember those anonymous text messages on your phone?"

She tensed. Not that again. "Of course."

"I got one this morning."

"What?"

"I got an anonymous text on my phone."

Her knees buckled but she managed to move to the card table and sink down into a chair. She put a hand to her forehead. Parker had gotten a text message like the ones she had?

"What did it say?" she asked.

"It said 'I have your daughter.'"

Was it from the same person? Had to be. No more esoteric musings like her texts. Just a straightforward gut punch. She didn't know what to say. She could hardly breathe.

"I need your help, Miranda," Parker said.

"My help?"

"I want you to help me find Gen."

"Me?"

"Yes, you. How soon can you be here?"

She looked around the apartment. There was nothing here to occupy her.

Gen was missing. Parker needed her help. She didn't even think about turning him down.

"I'll be there as fast as I can."

CHAPTER FORTY-TWO

Parker told her he wasn't at the Agency. He'd gotten a team together and they would be working at his penthouse, so as not to alarm the other employees.

Miranda made arrangements with Santiago and Lauderdale to handle the money exchanges later and drove down I-85 to Piedmont, relieved the traffic wasn't too bad this time of day.

Twenty-five minutes later she was pulling into the guarded parking deck of a gorgeous thirty-five story masterpiece that made the high-rise she'd gone to on Ponce de Leon yesterday look like a shoebox set on its side.

Somebody buzzed her in and she rode the elevator up to the top floor.

Butterflies were dancing a *pas de deux* in her stomach as she lifted her hand and knocked on the tall dark wood door.

To her surprise Becker answered. "Hi, Steele," he breathed.

"Hi."

He was in ragged jeans and a yellow T-shirt that didn't do much for his complexion. But it was great to see that long hair, those bushy black brows and that loveable big nose again. He looked a little shell-shocked, but the expression in his big brown eyes told her he was overjoyed to see her.

"So glad you're here."

He led her through a short white hall with a lighted niche filled with antique, hand-painted vases and into the main living space.

Wow.

Parker's new digs were more massive and ultra classy than she expected.

The air was clean, cool, comfortable. The floors were real hardwood—a deep glossy mahogany. The ceilings were high and dotted with muted lighting that gave off just the right amount of illumination. The décor was sheer male—slate blue and earthen tones against a creamy background.

Directly across from her, the far wall was all window—with a breathtaking view of every building in the city.

The thought struck her that Parker's father probably owned the building. Pays to have connections. And be loaded.

Recessed in a wall near the windows she recognized a sleek onyx desk and one of Parker's big screen monitors. He'd taken it from the mansion.

Off to her right stood a spiral staircase with a shiny chrome banister leading to an upper floor. In front of the stairs a blue marble support beam divided an area where two ivory sofas sat facing each other. At the end of the space was a floor to ceiling bookcase.

And standing beside the bookcase was Parker.

His jacket strewn across the back of one of the sofas, he stood in rolled up shirtsleeves, papers in his hands, his Glock holstered on his shoulder. His thick expressive brows were drawn together in deep concentration.

He was as heartbreakingly handsome as ever, but his dark, salt-and-pepper hair was disheveled and had more gray. He was still just as well-built and muscular as she remembered, but he'd lost weight.

He looked tired and stressed. Even from here she could see there were more distinguished lines in his gorgeous face.

He lifted his gaze from his papers and his gunmetal gray eyes fixed her with a look that went straight through her.

Parker stared at his wife—his former wife—feeling as if he were coming out of a nightmare and into some rapturous dream.

She was here.

And she looked so strong and so lovely. Those black, dagger-like lashes and lush, deep blue eyes he'd first seen glowering at him from behind the bars of a jail cell. That wild, unruly dark hair he used to run his fingers through. Her lean, firm body. That cocky demeanor. Emotion and memory of all they'd been together surged through him like a tempest.

It took all the strength he had to hold it in, to hide it.

She was dressed casually. Her pretty blue T-shirt read *Normal is Boring*. It almost made him smile. But it was her strong, confident stance that bolstered him.

Just what he needed now.

"Thank you for coming," he said.

"Don't mention it," she said, and the sound of her lovely voice raked over his heart like a claw.

He'd missed her. He hadn't realized how much until this very moment. But there wasn't time to think about his personal concerns now.

He gestured to the opposite side of the penthouse. "We're over here."

Miranda followed Parker beyond the sofas, past a section with marble flooring and four barrel chairs, and into a dining area.

Here stood a long, glossy table that could easily seat a dozen, surrounded by credenzas filled with modern art brick-a-brack. A huge abstract painting that went well with the décor hung on the far wall.

And at the table sat Holloway and Wesson.

Wesson had on a Kelly green jacket and black business slacks. As usual her luxurious amaretto red hair fell sensually over her shoulders. But her face was grim and her back rigid. She was in full work mode.

Looking lean and lanky as always, dressed in a tan coat and brown tie, Holloway shoved back his light brown hair and rose as Miranda approached. He extended a hand to her. Mighty formal of him.

"Glad to have you with us, Steele."

"Anything to help."

Wesson gave her a nod from her seat. "Good to see you."

"Likewise."

"We've missed you, Steele," Becker said as he eyed her and Parker slyly.

Miranda wanted to kick his shin. This wasn't the time for matchmaking.

Parker cleared his throat and took the floor. "As you all know, I've asked Miranda here to help us with this investigation."

"Yes, sir." All of them nodded in response.

"As you also know, I received an anonymous text message this morning."

Miranda turned to Parker feeling a little out of the loop. "Let me see it."

He reached into his pocket and handed her his phone.

She read the text.

Good Morning, Wade Parker. You may be interested to know that I have your daughter.

A shiver went through her. "He knows your name."

"And when Mr. Parker would see the text," Wesson added. "My theory is he knew when he would start missing Gen at the office and that was the time he sent it."

Miranda raised a brow. "So he's a planner."

"Would have to be. Gen isn't the type to just go off with someone."

"We believe she was taken this morning," Parker said. "She had stopped at the mall on her way in to work. Holloway and I made a quick run out there before coming here and found her cell and her car. The police are processing it now."

Probably wouldn't find anything. "So she's in another vehicle."

"Would have to be," Becker said, echoing Wesson.

Miranda thought a moment. "The mall has to have surveillance cameras."

Parker nodded. "My contact there will be emailing the recording from this morning to us shortly." Distress shadowed his face. "And speaking of surveillance recordings, I have a lot more to show you."

CHAPTER FORTY-THREE

They all crowded around the end of the long table, Miranda wedged between Wesson and Becker, while Holloway passed around soft drinks. Parker took Becker's laptop and explained what he'd been doing for the past several days—looking for the man who had sent Miranda those anonymous text messages.

Then he began to play a surveillance tape of one of the cube banks inside the Parker Agency.

Miranda tensed. She'd noticed those cameras when she'd worked there but had assumed they were fake.

Before she could decide how she felt about all this, her jaw nearly dropped at the image on the screen. "Is that my desk?"

"It is," Parker said.

A grainy grayish figure in a nondescript uniform stood in the still familiar aisle in front of her old cube. His head tilted, he stared at something as if mesmerized.

Her name tag.

He stood there for several long, uncomfortable moments. Then he plunged into her space. A second later came up with her phone. His arms and fingers bobbed this way and that.

"Is he doing what I think he's doing?"

"He's getting your number," Becker told her. "And probably some of your contacts. At least Mr. Parker's. This was the only lead we could find for anyone who got to your phone."

Miranda sat back, her shoulders sagging with shock.

She gestured at the computer. "Who the hell is that?"

"His name is Gabriel Anthony Pierson," Parker said in a low steady voice, tinged with simmering anger. "A cleaning man for Gypsum Management, the company that takes care of the Imperial Building."

Miranda stared at him open-mouthed. He'd been right. Some psycho had sent her those anonymous texts messages and this was the guy. "Have you tracked him down? Is he in jail?"

But how could he have sent that message to Parker's phone this morning? Had to be the same guy, right?

"I attempted to," Parker said. "I visited Diana Westbrook at Gypsum yesterday and got Pierson's employment records."

Miranda didn't know the woman.

"It seems Pierson has a very interesting address."

She frowned at him.

"A high-rise apartment on Ponce de Leon. Unit nine-twenty-nine."

"What?" She shot out of the chair and moved to the window.

That's where I was yesterday, she wanted to say. But instead she kept her mouth shut. She didn't want to go into the horrendous details of Hannah Kaye's case right now.

Hugging herself she stared out at the city. Gen's situation was getting more bizarre by the minute. The cleaning man who'd sent her those anonymous texts weeks ago—who presumably sent Parker that message about Gen this morning—lived in unit nine-twenty-nine? But that couldn't be true.

She paced back to the table and grabbed her soda for a fortifying swallow.

Parker watched her agitation. She had to know more about that apartment and the man who'd pretended to rent it. He prayed it was enough. "You've been looking for someone named Thomas Anthony Drew, haven't you?"

Miranda nearly choked on her soda. "How do you know that?"

"The landlord at the high-rise told me you were there asking about him yesterday. Just an hour or so before I was there asking about Pierson."

Miranda put a hand to her head to keep it from spinning right off her neck. "But Drew hadn't rented that unit. He gave a false address."

"As did Pierson."

"The same one?" Still holding onto her soda can, Miranda sank back down onto her chair.

"That's just crazy," Wesson said. She obviously hadn't been filled in on these details.

Neither had Holloway. "Are you sure there wasn't a misprint or something?"

"I'm sure," Miranda told him.

"Positive," Parker agreed.

Then he turned back to the laptop and went through Drew's history. Parker had already done a background check on the guy. And he'd found exactly what she had.

"The fact is Thomas Drew, the truck driver, had no history until three years ago. And the same is true of Gabriel Pierson, the cleaning man. The real Gabriel Anthony Pierson was a carpenter from Macon. He was eighty-five when he died three years ago."

"Oh, my God," Miranda murmured.

She thought again of her last case in Chicago and the ninety-one-year-old man in the nursing home named Adam Foster Tannenburg. But he wasn't the real Adam Tannenburg.

Parker continued. "Drew drove a light gray Hyundai which was impounded by the police two nights ago."

Miranda blinked at him in surprise. Parker must have contacted the police about Gen. He must have learned about the Hyundai from Lieutenant Erskine.

It was time to stop holding back. "I know," she said.

All three of her former colleagues turned to her in unison. Hey, it was Parker who was the clairvoyant here.

"One of my…client's men found the Hyundai that night," she told them. "That's where I got Drew's drivers license. How I dug into his background."

Holloway gave her a crooked grin. "Good going, Steele."

She didn't smile back. "I need to tell you about Drew." The things Parker didn't know.

She rose to her feet again, moved over to the abstract painting with the slate blue and earthen colored rings and cubes. She paced back and forth in front of the cherry credenza covered with globes and decorative metal pieces in the same colors. Parker must have hired a decorator.

How was she going to say this?

"So with the drivers license, I did a run on Drew and discovered he worked for a place called Phelps Supply Company. He was a truck driver, delivering medical equipment to places like Saint Benedictine Hospital."

Parker nodded sharply. "While you were in rehab there."

Of course, he'd known that, too. He'd run Drew's background himself.

Becker sucked in a breath. "Was Drew stalking Steele at the hospital?"

"Don't know for sure," she replied, trying to keep her voice steady.

But now that she'd heard the words out loud, they sounded all too plausible.

She took a deep breath and went on. "What I found was a bookkeeper who thought Drew had a fixation for her."

"A fixation?" Wesson asked.

"Hung around her office all the time. Got close enough one time to sniff her perfume. She said Drew looked at her once like he wanted to kill her."

Everyone stared at her.

Miranda licked her lips and began pacing in front of the credenza again. "I found the details on Hannah Kaye's car—that's the missing exotic dancer my client hired me to find," she explained when Becker frowned. "I put a GPS tracker on Hannah's car and got a hit yesterday afternoon."

"You found her?" Wesson said, wide-eyed.

"Yeah, I found her. She'd been missing since last Thursday." Her legs feeling shaky, Miranda pulled out a chair on the far end of the table and sat down. "I found her in a deserted place thirty miles east of the city. She was dead."

She told them the rest of it. All of it. Her drive to the grungy house in the woods. Her search that revealed the occupant was long gone. And what she'd found on the lower level.

Hannah Kaye's body strung up like a ham, with gory wounds and bruises covering every inch of her. The horrible smell. The insects. And the blood. So much blood.

When she finished, her colleagues' faces were as grim and somber as she'd ever seen them. Parker's eyes were moist and he looked deadly pale.

She knew he felt for Hannah Kaye, but right now his thoughts mirrored hers. What might Gen be going through this very minute?

"Wait a second." Wesson pressed her palms to her head. "I'm confused. We think Drew is the one who stalked Steele at Saint Benedictine's."

"Yes," Parker replied.

"But Pierson's the one on the surveillance recording from the Agency. The one who got Steele's number off her phone. The same guy who texted her and Mr. Parker this morning, right?"

"Correct."

"So are we looking for two killers? And which one has Gen?"

Miranda lifted her hands. She didn't even know Parker had come up with another guy until a few minutes ago. But he seemed to have an idea.

He took command of the laptop again, and she came around the table to see what he was doing.

"This," he said, "is Gabriel Anthony Pierson." He clicked on an icon and a photo of the cleaning man appeared.

Pierson had bushy dirty blond hair and blue eyes. His uniform looked tight over his bulky shoulders, or maybe it was his slouch that made him seem so uncomfortable. Or the mean look in his eyes that gave Miranda a chill.

Parker clicked another icon. "And this is Thomas Anthony Drew."

Miranda gritted her teeth as the face she'd been studying for two days came up on the screen. The dark wavy hair, the good looks, the pencil mustache. This was the man who had so brutally murdered Hannah Kaye.

He wasn't a man. He was an animal.

Parker moved the photos on the screen so they were side by side. And when he did, she felt her stomach twist into a hard knot that made her dizzy. There were differences but they looked so similar.

Parker watched his people as they studied the photos. He hoped they were seeing what he had seen.

"Drew's features are shaped a little differently," Holloway noted after a few moments.

Parker nodded. "True, but features can be altered. Let me remind you that both of these identities, Gabriel Anthony Pierson and Thomas Anthony Drew are stolen."

Miranda felt her blood go cold.

Becker's eyes went wide. "So we're dealing with…"

Parker nodded. "Someone else entirely."

Wesson pointed back and forth at the photos. "And these two could be…"

Becker gulped. "The same guy?"

CHAPTER FORTY-FOUR

Before anyone could reply to that, a window popped up on Becker's screen.
"It's the surveillance recording from the mall parking deck," he said, smoothly taking the laptop from Parker.

The place where Gen was snatched this morning. Miranda's heart beat in heavy thumps as he brought the film up on the screen, replacing the two photos of Pierson and Drew.

The view changed to gray, water-stained cement walls and vacant parking spots. The lighting wasn't great, but Miranda could make out enough detail to see the lot was empty.

"Scroll to nine o'clock," Wesson said. "That's when the stores open. Gen wouldn't have gotten there any earlier."

Good point.

Becker followed her command and let the film play.

For a long while the view remained static. Miranda studied the layout and the oil spots on the cement. At nine-oh-eight, an employee pulled into a spot, got out of his car and went inside. At nine-twelve he was followed by a woman in a Civic.

Finally, a sapphire blue Infinity turned the far corner and pulled into a spot.

Wesson came to life. "That's her."

Miranda inched forward and watched Gen get out of her car carrying three packages and head for the mall. "What's she doing?"

There was silence for a long moment.

Finally Parker spoke. "Returning anniversary gifts."

From their party? The one she'd never gone to? "Oh." She hugged herself tighter and kept her eyes on the screen.

Minutes passed.

Getting impatient, Becker fast forwarded. Then he went back. There was movement again. "There," he said pointing to a truck that had just pulled into view.

"Is that it?"

It was a rust red F-150 with an off-white stripe. Had a crew cab and a dent in the door. The driver didn't get out.

The room was silent while everyone stared at the screen and waited.

Finally Gen appeared again. She stopped to make a call on her cell phone.

That was when the driver got out of the truck. He didn't go toward the store. He moved toward Gen.

He wore jeans and a baggy gray T-shirt. He had a matching ball cap pulled down so you couldn't see his face, but he was muscularly built.

As soon as he reached Gen he grabbed her from behind.

She struggled, tried to kick, bite him. Good for her, Miranda thought.

But she couldn't escape that powerful grasp. He was too strong for her. He dragged her to the pickup, put a rag over her face. He was drugging her so she wouldn't fight.

Her body went limp. She was out cold. He tossed her into the back seat, climbed inside and drove off.

"This way," Becker cried. "Turn this way."

And as if he had cast some sort of spell over the footage, the truck turned toward the camera. And as it curved, the license plate came into clear view.

"Stop the film!" Parker cried. His voice was raspy. Miranda had never seen quite that much agony on his face.

But Becker had already paused it. The number on the plate was blurry but readable.

"I've got a GPS tracker," Miranda offered. "But it's slow as Christmas."

"We have the Agency's tracker," Parker said. And he grabbed Holloway's laptop, brought up the program, and entered the truck's information as fast as he could.

Miranda watched the tension in his shoulders as he worked and her heart broke for him. She couldn't stand seeing him in this much pain. She hoped the Agency's program was as fast as she thought it was.

He had the tracker up and running within two minutes, but it would still take time to process.

"We've got it, sir," Becker assured him. "We'll find her now."

Miranda prayed Becker was right.

CHAPTER FORTY-FIVE

Gen's eyes fluttered open and then shut again. How much had she had to drink at the club last night?

Only a few zombies. And she'd left half of the last one.

Still her head pounded and swirled as if her brain was about to explode. Her tongue was so dry it felt like overused sandpaper. She'd never had a hangover this bad. Was she getting the flu?

She wrinkled her nose.

What was that awful smell? Musty, moldy, like an old locker room. Wow, what a dream she'd had. She thought someone had grabbed her at the mall. Enough of that. It was time to go to work.

She reached over, she felt for her alarm clock but instead of the snooze button her fingers touched something hard and cold.

She opened her eyes and let out a scream.

It was a cage. She was inside a cage! How did she get in here? She tried to sit up and bumped her head on the top of it. Dear God. What was going on?

There was a door. She tried to push it open with her hands, but a padlock held it firmly in place. She pushed harder, harder. Until the whole cage rattled. Open. C'mon now. Open.

She looked down at herself. All she had on were her panties and bra. Where were her clothes?

She peered through the wires of the cage and saw she was in some strange place. It looked like a basement of some sort. There was padding on the walls. Paper lanterns with candles in them lined up along the floor.

Overhead wooden beams ran crosswise along the ceiling. And over one of the beams hung a pulley with thick ropes suspended from it.

What the hell was that for?

And then she heard footsteps. She craned her neck upward and saw a man coming toward her. Large feet clad in running shoes. A pair of baggy jeans frayed at the hems. His T-shirt was baggy, too. And gray.

His hair was shaggy and light colored. She'd never seen him before.

He leaned down and grinned at her. "Well, hello there sleepy head."

The sound of his voice made her cringe. "Let me out of here," she demanded.

He pouted with a frown. "Is that anyway to greet your host?"

Host? He wasn't her host. "You'd better let me out of here right now."

He chuckled to himself.

Her heart started to pound. "Who are you?"

He didn't answer. Just kept laughing.

"You won't get away with this, you creep. My father's the best investigator in the southeast. He'll find me and when he does, there'll be hell to pay."

The man stopped laughing and leaned down as if to get a better look at her. "Oh, I know who your father is. Wade Parker."

She stifled a gasp of surprise. "Then you know what he'll do to you when he finds you."

"Oh, he'll find us all right. And so will Miranda Steele. And when they do, the party will start."

What? What did Miranda Steele have to do with all of this? Was this her fault? How did this guy know about her? How did he know they were coming for her? Nothing made any sense at all.

All she knew was that she was dealing with a crazy man.

"Look," she said to him, trying to keep her voice calm. "Let's be reasonable about this. We both know once my father gets here, you're going straight to jail. But if you let me out of here now and give me my clothes, I promise I won't press charges."

He laughed again.

What the hell was so damn funny? "I'll tell them to give you a light sentence. I'll tell them it was all a…a misunderstanding."

He squatted down in front of the cage and took a key from his pocket. He began unlocking the padlock.

Had her promise worked? Was he going to let her out? He was. Thank God, he was!

He opened the door.

She tried to climb out but he blocked her with his legs. It was then she saw he had a water bottle in his other hand.

"Are you thirsty, sweetie?"

Thirsty? Hell yeah, she was thirsty. Her mouth felt like she'd been stranded in the desert for a week. But she didn't dare drink anything he gave her.

"Here you go." He twisted open the lid and she saw it had already been opened.

More alarm bells went off in her head.

He put the bottle close to her face. "Here, sweetie. Have some water."

Instead she clutched his pant leg and gave it a yank, trying to throw him off balance. It almost worked.

But he reached inside the cage and grabbed her by the hair.

"Now that's not very polite of you." He forced her head back and poured the water into her mouth.

She fought and spat and tried to keep her mouth closed, but he was too strong. He got the water between her lips, her teeth. It tasted good. She was so thirsty.

But there had to be something in it. Her resistance caved almost immediately.

Her jaw relaxed and he poured the rest of the water down her throat without a protest.

As she swallowed the last of it her eyes shut and once more her muscles went limp.

Through a thick cloud she heard his voice again. "And when your father and his whore get here, I'll make you pay for trying to escape."

Her head felt like it was filled with cotton. The room began to spin.

And the last thing she heard was him re-locking the cage.

CHAPTER FORTY-SIX

While they waited for the GPS tracker to work everyone got busy around the fancy dining room table.

Parker watched anxiously for results on the screen, Holloway and Becker fiddled with something on his laptop, and Miranda reviewed all the new data she'd learned and wrote up a report with Wesson on her machine.

An hour went by. Two. Still no results.

Parker ordered a pizza and they all chowed down while they kept working. But even though they were busy, Miranda felt they were getting nowhere.

She hated just sitting here, but it would be pointless to go off on a blind hunt. Gen could be anywhere in the state of Georgia by now.

Or beyond.

She needed a break. Getting up she stretched, then strolled into the area where the barrel chairs were. This place was as fancy as the Parker mansion. The man had taste. She wondered if there was a gym. She longed to go for a nice long run to burn off the tension. But there was no time for that now.

She ran her hands over her face. If only she had gone to Parker when she'd first gotten those anonymous texts on her phone. If only she had taken them seriously. Was it her fault the love of her life was going through such agony right now?

And what if they didn't find Gen in time? Like she hadn't found Hannah Kaye in time. Would they find Parker's daughter in the same state?

If that happened, she'd never forgive herself.

She was about to return to the table when her phone rang. She pulled it out and checked the display. It was Chambers.

"Steele," she answered.

Chambers' slow southern accent had an edge to it today. "You're not going to believe this."

She listened to him for a moment then stopped him. "Wait. I'm working with some colleagues from the Parker Agency. I'm going to put you on speaker so you can repeat that."

She hurried back to the dining area. "This is Detective Chambers from APD," she told everyone as she pressed the button and set her cell on the table.

Everyone turned to look at the phone as Chambers' southern voice echoed into the open space of the penthouse.

"What I said was the CSI guys found some tire tracks yesterday behind the house going into the woods."

"The house where Hannah Kaye was found," Miranda clarified.

"Right. The killer must have escaped that way. We don't have a timeframe on that, but we did run the tracks and have a lead on the vehicle."

Miranda sucked in a breath. "Let me guess. Rust-and-cream F-150 with a dent in its side."

Chambers let out a squawk. "Steele. How the hell do you know that?"

For a moment she caught Parker's eye and they shared a rueful smile. "We spotted it a little while ago on a surveillance recording from the mall. We're tracking it now. The driver of the truck seems to be the same guy who kidnapped Gen Parker this morning."

"Hold on a sec. Wade Parker's daughter has been kidnapped?"

Parker picked up the phone. "Detective Chambers, this is Wade Parker. I spoke to Lieutenant Erskine about this matter earlier today."

Chambers stammered a moment. "He hasn't said anything to me, but I'll be sure to check in with him and coordinate. But...I have some bad news."

Miranda felt her stomach twist inside her. "What is it, Chambers?"

"First—I hate to tell you this—but we found semen in the vic's body. Quite a lot of it, I'm afraid. We're running it through the databases."

So he'd raped her before he'd strung her up. Sounded like repeatedly.

"And secondly, we've been looking into murders like the one we saw yesterday, casting a wider net. Nationwide, in fact." He cleared his throat.

"And?"

"And it looks like our guy has been at this game a while."

He meant the grisly murder game of torturing and killing young women.

"I found over thirty cases of similar killings all around the country over a span of fifteen years. Earliest was in Downers Grove."

A cold chill went through her. That was near Chicago. A few suburbs away from where she grew up. Where she'd lived with Leon.

"All of the victims were blond," Chambers continued. "Early to late twenties. Many were hookers or strippers, like the vic yesterday."

But Hannah Kaye had been more than that. The other victims had been, too. All of them had lives and backgrounds and families who now mourned for them.

But her earlier instinct had been right. This was a crazed serial killer with a specific M.O.

"Anything else, Detective?" Parker asked.

"That's it for now. I'll keep you posted on any developments."

"Thank you."

"And Mr. Parker?"

"Yes?"

"I want you to know I'll do my damndest to find your daughter."

"I appreciate it."

Miranda took the phone out of Parker's hand and hung it up. He looked worse than before. Worse than she felt and that was horrible. She couldn't look at him anymore.

She sank down into her chair and stared into space. If only she could do something. But all she wanted to do was put her head down on the table and weep.

"Got it," someone said.

It was Becker. She scowled at him. "What are you talking about?"

"Holloway and I have been playing around with these photos. The ones of Pierson and Drew?"

Miranda blinked at him. "Yeah?"

"You enhanced them?" Wesson was already looking at the screen.

"Sort of. We took out the things you could add if you wanted to disguise your appearance. For instance Drew could have altered the shape of his chin with a bit of cotton between his gum and cheek. And Pierson's nose. Just looks like there's some putty on this ridge. And so I took some of those features out with the software, and voila."

He turned the screen around. Except for what they were wearing, the two photos of Drew and Pierson were nearly identical. He'd even removed Drew's mustache and changed the hair coloring.

Wesson gasped. "It's the same guy."

Miranda jabbed a finger at the screen. "Why'd you pick the blond hair?"

Becker shrugged. "The guy in the mall tape is blond. Plus it's easier to dye your hair a darker color if you're blond than the other way around. And you can always grow or shave off a mustache."

Good point. "You think this is the man's natural appearance?"

Becker nodded. "That's my best assessment."

So Pierson and Drew were one and the same. It was all clicking into place, but it made less sense than ever. Why pretend you're two people?

She felt Parker touch her arm.

"I need to speak with you in private a moment, Miranda."

His face was so serious she couldn't refuse. "Sure."

CHAPTER FORTY-SEVEN

Parker led her across the floor toward the window and through a glass door to a patio.

She stepped onto the terracotta surface where a glass-and-steel rail formed one edge of a large triangle overlooking the city. In one corner sat a glass outdoor table with chairs in a fancy swirling wrought iron design.

Miranda rubbed her arms as a light breeze swept through her hair. It was almost chilly up here.

In the distance, past the tall buildings, the sun was getting low. Soon it would be flooding the horizon with color. It had been twenty-four hours since she'd driven west and found Hannah Kaye's body. It would take a lifetime to forget the image of it.

"Miranda," Parker began.

"I need to say something first," she blurted out. "I'm sorry." She didn't turn around to face him. Didn't have the strength to.

"Sorry?"

"I should have listened to you when you told me those text messages on my phone were dangerous. I should have told you about the first one when I got it. I'd give anything if I could go back and change that now."

He didn't speak.

Now she did turn around and dare to look into his handsome face. There was such pain in it, such feeling, it broke her heart in two.

"Whatever happened between us, I want you to know that."

He nodded and for a moment seemed as if he wanted to lift a hand to her face and touch her. Then he must have thought better of it.

He turned away to lean over the banister. "I have a confession to make as well."

She couldn't imagine what he meant. "Okay."

"It's about when we were in Chicago."

"When we were working the Sutherland case?"

"You were working the Sutherland case. I was trying to find…"

"Yes, I know." He'd been trying to find the man who'd raped her fifteen years ago. The man who Mackenzie was looking for—her birth father.

"I went to Florida."

"I remember." She'd thought he'd run out on her. He'd lied to her and said he'd been interviewing prospective employees for the Agency. It seemed like ages ago.

"The reason I went to Florida was because of something I found at Cook County Jail."

She put a hand to her head. "You went to the Cook County Jail?"

He nodded. "I was looking in the archives for men who had been arrested fifteen years ago."

For rape, he meant.

"What I found was that Adam Tannenburg had been brought in on February first of that year."

Folding her arms she thought back to the case.

Lydia Sutherland, a pretty young blond art student had been strangled and set on fire in her own home. The police hadn't been able to find her killer and the case went cold. Parker had picked up the case as an excuse to get to Chicago.

Miranda had worked it hard. She'd discovered Lydia had had a lover. A boy of nineteen named Adam Foster Tannenburg. He went to art school with her. He played the clarinet. And according to one witness he was with her the night of the fire.

A year later his own mother had also died in a house fire, the Tannenburg family estate. She and Parker had visited what was left of it now. Miranda had been there with the detective she'd worked with in Chicago, as well.

But after the house fire Tannenburg had disappeared.

Miranda had thought the boyfriend was Lydia's killer but evidence proved it had been someone else—Miranda's ex-husband, Leon Groth.

She rubbed her forehead. The details had come back to her. "That date can't be right. Lydia died the night of December eighteenth. Tannenburg was brought in the next day."

"And released," Parker said. "But he was brought in again later."

She frowned. "We never found any record of that." She'd worked with a police detective in the Larrabee station who'd had access to those records.

Parker shook his head. "The record of it was expunged."

"What do you mean expunged?"

"It was erased. All except a small note. One line indicating a single person who had visited Tannenburg in jail."

"Who?"

"Leon Groth."

Her ex-husband? She let out a smirk. "Wait. You're saying Leon visited Tannenburg? How did he even know him? He wasn't involved with the Sutherland case—except as the killer. He worked for the Oak Park police department."

"That's what I went to Florida to find out. I visited a corrections officer who'd been on guard during the night of Groth's visit to Tannenburg."

"What did he tell you?"

"That he spoke to Groth the night of the visit. Groth told him he had evidence on Tannenburg that could put him away for a long time."

"But it was Leon who killed Lydia Sutherland. Was he trying to frame Tannenburg for it?"

"I don't know, but the officer told me Tannenburg had been brought in for sexual assault."

Miranda shivered.

"After we learned it was Groth who had killed Lydia Sutherland, and that he had left his sperm in her that night, I believed Groth had been blackmailing Tannenburg."

"You mean Leon thought he could make Tannenburg pay for his crime?"

Parker nodded. "I thought Tannenburg had witnessed it. And so Groth made a deal with him. He'd get the charges dropped and the record of his arrest expunged if Tannenburg disappeared."

"And never tell anyone the truth."

"Yes."

Miranda let out a long slow breath. Was that why she'd never been able to find Tannenburg?

Parker's voice was low and soft. "I'm sorry, too."

"What?"

"I'm sorry I kept that from you."

She nodded, taking in the sorrowful look in his handsome gray eyes. She loved him so much. She always would.

"You never found a picture of Adam Tannenburg, did you?" he asked.

"No."

"I can't get it out of my head that this man we're looking for matches his description."

Miranda tensed. He had a point. The shaggy dirty blond hair, the muscular shoulders. It wasn't much to go on. A lot of men looked like that. But one of them was the guy in the photo Becker had doctored.

Before Miranda could say anything else, there was a knock on the glass door to the penthouse.

It opened a crack and Becker stuck his head out. His eyes were wide and looked a little wild. "Sorry to interrupt, Mr. Parker."

"It's all right, Dave. What is it?"

Excitedly he pointed back to the dining area with his thumb. "We got a hit on the tracker. We've located the kidnapper's truck."

CHAPTER FORTY-EIGHT

This time he'd gone southeast.

Nearly fifty miles southeast, the bastard. It would take them an hour to get there.

They packed up the laptops, piled into Parker's Mazda, and took off. Parker flew down surface streets to 285, then spun onto I-20. He whizzed around the traffic, driving like a madman.

Miranda couldn't blame him, but she wished she had offered to drive.

Too late for that now. She knew he wasn't stopping.

On and on they went. Mile after mile. They passed Snapfinger and Redan and Lithonia and Conyers, strange sounding names of surrounding southern towns. As they neared Covington they took an exit and raced down the two-ways, Parker not caring if the small town police came after him for speeding. They headed towards Mansfield, Newborn, deep into the country.

Miranda watched the fields and trees whizz by her window, nerves dancing in her stomach.

This was a replay of yesterday. Follow him deep into the woods, find him, see what he'd done. No, he'd only had Gen since this morning. He hadn't had time to do what he'd done to Hannah Kaye.

But he'd had time to start.

Holding her breath she felt that strange sensation along the back of her neck. Insects crawling up and down her vertebrae. And she felt as if she were being manipulated. Pierson or Drew or Tannenburg or whoever this creep was, was luring them into his trap just when he wanted them to get there.

That thought only made the sick knot in her stomach tighter.

Twenty minutes later Parker pulled onto a dirt lane in a grassy wooded area.

Just like yesterday, Miranda thought. Though this time instead of storm clouds, the sun was setting at their backs, flickering through the oak leaves and pine needles.

"We're in Jaspar County," Parker murmured. "My father took me here as a boy. To Monticello to see the old mansions."

Might as well be on the other side of the world.

In the backseat, Wesson was glued to her phone. "I've contacted Lieutenant Erskine and Detective Chambers, sir," she said. "They're on their way. They'll contact the local police when we're ready."

Keeping his gaze fixed on the dirt road, Parker nodded. "Thank you, Detective."

They bumped down the path, kicking up a cloud of red dust as they went. As the trail curved this way and that Parker steered the car right and left. Miranda thought she was going to be sick.

And then she saw it.

A lone house with a rust-and-cream pickup truck parked beside it.

There he was. Same as yesterday. Nothing around. No neighbors. Nowhere to go for help.

But yesterday he'd been gone. Deep in her bones Miranda knew he'd planned that. Just as he'd planned to be here today.

After all it wasn't that hard to block a GPS signal. He hadn't done that. Hadn't even made an attempt. He'd made sure they had a way to find him. He'd made sure she'd found Hannah Kaye's car yesterday. After he was done with her. He'd wanted her to find her hanging there.

To rattle her? He'd done a good job of that.

She had no idea what kind of greeting he had in mind for her this time, but her only focus now was to find Gen and get her out of here.

Parker pressed the brake and came to a stop. He stared at the place. "We need a plan."

"We can surround the house," Holloway suggested.

That would be a start.

"Inside surveillance would be nice," said Wesson.

Becker agreed. "Maybe one of us can slip through a window and plant a hidden camera. I have one in my briefcase."

"I can go in," Holloway offered.

Becker shook his head. "I'm the smallest."

"No," Miranda said sharply.

She didn't want Becker in there. Not after what he and Fanuzzi had been through in Paris.

"Going inside is too risky," Parker said, command in his voice.

"He's right," Wesson said. "Maybe we can get something through the roof or the duct system. Let's check out the place first."

The others nodded.

Each of them got out of the car and quietly closed the doors. They scurried to the far side of the truck and crouched there, using it for cover.

From that spot they surveyed the place. The sun was waning, but they could still make out the basic features in the dusky light.

The house was painted an ugly yellow. It might have been pretty twenty years ago but that would have been before at least two decades of neglect. It had a basement. Miranda could tell by the openings in the cinderblock along the foundation. It could have been just a crawlspace, but that wouldn't fit the bill for this killer.

The grass around the house was overgrown and looked snake-infested. A screened-in porch hung from the side looking as if it was about to fall off. A window that looked like it had been painted white before the Civil War was half open. Had to be stifling in there.

No curtains. No faces peeking out.

Becker waggled a finger. "See that window? I could climb through it, sir."

"No," Miranda hissed at him. Then she caught Parker looking at her with something like gratitude.

"Holloway," she whispered.

"Yes, Steele?"

"Let's you and me go around the back and check it out. Everybody else stay put."

"Roger that," Holloway murmured under his breath.

And the two of them crept out from their hiding place.

They found a path that wasn't so overgrown leading to the back of the house. Finding a clump of gnarled bushes they crouched behind them and checked out the place.

This side was even worse.

Trashcans and buckets of junk were piled up along the cinderblock, casting weird shadows in the grass. The siding was in ruins. The familiar black mold grew between the boards, under the eaves, along the foundation. A sheet of asphalt on the roof was torn and hanging down over the side.

"What a mess," Holloway whispered.

She nodded in agreement.

What was this guy doing? Buying up repossessed houses like a real estate agent?

"C'mon," she said to Holloway. "Let's get back to the others."

They scampered back to the trunk and found everyone waiting there looking hopeful.

Miranda shook her head. "That roof isn't stable enough to hold any of us."

Becker stifled a groan. "That's why I should go through that open window."

Miranda stared at it a while, thinking about the house on the east side. Yesterday the door had been left wide open. She knew now that had been deliberate. This door was probably open as well.

And if that were true, then this was personal. It wasn't about Gen or Parker. It was about her.

Why, she wasn't sure. But she knew it was definitely about her.

Suddenly her spine and the back of her neck went crazy with that awful sensation. Stronger than she'd ever felt it before. As if a thousand beetles were crawling all over her. It was a harrowing feeling, but one she knew well.

And she knew it was telling her exactly what she had to do.

"I'm going in."

Becker let out a quiet gasp. "No, it has to be me."

"You can't do that, Steele," Holloway said.

Wesson shook her red hair vehemently. "No, you're not."

For once Parker was silent. His jaw was clenched tight but he wasn't protesting with the others.

She tried to explain. "I think all this—this whole elaborate cat-and-mouse game with Hannah Kaye and Gen—is all a ruse. A sick one, but a ruse nonetheless. I think it's me this guy really wants."

Holloway's mouth opened in shock. "You don't know that, Steele."

"My instincts do. Hasn't Parker always told us to trust our instincts?"

Holloway was silent.

"And if I'm right. If this guy wants me, maybe I can trade myself for Gen."

Now Parker came to life. "I can't let you do that, Miranda."

She locked her gaze on him, drank in his pain and sorrow, wishing she could take it all away. If she did this one thing, maybe she could. "It's not your decision to make, Parker."

Stunned he gazed back at her for a long moment. But he didn't reply.

It was true. She no longer worked for him. They were no longer truly married. There was nothing he could do to stop her.

He breathed out a frustrated breath. "Wear a wire, at least."

That was a good idea. "Okay."

He turned to Becker. "You brought one, didn't you, Dave?"

Becker grinned. "Always at the ready."

In true nerd spirit, he'd brought his briefcase along, too, when they'd gotten out of the car.

He pulled out a small contraption with a lot of sticky stuff on it and began checking it out. "It's wireless," he whispered. "Made of spool metal wiring, kind of like electronic yarn." He went on for a while, jabbering out geek talk. Finally he handed it to her.

It looked like a small white button.

"Checks out fine," he said. "Just put it under your clothes somewhere."

"Thanks." She lifted her T-shirt and stuck it under her sports bra. "Okay, I'm ready."

Parker touched her arm. "We need a signal in case you get in trouble."

"Like a special word or something?"

"That would do."

She thought a moment. "Penthouse," she said.

Parker's eyes narrowed and he nearly smiled.

She smiled back, her heart melting. Then she took a deep breath. "Here I go."

"Good luck, Steele," Wesson said.

"We'll be right here listening to everything," Becker reminded her.

Holloway gave her a thumbs up. "Don't forget to use the signal."

She nodded and turned toward the dilapidated house.

CHAPTER FORTY-NINE

She picked her way across the yard, managing to avoid getting snake bit, and reached the creaky porch after what seemed like an eternity.

Carefully, she reached behind her and drew out her Beretta from where she'd shoved it under her waistband that morning. She studied the construction.

Four steps up to the screened-in porch. It looked like the whole thing would collapse as soon as she put a foot on it.

She recalled how rickety the entrance of the house in the west had looked yesterday. But it had held. Somehow she knew the guy who had Gen would have made sure the way inside this place held today, too.

She took the first step and found it more solid than it looked. Three more steps and she was at the front door.

Like yesterday she could see it had been left unlocked and ajar.

Beretta raised, she nudged the door open.

She stepped into a large empty room with a grungy carpet-less floor and two ceiling fans. The single half-open window Becker had wanted to climb through was situated near her in a wall that was painted an ugly hot pink.

On the far side of the room Miranda could see a hall that led to the kitchen and another opening with stairs leading to the upper floor. But today she didn't bother to search the place.

She turned to the door on the adjacent side of the room, strode to it quickly and turned the knob. Just as she thought. The stairs to the basement.

The air smelled musty but she didn't catch the foul odor of death she had yesterday. A hopeful sign.

Taking a deep breath, down she went.

CHAPTER FIFTY

It was hot on the stairs and the air had that familiar mildew scent.

Miranda felt sweat bead up on her skin as she descended. It took a while for her eyes to become accustomed to the dim light. But there was light here.

As she neared the end of the staircase she saw it came from a row of half a dozen paper lanterns—candles in a bag—placed along the edges of the floor, outlining the room.

The lanterns cast eerie shadows against the walls, giving the place a weird feeling. Like some sort of ceremonial tomb.

Just like yesterday the walls were padded with acoustical foam to block the sound of female screaming. Overhead were the reinforced beams, the ropes, the pulley system.

Except here there were two of them, placed about five feet apart.

She knew it.

This guy had a plan and she was at the center of it. Well, he was in for a surprise because she was going to ruin that plan.

Despite her resolve, as she stared at the pulleys and the thick ropes hanging from them, the image of Hannah Kaye's mutilated body came to her. Fear clawed at her stomach, but she fought it down.

No time for that. She had to rescue Gen.

Somehow she had to get her away from this creep. Then Parker and the team and all the police in the southeast could swarm down and do whatever they needed to this guy.

Three-quarters into the room stood a short waist-high divider. Across from it in a shadowy corner near the back she spotted a wire cage. Same size as the one she'd seen yesterday. The type you'd keep a big dog in.

Miranda's breath caught.

On the floor inside the cage she caught sight of Gen's short, white-blond hair. The sick bastard had her locked up in there.

Miranda dared a step toward the cage. Gen didn't move. She took a few more steps.

She blinked hard trying to make out more detail and noticed a strange odor in this part of the room. She couldn't tell what it was.

Gen's eyes were closed. He had her down to her underwear. Miranda hoped that meant he hadn't touched her yet. She didn't dare call out to her, but she could see her back gently moving up and down.

She was sound asleep. He must have kept her drugged all this while. She hoped he'd had to because Gen had given him a hard time.

And where was he?

Maybe she should have checked the rooms upstairs. She might have caught him up there. Too late now.

If she could just get that cage open and get Gen out of here before he came back, they'd be home free.

She took another step forward and saw there was a padlock on the cage's door. She'd have to get that open fast. But what was that on the top?

Two leads, like the type used to start a dead car battery. Jumper cables. One hooked to the cage's top, the other to its side. Miranda followed their cords with her gaze and saw what they were connected to.

A charger. A big one.

She hadn't quite reached the divider yet. But turning her head she could see an opening in the wall behind it. Looked like it led to a side room.

Suddenly she heard footsteps inside the room. She scrambled to hide behind the divider but it was too far away. Before she could get there a shadow fell across the floor and a man appeared in the opening.

He stared at her.

He was in the same jeans and baggy gray T-shirt she'd seen in the surveillance recording from the mall. Tall, big shouldered, shaggy dirty blond hair that came just under his ears.

He looked exactly like the photo Becker had doctored.

He hadn't been upstairs. He'd been in that side room the whole time.

Waiting for her.

He looked at her with eyes as green as well fertilized grass and gave her a sickly grin. "Hello there, Miranda Steele."

CHAPTER FIFTY-ONE

Her heart banging in her chest like a noisy water pipe, Miranda raised her Beretta and pointed it straight at the guy's chest. "Hands up, Drew."

He chuckled. "Do you still think my name is Drew? And you call yourself a detective?"

He was trying to rattle her. "I said hands up."

He shook his head at her as if she were a stubborn child who wouldn't go to bed on time. Then he grinned again and pointed at her. "Interesting T-shirt. A philosophy I agree with."

Don't look down, she thought. He's playing with you. Then she remembered what her shirt said. *Normal is Boring*. Not a great thing to wear when you're going after a serial killer.

She took a half a step toward him and put a growl into her voice. "I'll give you one more chance, you sonofabitch. Get your fucking hands up!"

Now he laughed out loud. A low sick guttural laugh that turned her stomach. This guy was certifiable.

Still laughing he shook his head. "No, Miranda. It's you who must put down that gun."

"Don't think I won't shoot you." She braced herself, ready to do just that.

"I know you won't." He snickered as if he'd just told a very funny joke. Then he raised his hand. Between his fingers was a small black plastic case about the size of a cell phone. "Did you know these things work remotely?"

"What things?"

"Why, the battery over there, of course."

He nodded to the car charger. The one hooked up to the cage Gen was asleep in.

"You see, when I press this button the battery will send a charge to that cage in the corner."

The one with Gen in it.

He turned the thing in his hand. "It's a very interesting device. Did you know it's not the voltage that kills but the amperage? Fascinating, don't you think? It takes only .65 amps to stop the human heart. This one is rated 700 amps. Of course, there's the resistance of the body, but still it will do the job nicely."

Was he going to electrocute her? That wasn't his M.O.

Miranda's mind raced. He had to be bluffing. There were a lot of urban myths around car batteries and whether they could kill you. But for the life of her right now she couldn't remember any of them.

"Care to press your luck?" He held up the device and poised a finger over it.

She didn't lower the gun. But a shiver went through her as she remembered how intelligent Adam Tannenburg was. He'd made top grades all through school.

"Oh, I see. You don't believe me. That's right. Good detectives are skeptical. Well, of course I'd test it thoroughly first. I was working on a specimen about an hour ago. Here it is."

He gave a kick and something furry flew out from behind the divider and landed near her foot.

Keeping her gun aimed at his chest she risked a glance downward.

It was a dead squirrel. That was the odd odor she'd smelled.

Had he really killed it with that battery? Would it work on a human? She couldn't take that chance. Even if the charge didn't kill Gen it might do some serious damage.

"Now, let's try this again," he said in the tone of a kindergarten teacher. "Put down the gun."

Suddenly Miranda remembered Parker and her colleagues were listening to all this. But the sound only went one way. If only she could talk to Becker and get his opinion on car batteries.

"Very well." Drew raised the switch in the air. "Say good-bye to your stepdaughter."

Miranda held up a hand. "No. Stop. I'll do what you say." Slowly she bent down and laid the gun on the floor keeping it as near to her as she dared.

Drew clucked his tongue at her. "You know better than that. You're an ace detective, aren't you? Kick it over here to me."

Feeling helpless she did as he said.

"Very good. Now sit down on the floor over there." He pointed to the far wall, near where the pulleys hung.

She didn't want to go over there, but she obeyed and sat down against the foam insulation about three feet from Gen. The mold smell was thicker here. She could feel the moisture of the cement floor through her jeans.

She could still see her Beretta on the floor near his running shoes. He hadn't picked it up yet. Awfully sure of himself, wasn't he? Maybe she could use that to her advantage.

She gestured at the room. "Pretty elaborate setup you've got here."

The side of his mouth turned up in a crooked grin of pride. "As was the one you saw yesterday." He watched her closely to see her reaction.

She kept her face still.

"You know, it isn't very difficult to remove a GPS tracker and toss it into a dumpster somewhere."

She had realized that. Too late, though.

"And even though you and your husband are supposed to be such smart detectives, you couldn't figure out I wanted you to get here. Oh, I know he's outside. That was part of the plan."

Miranda gritted her teeth, tried not to show fear. She hadn't noticed any surveillance cameras on her tour of the place with Holloway. But maybe he was making an assumption.

It made sense. That was why he'd taken Gen. He'd used Gen to draw both her and Parker to him. Of course, Parker would be here.

He planned on stringing both her and Gen up and torturing them while Parker stood outside helpless.

But he didn't know the rest of the team was here. Or that she'd faced insane killers before. Or what was in her past that gave her the strength to face them down.

She scanned the perimeter of the ceiling. The basement windows she'd seen from outside were covered with the acoustical padding. Otherwise Holloway or Wesson could crawl around to the back and take a clean shot.

She'd have to think of something else.

Keep him talking, she decided. Becker was recording everything this guy said. If nothing else, she could get a confession out of him and send him to prison for the rest of his life.

Start by playing dumb. "Did you say your name's not Drew?"

He bent down and smiled at her as if she were a child. "You found the fake drivers license I left in that Hyundai, didn't you? I left it there for you to find the night I took Hannah."

"Somebody said she was in love with you."

"She was in love with herself. She was a whore. She kicked me. See?" He turned his head and showed her a bruise on his jaw.

So Hannah Kaye had put up a fight. Gen would have, too. No wonder he'd resorted to drugs to keep her quiet.

"You were going by another name, too. Gabriel Anthony Pierson."

Scowling he motioned with his finger in the air like a schoolteacher. "Thomas Anthony Drew. Gabriel Anthony Pierson. The middle initial is the same."

And maybe the same as his first name.

"That was a gift. Did you find it helpful?"

Miranda didn't answer. The look in his eye was getting unbalanced.

He took a step closer to her. "As Drew I watched you while you were doing rehabilitation at Saint Benedictine's. As Pierson I emptied your trash at the Agency."

And got her phone number.

Miranda took a breath to steady her nerves. "You sent me text messages."

His green eyes sparkled with near admiration. "Very good. *I know who you are. I know where you are. I know what you are.*"

Confession number one. "And the one Parker got this morning?"

"Exactly. *Good Morning, Wade Parker. You may be interested to know that I have your daughter.*" He giggled as if delighted with his own cleverness. "As you can see, I wasn't lying."

She needed more. "But those names, Drew and Pierson. They belonged to other people."

His eyes widened. He was surprised she knew that. Then he waved a hand to dismiss it away. "They were just names I found. Silly old men who died a long time ago. Like my father."

Miranda recalled the neighbor in Evanston saying her suspect's father had died when he was nine.

Was this man standing before her Adam Tannenburg?

How had the young boy who'd been in love with the art student who'd died in a house fire turned into a monster like this?

"Who are you?" she dared to ask.

"That reminds me." Without answering suddenly he bent down and reached for something behind the wall divider.

Go for the gun, Miranda thought. But he was still holding that remote.

He popped up again. He put the remote into the pocket of his T-shirt. In both hands he held a long thin object.

A baton?

"Do you know what this is?"

She nodded. "Music conductors use them."

His brows went up in surprise. "Correct. They conduct the orchestra, keeping time with these." He waved it in the air and hummed some classical piece she didn't recognize.

Then he stopped. He stared at her and his green eyes seemed to take on an eerie glow. "But this one has a point. I sharpened it myself. See?" He touched the end to his fingertip and drew blood.

Miranda felt her breath grow shallow. Was that what he'd used on Hannah Kaye?

"Mother was a musician," he said, delicately sucking the end of his finger. "She played the clarinet. But she also had batons. So many batons."

Miranda felt her stomach twist at the way he'd said that. The strange glaze in his eyes glowed greener.

He took the stick and slapped it against his palm with a snap. "She used to punish me with them when I missed a note. Three strikes for every missed note. Four for every missed beat. I had to be careful. I had to be perfect. And I was. I was excellent."

Adam Tannenburg had played the clarinet like his mother. He'd earned a music scholarship to Northwestern.

"But it wasn't enough. It was never enough for her." Agitated, he began to pace back and forth in front of the divider. "Even when I was a little boy she would take me to her room and make me take off my clothes and lie on the bed. She would touch me with her clarinet while she played Stravinsky."

Miranda could only imagine where she'd touched her son. Instinctively she inched away from him on the floor.

"She would take her hand and grab me so tightly I would cry out in pain. Then she would tell me to be quiet. But I couldn't be quiet. And when I kept screaming and crying she would hit me and poke me with her baton. Over and over and over. I still have the scars." He lifted his T-shirt over his stomach. It was covered with old welts.

Dear God. His mother was a monster. And she'd created another monster in her own image.

Miranda stared at the man. He was in another world, reliving his nightmare. Was he incoherent enough for her to get to the gun and shoot before he used that remote?

Suddenly he came out of the trance with a shrug. "But I paid her back. I killed her." He said it as if he were talking about turning off the TV for the night.

Miranda started. Was this the same guy she'd been looking for a month ago in Chicago? How could it be?

She had to know the truth. "Your mother died in a house fire, didn't she?"

A broad smile crossed his face. The pride was back. "A fire I set." He laughed again.

A low guttural laugh. A sick, painful laugh that would have torn her heart out if she didn't know how insane, how deadly he was.

"It was easy. I mixed sleeping pills in her wine and when she'd fallen asleep on the sofa, I poured gasoline on her and set her on fire. It burned down that whole awful place with all those awful memories. But before I did that I tampered with the wiring to make it seem faulty. The police fell for it. They declared her death an accident."

It was him. "That house was in Evanston, Illinois."

He blinked at her as if she were the crazy one. "Well, you know that. You were there just a little while ago, weren't you?"

How the hell did he know that?

He stepped a little closer to her. "I was there, too. Don't you remember the feel of my arm around your neck?"

Did the floor just quake? Were the walls coming down on top of her?

Suddenly she was back in that mansion in Evanston. Standing in its ruins in the middle of the night. Picking through the rot and the ash looking for evidence. She'd sensed someone behind her. A rotten rafter overhead had snapped and tumbled to the ground. It would have crushed her but someone threw an arm around her neck and pulled her out of the way.

But the grip around her throat had tightened and tightened until she passed out.

It was him. This was Adam Tannenburg. And he'd almost killed her that night.

CHAPTER FIFTY-TWO

So why hadn't he killed her?

Again she looked at the room. The paper lanterns, the padding, the pulleys, the cage with Gen inside it.

This was why. He was waiting for this.

Miranda's heart began to beat with fear. But why her? Why Gen? Why Parker?

Adam Tannenburg had had a sweetheart. Could she appeal to that side of him? The nice young man she'd learned about in Chicago? Find it buried inside the killer?

"Tell me about Lydia," she said softly.

He glared at her. "Do not speak her name. No one is allowed to say her name but me."

So he still cared about her. "You were in love with her."

His eyes glowered as he stared at her. "You already know. You know we met in art school."

He had stalked her in Chicago. How had he known she was there? A chill went through her. Because he had been Gabriel Pierson, the cleaning man. And after that he'd been Tommy Drew, the delivery man at Saint Benedictine's. He'd stalked her in Atlanta, too.

"I fell in love the instant I saw her," he continued, his voice dreamy. "She was so beautiful. All that luscious blond hair. That perfect skin. Those big bright hazel eyes."

Just the way Lydia Sutherland had looked in the photo Miranda had seen in her case file in Chicago.

"And she fell in love with me, too. We spent every spare moment together. After only two weeks I asked her to marry me. She said yes. We would have been so happy together."

"What happened?"

"You know what happened," he shouted. But he told her anyway. He needed to tell someone. "It was the middle of December. Just before the holidays. She asked me to stay overnight at her house. I drove her there in my Mustang. She made us hot chocolate with rum. We drank it together, then finished the bottle of rum. And a second one. We smoked some weed, talked about school, our future."

He smiled, reliving the best part of his past.

"We lay together in her bed but I didn't touch her that night. We were both too intoxicated. We fell asleep." He ran a hand through his hair, growing agitated again. "It must have been around two in the morning when I woke up. I heard someone breaking in the door. I was going to get up to find out what was going on but before I could, *he* came into the room."

He? Who was he talking about?

"I shot out of bed. Told him to leave. He stood there yelling at Lydia. I tried to fight him but he was better trained. He threw a hard punch and hit me on the jaw. I fell to the floor. I hit my head on a table and passed out."

Dear God, was that what had happened that night?

"When I came to, at first all I could hear was screaming. I opened my eyes and saw him on top of her on the bed. 'What are you doing with him, you bitch?'" he cried. 'Don't you understand you belong to me?' I tried to get up but the room was spinning."

He struck a fist into the air as if he could punch the man now.

"'I've been following you for weeks now,' he said. 'You've been fucking him, haven't you? Haven't you?' And then…I watched him rape her. She cried out, told him to stop, but he wouldn't. I saw him writhing over her body on the bed. Holding her down. Taking her from me. He kept yelling at her. 'Whore! Whore! Whore!'"

Miranda felt numb. It was Leon. Leon was the one who'd killed Lydia Sutherland.

"He had his hands around her neck. He was shaking her and shaking her. I watched her go limp in his hands but he just kept shaking her. And then finally he stopped. He'd strangled her. She was dead." The man before her began to whimper in agony. "I watched him climb off of her and stare down at her body. I was so afraid I pretended to still be out. I huddled on the floor and hoped he'd go away so I could mourn my Lydia. But he'd come to his senses by then. He knew he'd be charged with murder. If anyone found her."

Oh, my God.

Adam wiped his tears away with both hands and sniffed. "He ran into the kitchen and got some gasoline or something. He kicked over Lydia's space heater and poured the liquid over it. It went up in a burst of flames."

Exactly the details the fire marshall had determined.

"Then he ran out of the room. I followed him out. I knew I'd be burned and die with her. I saw him go out the back door so I ran toward the front. I was so afraid. I got outside and into my car and drove away as fast as I could."

So Lydia's neighbor had been right. Adam Tannenburg had been with Lydia that night. And he'd driven away in his Mustang after the fire started.

"The next day the police picked me up and questioned me about what happened. I lied and said I wasn't there that night. They let me go." He inhaled a raspy breath. "Then a month and a half later, they picked me up again. On sexual assault. But I had never been with anyone but Lydia."

A month and a half. He had been arrested in February. Just like Parker had told her today.

"It was that night I learned who I truly was. What I was meant to be."

From Leon's visit to his jail cell?

Leon had turned into as sick a psychopath as any Miranda had known. He'd stalked her for years and tried to kill her. Had he somehow passed on that legacy to Tannenburg? How?

"He told me what a slut Lydia was. How she'd fucked so many other guys before me. And he had had her more than any of them. She was a whore. She deserved killing. My sweet, gentle Lydia. I loved her so, but she used me. She hurt me. More than Mother ever had."

He began to weep. He wasn't looking at her now. He was lost in his past. If only she could get him away from that remote and get to her gun.

She dared to move her butt a little closer to where it lay near his feet. He didn't see her.

He drew in a breath and raised his eyes to the ceiling. "And that was when we made the deal."

"Deal?" To leave town, right?

"He said the police had physical evidence. They knew I was at Lydia's house the night of the fire. He reminded me they had already charged me of raping her and that they were about to file murder charges against me."

It wasn't true. She knew that from the case file. There hadn't been any physical evidence against Tannenburg. Leon had pulled strings with his buddies just the way he had when he took her daughter and put her up for adoption without her knowledge.

"He told me I just had to do this one thing."

Leave town. Disappear and never come back. Miranda waited, not daring to prompt him. She watched his chest heave up and down as he relived his past. He'd confess it all soon. Tell her where he went, how the killings started. Who and how many.

He calmed himself and turned to her with that frightening grin. And when he spoke, the sound of his voice suddenly became all too familiar.

"He said he had a wife at home who needed to be taught a lesson. He wanted me to rape her."

CHAPTER FIFTY-THREE

Outside the house the sun had set and fireflies and insects buzzed through the thick humid air.

Still stationed behind the kidnapper's truck, in the dark Parker pressed the bud into his ear and watched the screen on Dave's computer as it recorded the conversation inside.

This couldn't be right. There must be a malfunction in the system. But he knew that thought was his own denial.

Denial of what he'd just heard over the wire.

The man inside, the man who had kidnapped Gen, the man who had taken Miranda's gun was Adam Tannenburg. And it was Adam Tannenburg who had attacked Miranda one wintry Chicago night in February fifteen years ago.

It was Adam Tannenburg who was the man Mackenzie had been looking for. Her birth father.

Dear God in heaven.

How could he have been so wrong about this man? Why didn't he see it when he'd discovered Leon Groth's visit to Tannenburg's cell fifteen years ago?

If he hadn't been so obsessed with protecting his wife, maybe he would have been able to think clearly. Maybe he would have put the pieces together before now.

But how could he? It was so bizarre, so evil, even for a man like Groth—to blackmail someone into raping his wife?

Thank God Groth was dead.

But Tannenburg was very much alive. And he was about to do to Miranda and Gen what he did to that poor college student.

Not if he could help it.

He turned to Becker and whispered low. "Man the station here, Dave."

Becker looked at him with questioning eyes. "What do you mean, sir?"

Parker drew the weapon he was carrying in his shoulder holster. "I mean I'm going in there. Holloway, Wesson, cover me."

CHAPTER FIFTY-FOUR

The dank ugly basement with its padded walls and lanterns and pulleys receded into a dream. No, not a dream. A far worse nightmare.

Miranda wasn't here anymore. She wasn't in Georgia. She wasn't in Jaspar County. She wasn't in this house.

She was back in Chicago on that awful night fifteen years ago.

She saw the shadows of the convenience store and the warehouse and the cold dark alley they formed. She saw the black ski mask hovering over her, felt the hands groping her, ripping off her clothes. She felt her flesh tearing on the icy pavement. The bitter wintry February cold on her bare skin. Heard his sickening grunts as he took her. And her own helpless screams.

And she smelled the nauseating odor of cheap cologne.

She raised her head and saw Tannenburg staring at her. He was smiling.

He wanted her to relive it. To feel what she was feeling right now. He was a sick, sadistic bastard. He was the monster in her head. The demon who had haunted her dreams for fifteen years.

His mouth was moving. He was speaking to her. She hadn't heard it all, but now his words were clear.

"I saw you on the news in Lake Placid," he said. "I knew then I could find you and finish the job."

"What?"

"He wanted me to kill you that night in February. He said he'd send you out for ice cream and he didn't want you to come back. But I couldn't do it. I was too weak then. I went back home and hid from him for awhile. I thought he would kill me. But Mother wouldn't leave me alone. That was when I knew I could become what he wanted me to be. It took me months to come up with the plan, to work up the courage to set her on fire. But after I did that, I knew I could do what he wanted. But I couldn't find you. And so I had to find others to replace you."

Miranda thought of the dozens of murder cases Chambers had found.

"My first was in Downers Grove. That was when I came into my own."

When he'd started on the path he was on now, he meant.

"But my first lasted only a few hours. I honed my technique. I became an expert. It's taken me years. And now I can make them last days." His breath grew ragged, like a hungry wolf.

Slowly he turned to her. "And all this time I've been looking for you. Waiting for you. Getting ready for you. And now?" His teeth glistened with his ugly smile. "It's high time we got started."

He moved toward her, pointing that awful stick at her.

She shot to her feet and stepped back. "No."

"Don't worry. I'm going to do her first." He nodded toward the cage with Gen in it. "But I want you to watch. It will bring back memories of me."

She'd had enough memories of him. She wasn't going to let that bastard get to Gen. And she wasn't going to let him touch her either.

"Get away from me." She used the commanding tone she should have used that night. The one she'd learned in the dozens of self-defense courses she'd taken since then.

He chuckled, took another step toward her. "Oh, my. Aren't we bold."

She glanced down. He was as far from her gun as she was now but that electrical remote was still in his pocket.

"I know you killed him," he said.

"Who?"

"Him. I saw that on the news last October. Lake Placid."

He meant Leon.

"He was right about you, you know." He took another step.

She braced herself. "Get any closer and you'll be sorry." She still had the martial arts skills she'd been honing for fifteen years.

But again he only laughed. "You might have killed him, but you won't kill me. That will be my job. After I'm done here."

Was he talking about suicide? Along with a double murder? He was going for all the glory, wasn't he?

He lunged forward with the baton. She tried to bat it away but he was too fast. He stuck her in the breast with it.

Damn. It was sharp as a dagger and it stung like hell.

She felt blood stain her T-shirt. *Normal is Boring.* What she wouldn't give for normal now. A normal afternoon with her daughter. Dear God. She just realized this madman was Mackenzie's father.

As if he were fencing he charged in and stabbed at her again. This time she managed to block the full force but he nicked her upper arm. More blood oozed into the short sleeve.

He lunged again and she whacked the stick away.

Another swipe and he got her in the stomach. She could smell him. That sour odor of cheap cologne. She felt herself going under again. Back to that night. That time when she was so weak and defenseless.

Keep your head, dammit. She wasn't that woman any longer. Hadn't been for a long time. She'd battled her demons. They might keep coming back, but she kept beating them down.

She'd do that to this monster, too.

She danced away from him and took stock of her position. One solid roundhouse kick to the head and she could knock him out. Or at least stun him enough to get that remote away from him.

And that stick.

But she didn't have enough room. She was too close to the wall. He was going to pin her to it soon.

She thought she heard a step groan on the staircase. It was her mind playing tricks on her again. Focus.

She stared him down. Right in his sickly green eyes.

He stared back, smiling. As if he knew he was going to win.

Think again, you sonofabitch. She wasn't going to let him take her down this time. Not without a fight. She'd bite off his nose, gouge out an eye. She didn't care what he did to her with that stick.

And then she remembered something.

A secret weapon she'd had on her the whole time. If there was any time to use it, it was now.

"Hey, Adam," she said as cockily as she could. "I've got a present for you."

For a moment he blinked at her stunned, confused. "What is it?"

She shoved her hand into her pocket and pulled out the ankle bracelet. The one the police detective had found on the Tannenburg estate the night he'd put his arm around her neck. The one she'd kept. The one she'd been carrying around for days.

She held it up so that the light of the lanterns caught the sheen of the pendant.

The golden heart with the initials A.T.

"Remember this?"

His eyes filled with sudden tears. "Lydia. My love. My own."

She knew he'd given this to her. And he still loved her. "Here catch." She tossed the bracelet into the corner as far away from her gun as she could get it.

It worked. He dove for it.

And she dove for her gun. She scrambled across the floor and scooped it up, came up just in time to see him on his feet again.

"You forgot about this!" He screeched.

He was holding the remote in one hand over his head. But he had the bracelet in the other hand. It would take a second or two before he could push the button now.

As she aimed the gun at his chest, she heard clattering on the stairs. No time to wait. No time to think.

She fired.

Her gun seemed to go off twice, as if two loud bombs had exploded in the room.

Her bullet hit its target. Tannenburg's body jerked back, blood spewing from his chest. Then he jerked forward, blood and brain matter shooting from his forehead. He swayed to the left, to the right. Then he stumbled over to the wall.

His green eyes glowered at Miranda. He gave her one last vicious look. He held up the remote. It slipped from his grasp, and he slumped to the floor.

Ears ringing from the shots, Miranda looked up and saw Parker on the stairs with his Glock drawn. He was the one who had fired the other shot.

"You killed him," she said.

"We killed him," he corrected.

But it wasn't over. Suddenly she smelled smoke.

She turned her head and saw the acoustical padding on the wall go up in flames. Tannenburg had fallen on top of the lanterns.

CHAPTER FIFTY-FIVE

Flames whipped up the side of the basement.

Miranda spun around and ran. She was the first to Gen's cage. But Parker was there before she could get her picks out.

He holstered his weapon and took them from her. Better that way. Her hands were shaking.

He had the padlock open in an instant.

Gen was just rousing. Had she seen the shooting? Did she know they had to get out of here now?

Miranda couldn't tell. Gen couldn't keep her eyes open. It was just as well.

Holloway and Wesson had come down the stairs, weapons drawn when they heard gunfire. Now they stood batting away the flames along the wall with their jackets.

"Get out of here!" Parker called to them as he lifted Gen in his arms and hurried across the floor with her.

Wesson stopped fighting the flames and draped her jacket over Gen, then they all raced up the stairs and out of that house of horrors.

Becker had called the fire department. And the cops.

Sirens blaring, lights flashing, the fire truck barreled into the yard and began hosing down the house. The local police arrived on the scene, accompanied by Erskine and Chambers.

Chaos ensued.

While the firemen worked, the cops demanded statements. They were very interested in Becker's recording of the conversation in the basement, But they wanted to talk to Gen.

Parker told them no. He was taking her to the hospital first.

Miranda told Chambers she'd talk to him later and climbed into Parker's Mazda while he gently laid Gen in the backseat. She had to get away. Becker and Holloway and Wesson stayed back to give statements. They'd get rides with Erskine and Chambers when it was all done.

Feeling as if she had escaped from hell, Miranda rode off into the night with Parker at the wheel.

CHAPTER FIFTY-SIX

Dr. Taggart, Parker's trusted friend, took over when they reached the hospital.

He put Gen in a room, ran tests to find out what she had been given, and pumped her stomach. Two hours later Gen was resting in a bed with Parker beside her, holding her hand.

Miranda should have felt nothing but relief. And she did. She was so happy Parker had his daughter back. He didn't deserve to be hurt any more.

But the thought of the life she could have had with him made her sad. And the death of that crazed killer—the man who had raped her so many years ago—made her too somber for words.

She slipped out of the room and wandered into the waiting area.

She'd wait for Parker. Tell him how she felt. Wish him the best. Tell him if he wanted her to sign divorce papers she'd be available anytime.

To keep her mind off what she'd been through tonight she sat down in a colorful chair and took out her cell phone. She scrolled to her messages. The first was an update from Chambers at the scene.

The fire had been put out after about half an hour. There hadn't been enough air in the basement to spread it. Good thing because they'd had to use the tank in the fire truck. Most of the evidence of the crime scene was intact. Tannenburg's body had been singed, but there was still plenty left of him for DNA testing.

She was glad. That would bring closure to the loved ones of all those other victims.

The next text was one from Wendy.

OMG. Timmy dumped me for Leslie! She's the 'popular' girl. Can you believe it?

Timmy was the boy Wendy and Mackenzie had fought over weeks ago. The one that had destroyed their friendship.

But guess what? I went over to Mackenzie's tonight to tell her. And she got mad and said he was a total jerk for doing that. She hugged me and said she wanted me back as her friend and was sorry she'd ever let him come between us!

Well. Would wonders never cease? Miranda couldn't help but smile.

We're going to the skating rink tomorrow after school and she's going to show me some moves she says will put me over the top at Regionals next year. Can you believe it?

Wendy was right. She couldn't believe it. But it was true. Her girls were back together. At last.

With a big grin, Miranda thumbed back a text. *You made my night, kid.*

With a sense of deep satisfaction she leaned back in the chair and closed her eyes.

It couldn't have been five minutes later that she heard Parker's rich, deep voice.

"So this is where you went off to."

She opened her eyes and sat up. "I thought you could use some privacy."

He nodded.

"Look." She held up her phone.

He took it and read the message from Wendy. He smiled. "I'm so glad they've come to their senses."

"Me, too." Then she caught his gaze. "We can't tell Mackenzie about tonight."

"No." He moved to the chair next to her and sat down.

"She might hear it on the news."

"I'll speak to Colby. I'll make sure she doesn't let her see it."

If a parent could accomplish that. But maybe Wendy would keep her mind occupied and off the news for a few days, as well as off her father.

Parker was quiet a long time. Finally he spoke. "I'm afraid I owe you a debt of gratitude I can never repay."

Did he mean for saving his daughter's life? He had a hand in that, too.

She shrugged. "I can send you a bill."

He didn't smile. "Miranda, if you hadn't gone into that house. If you hadn't gotten that confession. If you hadn't faced down that madman, Gen might—"

She held up a hand. "But she is. And she's going to be okay."

Though she might need a few visits to Dr. Wingate. But then who didn't after today? Miranda was ready to book appointments for the rest of the year. She knew she had more emotional fallout to deal with. Fallout she was suppressing at the moment.

Parker studied her intently. "I'd like to discuss something with you."

Uh oh. Here it comes.

Nerves bouncing in her stomach Miranda got up and strolled to the window. She gazed out at the city bathed in light. It was in a hospital like this where she learned her destiny. Where she thought she and Parker had made a pact to work together.

But it wasn't to be. Now it was really over.

She hugged herself and braced for his next words.

Parker gazed at the strong, lean body of his wife in the window, her T-shirt stained with her own blood. What a sacrifice she'd made for him tonight.

What a woman she was.

Why couldn't he have seen it before? She was worth so much more than he'd ever realized. Not only to him but to every victim whose case she took on. How could he have been so selfish?

He rose and moved to her side. He longed to touch her but didn't dare.

Miranda sucked in a deep breath. "Just say it, Parker."

"Say what?"

"What you want to discuss with me. The divorce." There. She'd said it for him.

He didn't answer. She turned to him and gazed into his deep gray eyes. There was a world of emotion there. Because of what he'd just been through.

"I was going to say that I saw you in a new light today."

That made her frown.

"You've said this life is your destiny. For the first time I'm beginning to understand what you mean."

"Okay," she said cautiously.

She wondered if he was being his classy self. Softening the blow with flattery and sweet talk. But he was only making things worse. She wished he would get to the point.

"I understand now," he repeated. "You have to do what you do because it's who you are. And you're one of the best."

Involuntarily her insides fluttered. She'd always been a sucker for his compliments.

She shrugged. "You're not so shabby yourself."

The corner of his mouth turned up in a smile. "It felt good working as a team again."

"Yeah, it did. And it was great having Becker and Holloway and Wesson there. And you, of course. And your Glock."

His eyes twinkled. "And so I've been thinking."

"About what?"

"What if instead of closing down Parker and Steele Consulting we expand it?"

She took a step back from him feeling as if he'd punched her in the chest. "What?"

He raised a brow. "You don't care for the idea?"

She stammered a moment. "I—I can't believe it came out of your mouth."

"Well, it did." He stepped close to her, dared to take her hand in his. "You've taught me a great lesson that I forgot along the way."

"What's that?"

"Risking it all is better than losing it all."

How true. But did he really mean what he was saying? "So you want to form a team?"

"Yes, I do."

"Safety in numbers, huh?"

"Something like that." He ran a thumb over her fingers, making her stomach quiver. "I can't promise I won't worry about you. Or be overprotective at times. But I do promise I'll never demand you stop being who you are again."

She stared up at him, hoping what he was saying was true. Hoping she wasn't dreaming. "Do you really mean that, Parker?"

In reply he took her into his arms and pulled her close to him.

The strength of his arms around her made her melt. She pressed her face to his muscular chest and breathed in his masculine scent.

He smelled so good.

He kissed her hair. "Come back to me, Miranda. I love you so."

He wanted her back? It wasn't the end? Her eyes filled with sudden tears. They ran down her cheeks and onto the floor and she didn't give a whit.

She lifted her face to him and smiled through the tears, her heart now melting into a soft, gooey pool like butter on a hot Georgia afternoon. "I love you, too, Wade Parker," she sniffed. "I guess fulfilling your destiny isn't so fulfilling if you have to do it alone."

"A wise thought indeed," he said.

And he drew her to him and pressed his lips to hers in a kiss that was more intense, more meaningful than all the others he'd ever given her.

He loved her. Just as she was. He wasn't going to change her ever again.

It was all she ever wanted from him. They were back together. Parker and Steele. And their friends.

As she threw her arms around his neck and kissed him back, she knew together they were going to make one unstoppable team.

THE END

ABOUT THE AUTHOR

Writing fiction for over fifteen years, Linsey Lanier has authored more than two dozen novels and short stories, including the popular Miranda's Rights Mystery series. She writes romantic suspense, mysteries, and thrillers with a dash of sass.

She is a member of Romance Writers of America, the Kiss of Death chapter, Private Eye Writers of America and International Thriller Writers. Her books have been nominated in several RWA-sponsored contests.

In her spare time, Linsey enjoys watching crime shows with her husband of over two decades and trying to figure out "who-dun-it." But her favorite activity is writing and creating entertaining new stories for her readers. She's always working on a new book. For alerts on her latest releases join Linsey's mailing list at linseylanier.com.

For more of Linsey's books, visit **www.felicitybooks.com** or check out her website at **www.linseylanier.com**

Edited by

Editing for You

Made in the USA
Monee, IL
06 December 2023

48399259R00120